A Scandalous Deception

AVA STONE

Night Shift Publishing

AVA STONE

ISBN: 1500817988
ISBN-13: 978-1500817985

Dedication

For ~ Tori Baker, Jane Charles, L.j Charles, Caren Crane, Claudia Dain, Tammy Falkner, Catherine Gayle, Samantha Grace, Sabrina Jeffries, Julie Johnstone, Jerrica Knight-Catania, Deb Marlowe, Joanne Repinecz, Stephanie Shaprio, DeShelia Spann, Michelle Tartalio, Becky Timblin & Tyler Woods

As I wrote the last words in A SCANDALOUS DECEPTION, I realized there was quite a bit of myself in Lady Felicity Pierce. And while that is often true for any number of characters any author may write over his/her lifetime, Lissy is very close to my soul, and a number of her thoughts were certainly things I have though myself over the years. But while Lissy had to go most of her journey alone, I am very fortunate to have had each of you help me along my path when it got dark and I wasn't sure what to do. Thank you for being there for me through the years. I love each of you and am so grateful to have had you in my life. ~ Ava

One

Astwick House, London – May 1816

Lady Felicity Pierce could not quite believe her eyes. Was that Phineas Granard? *Viscount Carraway*? At an actual ball? Heavens, was someone blackmailing Fin, or was there a dueling pistol to his back? He certainly wouldn't be here of his own volition, that was for sure. The overly serious viscount hadn't been remotely social in years, despite Lissy's best prodding that he stop sulking and get on with his life.

Fin started across the ballroom and greeted Lord Liverpool with an outstretched hand. Ah, that explained everything. Fin wasn't being blackmailed, and he hadn't suddenly become social. He was doing what he always did - politicking.

"The dolt is more starched than his cravat," came a deep voice from behind her.

Lissy glanced over her shoulder to find the decidedly

despicable Marquess of Haversham standing just a few feet away. Handsome devil that he was, the marquess' light blue eyes twinkled as he cast her a smug expression, one that a more foolish girl might have found charming. But Lissy had endured more than her share of that sort of man to last her a lifetime, so Haversham's attention was completely wasted on her.

She gave the marquess the back of her head, but said loud enough for him to hear, "I'm entirely certain Lady Astwick didn't invite *you*, my lord."

Lord Haversham chuckled, moving closer to Lissy, so close the scent of his citric shaving lotion invaded her senses. "She never does," he agreed.

"An intelligent man might make something of that. His continual lack of invite, that is." And yet the scoundrel attended every last event the dowager Marchioness of Astwick hosted anyway, as though daring the old dragon to personally drag him, kicking and screaming all the way to her front stoop.

Haversham laughed once more. "You are more direct than most chits your age. Do you know that?"

"My widowhood allows for a certain directness."

"Among other things," he added silkily. "But I imagine your directness stems more from being one of Prestwick's daughters. Not certain you're quite as direct as Lady Juliet, but she does possess a fortune you do not, doesn't she?"

Lissy didn't need her sister's fortune. Fin had made certain her allowance from Prestwick's holdings was more than generous. She glanced back at the staid viscount across the ballroom. He *was* starched. Haversham was right about that. And while she had accused Fin of that very thing herself more than once over the years, she hated hearing the disreputable Haversham voice the same criticism.

She tilted her head to the side in order to better see the marquess. "Shouldn't you be off chasing after Lady Staveley's skirts?" The lady in question wouldn't have a thing to do with him, but at least it would get the rogue away from Lissy.

Haversham's rakish grin spread wider. "I have no need to chase *anyone's* skirts, I'll have you know."

No, he probably didn't. The man was more than handsome with his dark hair and light, piercing eyes. He exuded masculinity and raw sexuality. Despite his fascination with Lady Staveley – a most happily married woman who was quite devoted to her husband - Haversham most likely had a throng of widows and unhappily married women lining up for a turn in his bed. *Widows.*

Lissy narrowed her eyes on the libertine. Her *widowhood* did allow for a certain directness. However, it also had been the source for more than one inappropriate suggestion to her over the years. "I am so happy to hear that, my lord. Perhaps you can go entertain one of your many paramours then and leave me to myself."

Haversham chuckled. "You are charming, Lady Felicity."

"And here I'm trying so hard not to be."

"A word of advice?" His light eyes twinkled once again.

"Could I possibly stop you?" she countered.

"If you smile a bit more, Carraway might actually notice you."

Lissy's mouth fell open. Did he think she wanted *Fin's* attention? Fin was like family. He *was*, in fact, her half-brother's uncle. He *had*, in fact, almost married Lissy's oldest sister before her untimely death. He would have been her brother otherwise. He *was* nearly like her brother as it was, for heaven's sake. A rigid, humorless brother who liked to tell her what to do, but a brother just the same.

"I doubt it would take much encouragement. You are supremely more beddable than Liverpool, after all."

What a perfectly ridiculous thing to say. "Well, I am so relieved to hear it as I'd considered Lord Liverpool my main competition on the marriage mart this year."

Haversham laughed once more, a sound Lissy was quickly coming to despise. "Something tells me the last thing you're looking for is another husband."

For a moment, Lissy's heart stopped, and a dreadful chill washed over her. At her tender age, everyone assumed she wanted to marry again, to have a second chance at a happily ever after, but even if that was a possibility, she would never willingly go through such an experience ever again. But how in the world did Haversham know that? Was she so very transparent to everyone or just to him?

"That is, I'd wager you're as anxious to find another husband as I am to find another wife."

"Your own wife or someone else's?" she asked.

"Touché." His eyes danced with mirth, then he sobered a bit, cocking his head toward the dance floor. "One of your suitors, I'm sure."

Lissy glanced in the general direction Haversham had indicated and suppressed a groan when she spotted Lord Richard Shelley approaching her.

"I'll give Carraway this. He's more interesting than *him*," the marquess said under his breath, just loud enough for Lissy to hear.

She looked up at the scoundrel beside her and said, "I'm not certain you're the best judge for what constitutes an interesting gentleman, my lord."

"My dear Lady Felicity—" he smirked "—I am more qualified than most to make such assessments."

"Lady Felicity," Lord Richard began softly once he reached her. "I had hoped I might persuade you to stand up with me for the next set."

Lissy smiled, as warmly as she was able, at the far-from-interesting gentleman before her. "Thank you, my lord, but I'm not dancing this evening. I am a bit parched however, if you'd like to bring me some punch."

A bit crestfallen, Lord Richard nodded and then started off for the refreshment table.

Haversham slid so close to Lissy she could actually feel him chuckle beside her. "I think you wounded that poor man's heart."

"I'm certain he'll survive."

"Heartless wench. I'm liking you better and better."

"Good God!" Phineas Granard, Viscount Carraway, couldn't quite see straight as the edges of his vision were tinged slightly red.

"Beg your pardon, Carraway?" Lord Liverpool replied, but Fin barely heard the Prime Minister.

Honestly, with the ringing in his hears, he couldn't even hear himself think. What the devil was Lissy doing? Had she lost her fool mind? Was she actually flirting with the Marquess of Haversham?

Fin gritted his teeth. Keeping that chit out of trouble was a never-ending chore. He cursed Lucas Beckford for holing himself up in Derbyshire. The blasted man should be here keeping an eye on Lissy, not playing nursemaid to Juliet. All right, so the man's wife *was* expecting, Fin begrudgingly acknowledged. Beckford did have a perfectly reasonable excuse not to be in Town for the season, but why the devil he and Juliet had allowed Lissy to stay in London alone made no sense at all. They knew what a flighty little thing she was! And now she was cavorting with Haversham, of all the damned people in Town.

Truthfully, Lissy probably didn't know how dangerous the marquess was. Very few ladies her age did, but she was most definitely aware Haversham possessed a blackened reputation. Everyone was aware of that. Good God, Georgie would roll over in her grave if she knew the company her little sister was keeping this evening.

Georgie.

Fin took a steadying breath. One would have thought that sometime within the last three years, he'd have gotten over her, that the pain of losing her would have dulled a bit, that he'd have made a step or two towards getting on with his life. But he hadn't. Fin wasn't certain how to move forward or if he even wanted to. Georgie had been everything to him. She was perfect. Perfect for him. He could search the world over a hundred times and he'd never find a woman like her in his lifetime.

Fin's gaze stayed on Lissy, her flaxen curls bobbing up and down as she laughed at something her scurrilous companion had said. How the devil she and Georgie were sired by the same man was a complete mystery. The two of them must have inherited the traits from their respective mothers. That was the only answer. They didn't think the same, behave the same or even look the same. Yet, Georgie had fretted over all of her younger siblings, more like a mother than a sister. If she were still here, she would have been more than upset by Lissy's sudden friendship with Haversham.

"I say, Carraway," Lord Liverpool's voice pushed through the deafening roar in Fin's ears. "Are you all right?"

Fin shook his head, not wanting to go into the particulars, but he didn't really have a choice. "It looks like my nephew's sister is in over her head, is all."

Lord Liverpool turned his attention towards Lissy and Haversham across the room. "Prestwick's sister?"

Fin nodded. "I am sorry, sir. I'd love to continue this conversation, but I really—"

"I completely understand, Carraway. I have female relations my own."

Lissy wasn't really his relation, but there was no point in wasting time explaining the intricacies of his connection to the chit. Not when she was looking up at Haversham as though he'd personally hung the moon in the sky. "Thank you. I'll see you soon, sir."

Fin started across the ballroom, his temper rising with each step. Foolish girl. What in the world was Lissy thinking? Was she even thinking at all, that was a better question! Spending time in

Haversham's company could ruin nearly any girl's reputation. Just because she was a widow didn't mean she didn't have her good name to protect.

"Lissy," he grumbled in way of greeting when he reached her. "What exactly do you think you're doing?"

"Carraway." Haversham nodded.

Fin speared the malevolent marquess with a look that said better than words ever could what the man could go do with himself, then he turned his attention back to Lissy, whose blue eyes flashed with something Fin couldn't quite identify. Annoyance, humor, mischievousness. A combination of the three, perhaps.

"Uncle Fin." She smiled innocently, though she knew full well he hated it when she called him that.

"I'm not your uncle," he said, and if he had a farthing for every time he'd had to utter those words to her…

"You can call *me* Uncle Marc, if you'd like," Haversham tossed in. The suggestive tone to the man's voice grated Fin's nerves like an electric jolt to his nether regions.

"She'll call you no such thing," Fin growled. He narrowed his eyes on the marquess. "In fact, she shouldn't even be seen in your presence." Then he gestured towards the main entrance with his head. "So why don't you take your leave, Haversham?"

Two

"Phineas Samuel Benedict Granard!" Lissy hissed.

Fin's arrogant brown gaze shifted from Haversham to Lissy. "Felicity Corinna St. Claire Pierce," he countered.

Oh! If they weren't in Lady Astwick's ballroom, she'd slug him in the chest. How dare he march across the room and behave like an angry guardian? She hadn't sought out Haversham's company, but even if she had, it was none of Fin's concern. He had no say in regards to which friends she could have, what she did with her time, or how she chose to live her life, for that matter. Controlling, overbearing, insufferable, starched stickler.

Lissy folded her arms across her chest. "I will thank you not to take that tone with me."

A muscle twitched in Fin's jaw. He grabbed her elbow in his hand and pulled her closer to him. "Come with me," he growled, and then towed her away from Haversham and towards the main entrance.

"Fin!" she complained once they reached the corridor. "What in the world do you think you're doing?"

"I could ask you the same thing," he grumbled, his eyes scanning the hallway as though looking for a safe place to talk. He started for an open doorway and pulled Lissy along beside him.

They entered a small parlor, which was thankfully uninhabited, and Fin shut the door behind them. Good heavens! He'd made much more of a scene dragging her from Lady Astwick's ballroom than Lissy had done by simply talking to Lord Haversham.

"If this is how you behave in society," she began, her ire building, "then it's a very good thing you never come out in it."

Fin's displeasure showed on his face, and he pointed in the general direction of the ballroom. "That man is a wholly unacceptable companion."

"One might say the same thing about Liverpool," she countered. "But I didn't stomp across the ballroom, behave boorishly, and yank *you* into a secluded parlor over it."

Fin's mouth fell open as though he couldn't believe she'd say such a silly thing. And Lissy was certain that was the precise thought going through his mind. He'd always thought her silly, incapable of making reasonable decisions on her own. Well, she wasn't a child, and hadn't been for quite a while.

"That is hardly the same thing, and you know it," he finally said.

Stubbornly, Lissy shook her head, even if no one in their right mind would compare the Prime Minister with the notorious marquess. "What I know, Fin, is that you have embarrassed me to no end. I cannot believe you just dragged me from that room in front of everyone as though I was an errant child in need of a scolding."

"If Georgie was here—"

"Georgie's *not* here. She's gone," she interrupted him. And for the first time since her sister's death, she felt no guilt in saying so.

No one could live up to Georgie's expectations, and Lissy refused to let Fin throw Georgie's would-be displeasure at her any longer. "And it's well past the time you should have started living your own life and stopped living hers."

The moment those last words were out of her mouth, Lissy wished she could call them back. The flash of pain that splashed across Fin's face tore at her heart. He loved Georgie, but only one of them had died all those years ago. If they were to talk about what Georgie would or wouldn't want, Lissy was more than certain that her oldest sister wouldn't want Fin to spend the remainder of his days pining away after her, mourning a future that was lost forever.

Lissy reached out a tentative hand, touching Fin's wrist. "I'm sorry. I didn't mean—"

"Don't you ever feel that way?" His dark eyes speared her. "Don't you ever lament the loss of Captain Pierce? Don't you wonder what your own life would be like if he'd lived?"

Only on the occasions when she suffered from nightmares. Lissy swallowed down the bile that rose up in her throat at the thought of her own husband. "I didn't know him as long as you knew Georgie," she hedged her answer.

Even still, her words were the truth. Had she known Aaron better than she had, Lissy would have never married the oh-too-dashing captain. Had she known the things Aaron was capable of, Lissy would have bolted as far away from the man as possible upon meeting him. In her darker moments, she wished she'd never met Aaron. If he'd never entered her life, she could actually enjoy a future now. But he had entered her life, and there wasn't a blasted thing Lissy could do about that. The past, as well as her future, was firmly etched in stone.

Though an actual future was not a possibility for Lissy, that didn't have to be the case for Fin. His stodginess aside, he was a delightful man. Kind, most of the time. Caring, even. If Aaron had been more like Fin...

"But you must have loved him, " Fin pressed. "Georgie showed me the letter you wrote."

The letter she'd sent from Boston. The letter she'd written on the day of her marriage before she realized the sort of man Aaron truly was. She hadn't had the heart to write again, she couldn't find the words to tell either of her sisters what a colossal mistake she had made. There was nothing either of them could do to rescue her from her impetuous foolishness, after all.

"I'd rather not talk about it, Fin," she said quietly. And she could go the rest of her life without talking about it, without ever thinking about it…

"You *never* want to talk about it," he interrupted her thoughts. "I've never seen you mourn, I've never seen—"

"No!" she blurted out, halting him mid-sentence. Lissy pushed past the panic that seized her heart and the shortness of her breath. She hated discussing Aaron. She hated it with every fiber of her being, and had ever since she'd returned to England. Lissy shook her head, hoping against hope that he'd stop his inquisition. "I won't live the rest of my life mourning his loss, Fin. I just won't. I'd rather look forward than back. And you should do the same." There! Perhaps now he'd leave the topic alone for a while.

⚜

Fin heaved a sigh and scrubbed a hand across his brow. Maddening chit. *He* looked forward. He looked forward everyday he was in the Lords. He looked forward everyday he tried to make England better for her people. He looked forward everyday he tried to be a good example for Edmund. Just because he didn't cavort with merry widows or spend his time chasing after this year's incomparable, whoever the devil she might be, didn't mean he was living in the past. He missed Georgie. He loved Georgie. He would until the day he died. But he was living in the present.

"If you're done scolding me," Lissy began, breaking into Fin's thoughts, "then I'd like to return to the ballroom now."

11

Fin scowled. Damnation, she could drive a saint mad. "I'm not scolding you. I'm trying to guide you."

Her pert little nose lifted high in the air. "The last I checked, Fin, you were Edmund's guardian, not mine. *I* don't need your guidance."

On the contrary, she was most definitely in need of a strong hand, something her father should have provided before his death, not that he could voice as much to her. "Then as Edmund's guardian, might I ask you to please be wary of the companions you choose? Your actions will, of course, reflect on your brother and his name."

"That is the most ridiculous thing I've ever heard." Lissy shook her head, and her flaxen curls bobbed against her shoulders. "Edmund is barely at Eton. I don't think his reputation is in any danger. Now, if you'll excuse me." She started for the door and turned the handle.

A moment later, she was gone and Fin was alone, like he had been for so long. He looked up at the ceiling above him as though guidance might come from on high. That was ridiculous, of course. But Felicity always vexed him, she always left him speechless and doubting his very sanity.

He did envy her ability to leave Captain Pierce and their dreams of a future that could never be behind her, however. He envied her ability to live every day with abandon. Fin could never do that. His obligations to his nephew, to his title, to his country weighed heavily on his shoulders. He couldn't even imagine living the carefree life Lissy led. But she wasn't thinking.

All of that aside, Fin did wish Lissy would take her role in society more seriously. Her actions would reflect on Edmund, no matter how much she protested otherwise. He needed to keep a closer eye on her, that much was evident.

※

Lissy stepped back into the Astwick ballroom, and her heart leapt to her throat. Good heavens! At the far side of the room, she spotted Mr. John Heaton from Boston, tall and handsome as always, talking with the aged Earl and Countess of Littleworth. What in the world was Mr. Heaton doing here? Lissy's breath shortened as she backed out of the ballroom, hoping against hope the American hadn't spotted her as well. If he had, how would she ever explain her presence, her living and breathing presence?

"There you are!" Phoebe Avery said from the ballroom entrance.

Several heads turned in Lissy's direction. Without a second thought, she lifted her skirts and bolted down the corridor.

"Lissy!" Phoebe called after her, and Lissy's heart nearly stopped. Of all the infernal times for someone to yell her name.

Lissy raced back towards the parlor she'd shared with Fin. She rushed over the threshold and was more than relieved to find the room empty. She shut the door behind her and sank against it. She had no hope of barring anyone from entering if they truly wanted to, but it made her feel a bit safer.

Three

Lissy stared at her reflection in the mirror. Heavens, she looked a decade older than her nineteen years. Of course, she'd tossed and turned all night long, plagued with nightmares and memories of her brief marriage.

The circles under her eyes spoke of the terrors she tried to keep hidden during the light of day, of the secrets she hoped no one would ever discover. She hadn't thought about Aaron in any real way for so long, it was almost as though he was, himself, a bad nightmare, a figment of the blackest parts of her imagination. She was certain her terrible night was all on an account of having spotted John Heaton at the Astwicks'. That, and Fin's incessant questions about her *dead* husband. If it *was* Mr. Heaton that she'd seen the previous night. She couldn't be entirely sure. Regardless, seeing the man, whoever he was, brought her mind shooting back to those terrible days in Boston and the truth that she had tried so hard to forget. Not that she could ever truly forget them, but the further she got from Massachusetts, the longer she'd been back in England, the easier it was to tell herself that those awful months had never really happened.

They had happened, however. No matter how much she wished they hadn't. Some scars could never heal, even if she pretended they didn't exist.

When a hand landed on Felicity's elbow, she yelped and nearly shot out of her skin. Her head spun to the side where she caught the frightened expression on her maid's face.

Annie touched a hand to her own heart. "Are you all right, my lady?"

Feeling like the biggest ninny in all of England for being frightened by the mere slip of her own lady's maid, Lissy took a steadying breath and patted Annie's hand. "I was just woolgathering. I didn't mean to startle you."

"I didn't mean to startle *you*," Annie insisted. "I am terribly sorry, my lady."

But it wasn't Annie's fault, so Lissy smiled her warmest smile and shook her head. "Nothing to apologize for. But I am hoping you can do something about these circles, Annie." She touched a hand to her cheek. "I look a fright, and I was supposed to go walking with Lady Arabella this morning."

"A bit of cucumbers ought to do the trick, my lady," Annie said as she started for the door. "I'll be back in a trice."

But there was no need to rush. Lissy didn't have to meet Bella for a few more hours, and though the idea of going out in public after spotting the man who looked so very much like John Heaton the previous evening twisted Lissy's stomach, she tried to push all thoughts of her former neighbor, of Boston and most especially of Aaron Pierce far from her mind. Mr. Heaton wouldn't be walking Rotten Row even *if* it was him she'd seen at the Astwicks' the night before. Besides, she wouldn't cower in the corner of her chambers the rest of her life all because of an *if* she wasn't entirely certain of.

Lissy leaned closer towards the mirror, her reflection looking back at her, a weary expression in her eyes. She did look a mess. Hopefully Annie would be able to work some sort of miracle this morning.

After but a moment, her maid scampered back into Lissy's chambers, a small bowl of cut cucumbers in her hand. "Do sit down, my lady," Annie said, gesturing to a chintz chair just a few feet away.

Dutifully, Lissy sat. She leaned back and closed her eyes. "I'd like my blue walking gown today too, Annie."

"Of course, ma'am. I pressed it yesterday." The first cool cucumber landed over Lissy's right eye. "Oh! Crawford says Lord Carraway sent a missive for you first thing this morning."

Lissy opened her left eye to look at her maid. "Tell him he can return it, unopened." Then she closed her eye once more.

"Unopened?" Annie asked as she placed a cucumber over Lissy's left eye.

"Mmm," Lissy returned. After the way Fin had behaved the night before, he could go hang. She wasn't about to dance to tear open his letter only to discover a fresh set of criticisms this morning.

Then again, it might be an apology…

Lissy nearly snorted at the thought. In all the years she'd known Phineas Granard, she couldn't recall him apologizing to anyone at anytime. Must be difficult being so blasted perfect all the time. Saint Fin.

"I don't think Crawford…" Annie began.

But Lissy cut her off, "Lord Carraway does not pay Crawford's wages." Juliet did, but that was beside the point. "And I don't particularly care what that starched viscount has to say this morning. So, please tell Crawford to return whatever pearls of wisdom Lord Carraway has thought to bestow upon me to the viscount. Unopened."

Besides, even if it was an apology, Fin should do so in person.

"Yes, of course, my lady."

Just as Fin stepped from his home on Charles Street, he spotted a footman in Prestwick livery hastening toward him. Monroe, if Fin wasn't mistaken.

"Good morning," Fin said with a nod.

Monroe's eyes dropped to the ground. "Sorry, my lord. I just meant to return this." He stretched his arm toward Fin, a letter clutched in his hand. The letter Fin had penned early that morning, by the looks of it.

Fin frowned. "My man delivered that this morning for Lady Felicity."

"Aye, sir." Monroe nodded, his eyes still on his boots. "She said to return it to you."

"Return it to me?" Fin grumbled, snatching the letter back from the servant. The damn thing hadn't even been opened. "She knew *I* sent it?" What a foolish thing to ask. Cleary, she knew he'd written it as she'd sent Monroe to return the blasted note.

The footman finally raised his gaze to meet Fin's eyes. "Aye, sir," he said, sounding most apologetic.

Fin crumpled the letter up in his hand and slid the envelope into his coat pocket. This sort of behavior was exactly why Lissy needed a keeper. Stubborn, petulant chit. Very well, Fin would just have to deliver his message in person and make certain she heard every last word. He nodded at the footman. "In that case, do tell her ladyship to expect me at Prestwick House this afternoon." Right after he met with Liverpool, he'd deal with Lissy.

Though Lissy was determined not to let Mr. Heaton, or who ever he was, interrupt her plans for the day, she couldn't help but scan Rotten Row for the American anyway. Just in case it truly had been him she'd spotted the night before. If it had been him, it would be best to see him before he saw her, after all. But as she'd expected, Mr. Heaton was nowhere in sight. He probably was a figment of her imagination. A play of the chandelier lights. Something.

Her friend, Lady Arabella Winslett, however, did seem as though *she* was bothered by something. The dark haired beauty continually bit her lip as she, herself, scanned Rotten Row as though looking for the devil himself. They couldn't possibly be looking for the same man, could they? What a foolish thought.

Lissy shook off her anxiety about Mr. Heaton and smiled at her friend, bumping Bella's shoulder with her own. "You seem a bit on edge. Is everything all right?"

Bella glanced over her shoulder as though to make certain neither of their maids, walking a few feet behind, could overhear their conversation. Then she threaded her arm through Lissy's and drew her closer as they walked.

"I need a husband!" Bella hissed urgently in her ear.

A husband! Lissy managed not to snort, but just barely. The last thing any intelligent girl needed was a husband. Until now, she'd always considered Bella an intelligent girl. "Why would you possibly want one of those horrid creatures?"

"Did you hear Lucinda Potts ran off to Gretna Green with Lord Brookfield?"

Who hadn't heard it? Considering Brookfield's blackened reputation, Lissy wasn't certain if the new Lady Brookfield would have been better off ruined than married to a man like him. Not that the girl in question had sought out Lissy's advice on the matter. "I certainly hope you're not considering something equally rash." For heaven's sake, who was Bella enamored with? Who did she want to elope with? For the life of her, Lissy couldn't come up with a name or a face. No one her friend had mentioned recently, in any event.

"I don't know that an anvil wedding is necessary," Bella added quietly. "A perfectly respectable wedding at St. George's will suffice. But I *need* a husband, or in the very least, a fiancé. And I need him quickly."

A memory of her own naïve exuberance at marrying a dashing American captain flashed in Lissy's mind, and her stomach turned. Naïve exuberance, indeed. She'd been a blasted fool. Lissy noticed a bench just a few feet away and stopped walking along the path. Then she glanced back over her shoulder at Annie and Bella's maid. "We're just going to sit a while."

She didn't wait for either servant to reply before pulling her friend toward the bench.

"Sitting isn't going to change my mind," Bella whispered only loud enough for Lissy to hear.

She shushed her friend and continued toward her destination. "Rushing into a marriage is the worst possible thing you could do, Bella. You can take that from me." She dropped onto the bench and tugged the brunette down beside her. "It's one thing to turn your life over to a man you love and trust, and quite another to do so with a man you barely know."

"I don't have a choice with the timing." Bella turned her gaze on Lissy, piercing her with her silvery grey eyes. "Besides, it'll be better with someone *I* choose rather than the awful man Grandpapa has in mind for me."

The Duke of Chatham was behind this insanity? Playing matchmaker hardly seemed like something the domineering duke would waste his valuable time doing. "Your grandfather?"

Bella nodded, her dark curls bobbing up and down, her brow etched with fear. "My cousin. Johann von Guttstadt, Count of Hellsburg." Then she shivered. "What a perfectly apt name that is, by the way. He is most definitely a horrid creature, as you say. And not one I want to spend the rest of my life with. So I have to find a husband quickly, before Hellsburg arrives in Town."

Rarely had Bella looked so serious and the fear she saw reflected in her friend's eyes was enough to alight Lissy's protective streak. "What about your father?" Certainly Lord

Aylesford wouldn't marry his daughter off to someone she despised, though Lissy's father had done that very thing years ago, with Georgie, hadn't he? She quickly pushed that thought away. Lord Aylesford wasn't like Lissy's father in the least; for one thing he was mild-mannered.

Bella shook her head. "Papa has never once defied Grandpapa. Not one time." She heaved a sigh, and her cheeks pinkened with panic. "So you see, I need someone to offer for me before Grandpapa declares an edict and it's too late."

What an awful predicament. Even if Bella got to choose her own husband, there was no guarantee what the man would be like after their vows were spoken. And a hasty marriage was the worst possible thing. Lissy heaved a sigh of her own. And then an idea hit her. She couldn't help but smile. "You just need someone to offer for you?"

Her friend nodded. "You look like you have an idea."

"Perhaps." Lissy shrugged. "Your cousin, this Hellsburg fellow, he isn't intent on staying in London, is he?"

Bella shook her head. "I believe he'll be returning to Prussia after he visits Grandpapa." Then she squeaked. "And I don't want to be *with* him when he leaves, Lissy."

"Or course not." Lissy's smile widened as her plan became a bit more solid in her mind. "So you don't really need a husband, just a fiancé. One you can break it off with after your cousin returns to the Continent."

The expression Bella cast her spoke more loudly than words what a ridiculous idea she found Lissy's suggestion. "Is that all? I just need a fellow who will willingly let me cry off?"

Which made all the sense in the world. There was no reason for Bella to look at her as though she was mad.

"I suppose any gentleman would gladly let me make a fool of him. Is that your idea?"

A fellow who didn't want to get married might be persuaded to help. "I'd offer up Edmund on a platter, but he's only twelve.

You don't think your grandfather would agree to that, do you? I mean, he *is* already a duke. That should count for something, shouldn't it?"

A shadow fell over the two of them, and Lissy tipped her head up to find Fin standing before them, blocking out the sun and sporting an annoyed expression on his handsome face. "What's this about Edmund?"

For the briefest of moments she was happy to see him, and then the memory of his behavior at the Astwicks' came rushing back to her mind. "Uncle Fin." Lissy's smile faded and she folded her arms across her middle. "What are you doing here?"

"Looking for you," he returned calmly. "And I'm not your uncle."

Blast him. He was always calm. He could criticize her, get her all wound up, and then just stand there, composed as could be, looking like the most well-behaved gentleman in existence. He was simply maddening. "You're looking for me?" She feigned a demure smile. "Come to apologize, have you?"

Fin's dark eyes narrowed on her. If he were a cruel sort of man, she'd have been intimidated by that scowl. But he wasn't cruel. He was Fin.

"Well, let's have it, then. My apology."

Fin's brow rose, as though he was surprised at her audacity. "Don't even think to distract me, Felicity. What are you offering up Edmund for?"

The problem with offering up her brother for Bella's ruse, she realized in that moment, was they'd have to go through Edmund's guardian – Fin, for any betrothal, fake or otherwise. And that was something she was certain Fin would never agree to. "Nothing that concerns you."

"On the contrary, anything that concerns Edmund concerns me."

Bella fidgeted on the bench beside Lissy, wringing her hands in her lap. "Honestly, it's nothing, Lord Carraway. We're just being silly."

"Silly, I believe." Fin's gaze never wavered from Lissy, which made her the slightest bit uncomfortable. All that scrutiny. "I sent you a note this morning."

"Did you?"

"You know I did. You had a footman return it. Unopened."

"Highly improper to send a girl who isn't your niece a note, my lord." She bit back a smile. "And I know how you regard propriety above all things." In fact, the oh-so-proper Fin was the perfect candidate to pose as Bella's fiancé, now that Lissy thought about it. Handsome, wealthy, powerful. Chatham couldn't possibly find fault with Fin. "Do you—"

"As your brother's guardian, I believe I'm granted some leeway in regard to my correspondence with you, my lady."

"Oh?" Lissy blinked up at him. "Has something happened with Edmund?"

Fin's eyes darted from Lissy to Bella and back again. "Might I have a word with you alone?"

He wouldn't leave until she gave it to him, that much was evident from his stance. There was nothing else for it. "Very well." Lissy heaved a sigh as she pushed off the bench. "I'll be back in a moment, Bella."

Fin offered his arm to Lissy, which she regarded with the warmth one might welcome an approaching asp. Begrudgingly, she took his arm anyway. It was, after all, the proper thing to do.

"What is it?" she grumbled once they were out of earshot from Bella. "Pray tell, Fin, what reprimand do you have prepared for me today? Let's get it over with, shall we?"

Four

Fin closed his hand over Lissy's fingers on his arm and directed her towards a copse of trees, not far away. Her delicate hand clutching the crook of his arm reminded him at once of the way Georgie had always held on to him, and that memory echoed though his soul, warming him from the inside out. Good God! What the devil was wrong with him? "You make it sound as though I'm forever reprimanding you."

"Because you forever are," she returned, not even bothering to look up at him.

A slight pain twisted Fin's heart. He didn't enjoy chastising her, but... Well, someone needed to rein her in, to keep her from destroying her own future. She'd received very little direction from her late father, and though Georgie had tried her best with Felicity, the flaxen haired imp had always possessed a stubborn streak and a mind of her own. A mind that he didn't understand the workings of in the least, and one he wasn't certain she used or heeded all the time. Lissy raced headfirst into one thing after another with very little, if any, thought to her actions. An impromptu trip across the Atlantic to visit her late mother's family, a hasty marriage to a man her sisters had never met nor approved of, and now cavorting with blackguards like Haversham. "I just want what's best for you," he said softly as he drew her to a stop and spun her to face him.

Lissy scoffed, but she did at least raise her cerulean gaze to meet his. "I am perfectly capable of taking care of myself, Phineas Granard."

That he wasn't so certain of. She might be a widow who'd seen more of the world than others of her age, but Lissy was still young and still rather flighty. "Perhaps," he agreed, just to appease her. "But all the same, it's not a good idea for you to be in London all alone."

"I'm not alone. I—"

"No, you're not." He squeezed her fingers. "You have me to look out for you."

"I don't need you to look out for me."

The one thing all three St. Claire women possessed was an unfortunate stubbornness they could have only inherited from their father. "Lissy," he pleaded, hoping she could see reason. "Be sensible. If Beckford and Juliet were in Town, I'm certain he'd see to your escort. Had things turned out differently, I'd be your brother, the same as he is. Besides, you're Edmund's sister. I just want to make certain you're safe."

Her pretty eyes softened, but just for a moment. "I am perfectly safe, Fin. I know you think I'm a ninny, but there's more to me than what you give me credit for."

"I don't think you're a ninny." Well, not all the time, though only a fool would say such words aloud. Fin shook his head, hoping to stress upon her the dangerous position she'd put herself in. "Did you even notice the way Haversham looked at you last night?"

Her brow furrowed. "Haversham again? Fin—"

"He looked at you as though you were a sweetmeat ready to be gobbled up."

"Is that supposed to be some sort of compliment? I hardly think I resemble a sweetmeat."

"Lissy!" Dear God, she could exasperate a saint. "While you're in Town alone, I'll be your escort. Period. Wherever you want to go, I don't care, and I won't hear any arguments to the contrary. Do you hear me?"

A mischievous smile settled on her lips. "That is so kind of you, Lord Carraway…"

There was a 'but' coming, he could feel it. She rarely called him Lord Carraway, and when she did there was always an impish tone to her voice.

"…But your services aren't needed."

"Felicity—"

"However, if you're so very anxious to play Sir Galahad," she continued without stopping to take a breath, "Lady Arabella is in definite need of a chivalrous gentleman."

"Lady Arabella?" He blinked at Lissy. The brunette chit she'd just been sitting with? His gaze flicked toward the lady in question. What the devil was Lissy up to now? They hadn't even been remotely discussing Lady Arabella.

"She's a delightful girl. Truly. You wouldn't really have to marry her, but if you could just ask her father for her hand, she'd greatly appreciate it."

If he could just ask her father for her hand? Fin's mouth fell open, and he redirected his attention back to Lissy. There was no way he'd heard her correctly. Even for her, that last statement was an outrageous thing to say. "I beg your pardon?"

"She'll cry off in the end," Lissy hastened to explain. "You'd only have to be betrothed until her Prussian cousin returns to the Continent."

Fin's head started to spin. He wasn't certain how to even reply to such a ridiculous suggestion. On occasion, Lissy made sense. This was not one of those occasions. "What in the world are you talking about?"

She gulped. "Bella doesn't want to marry her Prussian cousin, some hellish count, but her grandfather will force her to if she isn't already betrothed. *You* could pose as her fiancé. Not even the Duke of Chatham could find objection with you."

He wasn't sure if he should be flattered by that or outraged. His stomach, however, did plummet to his toes. "Did you tell that girl I'd ask for her hand?"

Lissy shook her head. "I hadn't thought of you yet. I thought Edmund—"

"Edmund!" he couldn't help but roar. "You thought to mix up your little brother in this madness?"

Her lip thrust out in a little pout that might have been endearing had he not been so thoroughly vexed. "It's not madness. It's inspired genius. I'd think you would know the difference."

What he knew was that Felicity Pierce could drive the sanest man mad. "You will not involve Edmund in any such scheme. And I will certainly not participate myself." Truly, Lady Arabella's plight was not Fin's concern in the least. He had his hands more than full trying to keep Lissy from ruining herself. He most definitely didn't need a fiancée, pretend or otherwise, demanding his time.

"Very well." Lissy tipped her nose in the air as she took a step away from him. "Then I'll just have to ask Lord Haversham to help."

Haversham! Fin reached for Lissy's arm to pull her back to him, but she backed away too quickly. He fell forward, and before he could right himself, he dropped to his hands and knees in front of half the park. A few gasps were heard, but Lissy's wasn't among them. She turned on her heel and stomped back towards her friend.

"Heavens, Lissy!" Bella touched a hand to her heart, her grey eyes wide. "Did you see Lord Carraway?"

Nearly fall on his face? Yes, Lissy had seen that spectacle out of the corner of her eye, but she wasn't about to give Fin the satisfaction of showing him any sort of a reaction. "Come along, Bella," she said reaching her hands out to her friend, still on the bench. "I think I know someone who will help us."

"You do?" Bella rose to her feet. "Who?"

"Cordie Clayworth," Lissy returned, threading her arm through Bella's. "She and her husband are fairly close to the Marquess of Haversham. And if there's a fellow who has no need for a wife, it's Haversham."

Bella looked aghast at the suggestion. "Haversham?"

Lissy shrugged. "I'd wager he could be convinced to help one way or another."

Bella shook her head as they started back towards their maids. "Even if he could be convinced, I doubt Papa would accept an offer from him."

Her friend probably had a point, but it was no matter. "Cordie has a calm head. She'll help us come up with something."

"I don't know," Bella hedged. "I don't really know Lady Clayworth very well."

Lissy grinned from ear to ear. "Well, luckily, I do. She's one of my dearest friends and she possesses a most devious mind."

"And you think she'll help me?"

Of that, Lissy was more than certain.

Fin heaved a sigh and dusted his hands on his knees as he watched Felicity and her friend make a direct path for the Park Lane entrance. How in the world was he supposed to make *her* see reason? He might as well have taken on the twelve labors of Hercules. After all, facing down a hydra had to be an easier task.

If she wasn't Georgie's sister, he'd wash his hands of her. If she wasn't Edmund's sister, he'd never give her another thought. If she... No, Fin shook his head. He couldn't lie to himself. Since the previous night, he'd been consumed by thoughts of Lissy, not because she was Georgie's sister, and not because she was Edmund's sister. Honestly, he wasn't certain why he couldn't shake her from his mind. Perhaps it was the panicked expression that had flashed across her face when he mentioned her late husband, an expression that reminded him of the one Georgie wore whenever her late husband was discussed. Perhaps it was because he'd always felt comfortable in Lissy's presence until now, which was odd, as he'd known her nearly all of her life. Perhaps it was just seeing her stare up at Haversham, depraved rake that he was. The last thing Lissy needed was to get entangled with Haversham.

"So nice to see you out of doors, my lord," came a melodic voice to his side. Fin pulled his attention from Lissy's departing form and smiled at Caroline, Viscountess Staveley, standing just a few feet away, her two daughters at her side. "I hope you had a delightful time at the Astwicks' last night."

And it was a good thing Caroline had talked Fin into attending that particular ball or he'd have never realized the danger Lissy was in. "My lady, it's always so nice to see you anywhere. Out of doors or otherwise."

Caroline nodded her head at the compliment. "You don't need to flatter me, Phineas. We might as well be family."

And they were family, in the most extended of ways. Caroline's brother, Lucas Beckford, was married to Edmund's sister, Juliet. But before that, before Luke's eyes had ever even fallen on Juliet, Caroline had been Georgie's oldest and dearest friend. "It's family I'm concerned about." He gestured toward the path Lissy had taken. "I don't know what to do with Felicity."

Caroline graced him with an ever-knowing grin. "You sound just like Georgie. If I had a farthing for every time she'd uttered those same words to me."

"She seems dead-set on landing herself in trouble."

Caroline agreed with a nod. "She was always the most adventurous of her sisters."

And she was. Georgie had been the steady, calm one, the one anyone went to if they needed an ear and solid advice. Juliet was the cynical one, the one who could size up a man within seconds of meeting him and put him perfectly in his place. And Felicity was the flighty one, the one who paid very little attention to anything around her, always consumed with her own ideas and very little else.

"But I'm sure she'll be fine, Fin," Caroline said, touching a hand to his arm. "She always is."

Fin snorted. "Because someone is usually around to yank her out of danger, but she's refusing to pay my council any heed these days."

"She's getting older," Caroline agreed. "It's natural she should come into her own, don't you think?"

Hardly. Fin shook his head. "You tell me, Caroline. Do you think she should involve the Marquess of Haversham in some featherbrained scheme of hers?"

All the color in Caroline's face faded away and a hand fluttered to her heart. "Haversham?"

"Exactly." Her reaction mirrored Fin's own thoughts on the matter.

"Mama?" Caroline's youngest daughter asked, tugging on the lady's skirts. "Who is Haversham?"

"A not very honorable fellow, Emma," Caroline replied, though her eyes stayed level on Fin.

"Indeed." Fin nodded. "I don't think letting Lissy come into her own is the best course at the moment."

"If *he* is involved," Caroline dropped her voice so low no one else in the vicinity could overhear her, "we can most certainly agree on that, Fin." Concern etched across her brow. "You should do whatever you can to direct her otherwise."

Which were Fin's thoughts exactly, though he had no idea how to accomplish such a feat. "Now if only divine inspiration would strike me."

Caroline heaved a sigh. "Let me think on it, and perhaps I'll come up with something."

Something was more than Fin had when he'd started out the day. Whenever Caroline Staveley set her mind on *something*, she always found a path that lead to success. "I'm certain Georgie would appreciate any help you can offer."

A sad smile lit Caroline's lips. "And I'm certain Georgie would be glad to know you're still keeping an eye on Lissy."

Which hadn't done him a bit of good. He might be better off keeping an eye on Haversham.

Five

Lissy beamed at the Clayworths' stoic butler as he opened the door. "Good afternoon, Higgins," she said brightly, pulling Bella along with her into the foyer. "Please inform Lady Clayworth that I'd like an audience."

"What if she's not here?" Bella whispered.

Lissy waited until Higgins shut the front door and started down the corridor to do her bidding before she turned her attention back to her friend. "She's always in. Ever since she became a mother, Cordie spends nearly every waking hour doting on her son." But mostly the countess had done so since her recent miscarriage, not that Lissy wanted to voice that last bit aloud.

"If she's always in, she might not be able to help," Bella said, her voice laced with panic. "Don't we need someone well connected? Someone—"

Lissy slid her arm around the other girl's shoulders to ease her fears. "Trust me, Bella. Cordie is better connected than either of us, and she'll know exactly what to do."

A moment later, Higgins returned to the foyer and gestured to a room right down the corridor. "Her ladyship is expecting you in the green parlor, Lady Felicity."

"Thank you, Higgins. You are a dear. " Lissy breezed past the butler, towing Bella along side her. As soon as they stepped over the threshold, Cordelia, the Countess of Clayworth rose from her spot on a brocade settee, tossed her dark tresses over one shoulder, and rushed to greet them.

"Lissy!" Cordie kissed her cheek. "What a surprise. What are you doing here?"

At once guilt washed over Lissy. She should have visited more often. Cordie was a dear friend, one of her dearest in the world. But ever since she'd lost her baby... Lissy pushed the thought from her mind before it had time to settle. "I'm so glad to find you in, Cordie." She gestured to Bella with a tilt of her head. "She needs your help."

"My help?" Cordie's green eyes flashed with surprise as she glanced from Lissy to Bella. "Lady Arabella, isn't it?"

Heat rushed to Lissy's face. "I am sorry." Where were her manners? Probably lying somewhere along Rotten Row, thanks to Phineas Granard. Blast him for flustering her. Starched stickler. "Bella Winslett, Cordie Clayworth."

"We met at Lady Eccleston's al fresco last season."

"Of course we did." Cordie smiled at Bella. "You wore a lilac spencer, and I remember thinking how adorable you looked in it."

"That is kind of you," Bella demurred.

Cordie gestured back to the settee she'd just abandoned. "Do have a seat, and tell me what sort of help you're in need of."

Bella followed Cordie to the settee, and Lissy dropped into a chintz chair across from them. "Tell her everything, Bella."

Bella gulped, nodded tentatively, then pressed on. "If I don't find a husband—"

"Fiancé," Lissy interrupted. "There's no reason to marry the man."

"Which man are we talking about?" Cordie asked, looking more confused by the second.

"Any man will do," Bella hastened to explain. "As long as he isn't my cousin."

"Her *horrid* cousin," Lissy threw in. She wasn't certain what made Hellsburg horrid, but if Bella thought he was, she must have good reason.

Bella nodded in agreement. "You see, my grandfather is quite adamant that I marry my Prussian cousin when he arrives in England." She snorted. "Says he has strong barbarian blood."

"There's something to recommend him," Lissy added, disliking Hellsburg more by the second.

Bella shrugged. "Grandpapa seems to think it's a noble trait. Johann certainly has the manners of a barbarian." A beleaguered sigh escaped her. "He has the coldest blue eyes. Looking at him makes me shiver. And he's impossibly mean. He barks and grumbles about nearly everything and..." Bella swiped at a tear. "Lady Clayworth, I'd rather convert to Catholicism and live the rest of my life out as a nun than marry my cousin."

"Well, I should hope it wouldn't come to that." Cordie smiled sympathetically and squeezed the girl's hand.

And Lissy took that break as the opening she needed to present her plan. "If Bella is betrothed before her cousin arrives, she won't have to marry her cousin."

Bella nodded quickly in agreement.

"All she needs is a borrowed fiancé, at least until her cousin returns to the continent."

"Borrowed?" Cordie's brow rose in surprise.

"Well, she may not want to keep him. I mean, what are the odds she'll find the love of her life in the next fortnight?" Lissy shook her head. "That would be as likely as finding a needle in a haystack. We'd be better off finding a gentleman who wouldn't mind being part of the ruse."

Cordie frowned a bit as though she was sorting something out in her mind. That could only be a good sign.

"So you see," Lissy continued, "I thought Lord Haversham might be convinced to be of service."

Cordie's frown transformed to a look of sheer horror in less than a second. "I hardly think he'd be a good candidate."

"But you and Clayworth are such good friends with him." And it wasn't as though the man was really in search of a wife. He wouldn't care one whit when Bella eventually cried off.

Cordie heaved a sigh and cast a rueful glance in Bella's direction. "I adore Lord Haversham. We both do. I owe him a debt I can never repay, but I'm certain Lady Araballa would like to leave this pretend betrothal with her reputation in tact."

To which Bella's eyes rounded in fear. "Most definitely."

"I'm certain Haversham could be convinced to help you, but he never helps without a cost, and I doubt you would want to pay his price."

Heavens! Even Lissy's face burned at the comment. Had Lord Haversham demanded some sort of payment from Cordie when he'd helped her a few years ago?

"No, I don't think I would," Bella finally breathed out.

Fine. Haversham was off the plate. "I thought about Edmund, but Fin refused to even listen to me."

"You talked to Lord Carraway about this?" Cordie laughed. "What were you thinking?"

"That he might, for once, not be so blasted stuffy," Lissy grumbled. "But, of course, he was. He doesn't know any other way to be."

Cordie quirked her a mischievous grin. "You're always so hard on him."

Someone needed to be. Saint Fin could do no wrong in anyone else's eyes. It was nothing short of maddening. "Not that it does either of us any good." Lissy shook her head as though to shake her annoyance with Fin from her thoughts. "But enough about him. We need to find a good candidate for Bella." She sighed. "If only Tristan wasn't already married."

A laugh escaped Cordie. "Yes, I don't think Phoebe would appreciate him taking a fiancée." Then her eyes lit with joy. "But I think I know the perfect man for the job."

"Who?" Bella asked, leaning closer to Cordie on the settee.

"A handsome fellow. Titled." The countess shrugged slightly. "He keeps mostly to his country estate, but he owes my husband a rather large debt."

"Who?" Lissy echoed Bella's question, as she couldn't imagine who in the world Cordie had in mind. If someone owed Clayworth a debt, why hadn't Lissy heard about it?

Cordie avoided Lissy's gaze, keeping her eyes on Bella. "Do you have aspirations for a love match?"

A blush stained Bella's cheeks. "Aren't such things fairy tales?"

Cordie's wasn't a fairy tale. The earl and countess' love match was something to envy, and Lissy's heart twisted a bit. How different her outlook on life would be if she'd met a man as loving, caring and devoted as Lord Clayworth. How different her life would be if Aaron had been who she thought he was.

"They don't have to be," Cordie said softly.

Bella shook her head. "I don't want to marry Johann. He's angry and unkind. Beyond that, if I end up married to a courteous man, that's all I require."

"I'll speak to the gentleman I have in mind then, and I'll report back."

"And he is?" Lissy pressed.

"I'd rather not say until I've had time to speak with him, but his name and reputation are in tact. Bella's family won't find issue with him, you can trust me on that."

Six

Haversham would have to make an appearance at some point. From what Fin understood, the marquess frequented White's as often as he frequented bawdy houses. Since Fin wasn't about to seek the man out in one of those locales, White's it would have to be.

The question plaguing Fin as he sat in one of the overstuffed chairs in the club, was what could he do or say to make the malevolent marquess swear off Lissy? After all, Haversham didn't have a care for his own reputation; he certainly wouldn't care about Lissy's. So what could Fin do in regards to the man? Threaten to call him out? Threaten to —

"I know that look," came a familiar voice, just a few feet away.

Fin turned his head to the right and smiled at his cousin, Sebastian Alder, the Earl of Peasemore. "What look is that?"

"The expression of complete frustration. Let me guess." A wicked glint flicked in Sebastian's eyes as he dropped into an overstuffed chair across from Fin. "Felicity Pierce is vexing you again?"

Fin couldn't help the chuckle that escaped him. "Hardly a lucky guess. When does the chit not vex me?"

Sebastian leaned forward in his seat, toward Fin. "Why don't you just bed the girl, and get it over with?"

Bed Lissy? Fin's mouth fell open. He could not have heard his cousin correctly. "I beg your pardon?"

"You heard me," Sebastian said, settling back in his chair. "When is the last time you bedded a chit?"

Fury coursed through Fin's veins. "In the first place, she's not some chit—"

"You're the one who just called her that."

That was beside the point. He was annoyed with Lissy; he hadn't intended to disparage her. "She's my nephew's sister."

"She's *Georgina Teynham's* sister," Sebastian added. "So I'm betting that's the real reason you haven't tossed up the girl's skirts yet. But Georgie wouldn't expect you to be a celibate the rest of your days, you know?"

Fin could hardly believe he was having this conversation. Of all the utterly ridiculous things for Sebastian to say. He'd never once thought about climbing into Lissy's bed or dragging her into his. He cared about her, was all. He didn't want to see her ruin her life or get hurt. That didn't mean he wanted to bed her. Just because Sebastian would have an ulterior motive in looking out for Lissy's best interests didn't mean Fin did. "She's a child."

Sebastian tipped back his laughed. Loudly. Then he wiped a tear from his eye, which was quite irritating of him, really. "Are you trying to convince me with that drivel or yourself?"

Drivel? Had Sebastian gone mad? Fin simply gaped at his cousin, at a complete loss for words.

"The *woman* has been widowed for three years, Fin. And one look at her *décolletage* makes it more than apparent that she's the furthest thing from a child."

Had Sebastian been ogling Lissy's bodice? Fin thought he might strangle his cousin before he took his next breath. "Stay away from her," he growled.

Sebastian laughed again. "Do you think I want the madness that swirls around her to encompass my life?" He shook his head. "But you, on the other hand, seem to thrive on it. So bed her and get it over with. It's the best advice you'll receive today."

"I will not *bed* her," Fin barked. "And I cannot believe you would suggest such a thing."

"You can't believe it? Shall I say it again?" Sebastian teased.

"Say it again and we'll be making a dawn appointment."

Sebastian's grin grew wider. "I just want you to find some happiness, cousin. Frustration doesn't look good on you."

"I am happy," Fin bit out.

"Oh, you sound it." Sebastian nodded toward a footman at the far end of the room. "Whisky." Then he turned his attention back to Fin. "At least think about it. You seem to have a taste for St. Claire women, and she does look like a tasty little morsel."

Before Fin could find the words to reply to his cousin, the Marquess of Haversham stepped into the club. It was about time the blasted man made an appearance. Haversham mumbled something to a footman and then started in the direction of the card room.

"Excuse me." Fin rose from his spot and started across the room to intercept the marquess before he escaped into the din.

"Fin!" Sebastian called after him, but he paid his cousin no notice. After the man's suggestion, he didn't deserve notice. Bed Lissy! Of all the awful thoughts to put into Fin's head. For God's sake, he couldn't even imagine kissing Lissy, let alone bedding her. She was like an errant little sister... Except she wasn't his sister.

A second later, he stood in the marquess' path. "Haversham," he greeted the blackguard with a nod. "I'd like a word with you."

"With me?" Haversham chuckled. "I'm the last fellow you

want supporting whatever act you want pushed through the Lords, Carraway. I haven't taken my seat for at least half a decade."

The last thing on Fin's mind was the treasury appropriations act. "Look here, Haversham, if Luke Beckford was here, he'd be having this conversation with you—"

The marquess' brow shot upwards, a bemused expression settled on his face. "Beckford is an old friend. I highly doubt he'd ever say to me whatever it is that's got you twisted up in a knot."

That was most likely true. Then again, if Beckford was in Town, Haversham might very well keep his distance from Lissy without being warned to do so. "I can't imagine that even Luke Beckford would want you spending time with Lady Felicity." And he wouldn't. Rogue that he'd been in the past, Beckford did seem concerned about his wife's little sister.

Smugness exuded from the marquess and Fin had the overwhelming desire to crash his fist into the man's jaw. What in the world was wrong with him? He was hardly the violent sort. Yet today he'd already threated to call Sebastian out and had the urge to punch Haversham in the face. Watching after Lissy was not conducive for one's health.

"Not that I have to explain myself to you, Carraway, but the lady and I were just talking last night. Nothing more. So you can turn your stiff arse around and get out of my way." Then he pushed Fin from his path and disappeared into the card room.

Fin stared after the marquess. Haversham might have just been talking to her last night, but Felicity was certain to approach the man with her mad scheme for Lady Arabella Winslett. And then what? She'd find herself a pariah, that's what. He started toward the card room himself, but a hand on his arm halted him.

He looked over his shoulder to find Sebastian standing there, shaking his head. "You're honorable. He's not. Don't start something you're sure to lose."

Fin scoffed. "I'm not about to let him ruin her good name."

"Then keep a closer eye on her, but don't engage *him*. Have you lost your good sense? He's not the sort of man you can reason with."

Reason had never entered Fin's thoughts. "I was trying to threaten him," he grumbled.

Sebastian shrugged just a bit. "If I didn't find your threat credible, neither will he. Besides, the last thing you want is to have your name splashed about the society pages as having been caught brawling with the likes of him. He never pays pointed attention to any particular lady, and he moves from one to another like a bumble bee pollinating a garden. He'll move on to the next flower in the blink of an eye. Just wait it out."

But he couldn't wait it out. That might have been an option if Lissy hadn't decided the villain would make the perfect candidate for her ridiculous scheme. Not that he could divulge that bit of information to Sebastian. He couldn't take the risk of putting Lissy or Lady Arabella in an unfavorable light. "I can't take that chance."

Fin shrugged out from his cousin's grasp and quickly entered the card room. Haversham sat at the far end of the room at a *vingt-et-un* table, a lit cheroot hanging from his mouth.

Fin took a deep breath and then stalked across the card room. He pushed Haversham's shoulder.

The man glanced up from his cards and scowled at Fin. "You are a nuisance, Carraway."

There were certainly worse things one could be called. "You have a daughter," he began.

"A fact of which I am most keenly aware," Haversham drawled.

"When she's of an age, you'll do your best to look out for her. I'm just doing the same."

"Except the lady in question isn't your daughter." Haversham's smug expression was more than grating. "Nor is she even a relation of yours."

"And yet I'm looking out for her anyway."

"And why is that?"

"Because someone has to," Fin replied.

"And Beckford's in Derbyshire."

"And Beckford's in Derbyshire," he agreed.

Haversham heaved a beleaguered sigh. "If you'll leave me alone so I can get back to my game, I'll promise to leave the lady alone."

"On your honor?"

Haversham chuckled. "I have no honor, but you'll have to take me at my word anyway as I have nothing else to offer."

That, Fin supposed was true, and likely the best offer he would get from the marquess. He nodded his head in acceptance. "In that case, I'll thank you and wish you good luck with your game."

An enigmatic expression crossed Haversham's face. "Very well, then I'll wish you good luck with yours. Whatever it might be."

Seven

Lissy pinched her cheeks as her reflection stared back at her, though she wasn't really seeing herself. Ever since she'd left Clayworth House, her mind had been a jumble. Which titled gentleman owed Lord Clayworth a debt? A debt large enough for Cordie to call in the fellow's vowels in order to help Bella? She said the man spent most of his time in the country. Who in the world could he be? Someone she knew, or…

A scratch sounded at her door and she automatically called, "Come."

"My lady," Annie said as she stepped into Lissy' chambers. "Crawford says Lord Carraway has arrived."

Fin! Hadn't she seen enough of him today? That was, of course, rhetorical. She'd seen enough of him in the previous twenty-four hours to last her a month, perhaps a year. "Please inform Crawford that I am not in at this hour."

Annie made a face. "He's not here to call on you, my lady. He's here to escort you to the Rotherbys'."

There were no less than half a dozen events that night. How in the world did Fin know she meant to attend the Rotherbys' soiree? She folded her arms across her middle. "That infernal man," she grumbled. Why was he so insistent on hounding her? She wasn't his ward. She wasn't his sister. She wasn't even his niece. No matter she'd known him nearly all her life, she wasn't anything to him. Not really. What she did and how she did it was none of his concern. "Please inform Crawford that I will be taking the Prestwick coach and that I am in no need of his lordship's escort."

Annie bobbed a quick curtsey, then slid back into the corridor.

Saying the words aloud had felt a bit liberating, but Lissy knew they were of no consequence. If Fin had come to Prestwick House, intent on escorting her to the Rotherby's, it wouldn't matter what she said. If she refused his carriage, he'd simply follow her there and watch after her anyway.

Heavens! Shouldn't he be focusing on some sort of legislation? Some sort of act? Some upcoming vote? She heaved a sigh and dropped onto the edge of her four-poster, waiting for Annie's inevitable return.

An intelligent woman wouldn't fight the unavoidable, but giving in to his will irritated her to no end. It was no wonder Georgie had refused him time and again... Well, up until she sent him a letter when he was in India, finally agreeing to marry him. Was it possible her sister had missed his overbearing ways after he'd left for Bombay?

Just like clockwork, a scratch came at her door. "Come," she called half-heartedly.

Annie stepped inside her chambers once more. "His lordship says that if you'd rather take the Prestwick Coach, he'll send his back home. "

"But he's escorting me, whether I like it or not."

Annie nodded, a pained expression on her face. "I am sorry,

Lady Felicity. Crawford tried his hardest to put his lordship off."

"But Lord Carraway is most determined. And stubborn."

Her maid nodded once more. "He is that, my lady."

Finally resigned to her fate, Lissy pushed away from the edge of the bed. "Then you'd better get your wrap, Annie. He'll insist you play chaperone." As though she could ever be in danger in Fin's staid presence. "I'll meet you downstairs."

~~✦❦✦~~

Fin paced Prestwick House's pink parlor. The room was an atrocity, something Juliet had designed years ago to thwart unwanted fortune hunters from calling on her. Why she'd never redecorated the room was a mystery. Not that Fin generally cared one way or the other about Juliet's decorating tastes, but this evening it gave him something to focus his frustrations on. Well, something other than Felicity.

All afternoon, thanks to his debauched cousin, he'd imagined pressing his lips to Lissy's. He'd wondered what it would feel like to pull her into his arms, have her lithe form pressed against his. And then he'd imagined more. How soft her skin was, the scent of her hair spread across him in his bed, the taste of her on his tongue, the gasp she would make and the look in her eyes as he thrust inside her.

Damn it all. It *had* been too long since he'd bedded a woman. Sebastian had been right about that. But how was Fin to know it would just take his cousin's flippant suggestion to start his imagination down a path he'd never traveled before?

He shouldn't even be here. He'd told himself it was to make certain Lissy was safe from the lecherous men of the *ton* and her own flighty ways. But who was going to keep her safe from him?

"Uncle Fin!" The waspish sound of her voice from the threshold made him stop mid-pace.

"I'm not your uncle," he repeated the words he'd said a million times over throughout the years. With all the thoughts darting in and out of his mind all day, thank God he wasn't her uncle. He was, apparently, depraved enough as it was. At least they didn't share any blood.

Fin turned on his heel to find her standing just inside the parlor, her slender arms folded across her middle, lifting her bodice and putting her charms on display. Damn it all, Sebastian had been right. Felicity was most definitely *not* a child. Her *décolletage* made him lick his lips, and would, no doubt be the cause of more than one sleepless night in Fin's future.

"Lissy." He cleared his throat, like a green lad might upon seeing his first pretty girl. Good God, he sounded like a dolt.

She heaved a sigh, looking more than a bit petulant. "What *are* you doing here?"

Hoping that she wouldn't be as radiant as she'd been in his daydreams, and failing miserably. "I—um—Well, I thought it would be nice to escort you to the Rotherbys'."

"Meaning you don't trust me not to get into trouble on my own."

Right now, he didn't trust himself.

"It's just a soiree, Fin."

Somewhere he found his voice. "You're the one forever telling me I should be more social."

She rolled her eyes, but her lips quirked up to a charming smile, the combination of which Fin found more than endearing. Dear God. His mouth went dry as he stared at her. Had she always been so lovely, right beneath his nose? If so, how the devil had he ever been so blind? Was it because he'd seen her so frequently over the years that he'd never noticed that she had, in fact, become a woman? A strikingly beautiful one at that?

Guilt and a bit of shame washed over him. Was he really lusting after *Lissy*? In the same home he and Georgie had made love? Damn it all, he was destined for hell.

"Fin?" Her voice was softer this time, laced with concern as she crossed the floor to stand before him. "Are you all right?" she asked, touching a hand to his cheek as though to determine if he was ill.

There was no need for her to check his temperature. He was nearly on fire, just standing there with her delicate hand on his face, her pretty blue eyes staring up at him. "I'm fine," he said, though he didn't shake her hand off, as he should.

"I think we should call for Doctor Watts." She frowned. "You don't look at all like yourself."

He didn't feel at all like himself, but the last thing he should do was make her aware of the fact. Fin stepped back from her and shook his head, hoping to find the bantering partner she so naturally was most days. "You don't think I'll fall for that, do you, Lissy?"

She blinked at him, looking completely bewildered. "Fall for what?"

He forced a smile to his face. "Trying to make me think I'm ill so I'll abandon you tonight. You'll have to do better than that."

Confusion flashed across Lissy's face, a frown settling on her brow, and Fin ached to take her hand in his and soothe away her worry. But that would be the worst possible thing he could do.

"Are you sure you're all right?" She stepped closer to him; her lilac scent swirled around him like a dream. "You don't seem like yourself either. Have you been imbibing?"

No, but that wasn't a bad suggestion. Perhaps a little whisky, or more than a little, would erase all the improper images Fin had floating about his head. He gestured to the doorway. "And you'll have to do better than *that*. Come along, your coach awaits, Felicity." There, perhaps thinking of her in a more formal way would help. Unlikely, but it was worth a shot.

"Very well," she said tentatively. "But if you start feeling strangely, I think we should call for the doctor."

Fin resisted the urge to snort. Feeling strangely, indeed. If he thought talking to old Doctor Watts would make him feel like himself again, he'd head straight for the man's home and plant himself on the front stoop 'til the doctor agreed to treat him. But there was nothing in Watts' black bag that would magically fix this problem.

He offered his arm to escort her and tried to ignore the warmth that coursed through his blood when she slid her arm around his. Lissy held him a little tighter than she had earlier in the day and his loins responded in kind. Hopefully, the short carriage ride would be long enough for his damned body to get itself back under control.

Eight

Something was most definitely wrong with Fin. Lissy stared up at him as they crossed the threshold into the Rotherby's drawing room. The entire carriage ride here he'd called her Felicity at every turn, and he'd shifted in his seat more than Edmund had on their last journey home to Derbyshire as though ants had taken up residence in his trousers.

Even Annie had noticed and cast Lissy more than one questioning glance along the way. All Lissy could do was shrug, however, as she had no idea what was wrong with the viscount. Perhaps some vote didn't have the support it needed to pass the Lords. Or perhaps he was anxious about some appointment. It could be anything, she supposed. After all, he very rarely spent time being social. Perhaps he just wasn't comfortable visiting one drawing room after another.

Across the room, Lissy spotted Mrs. Phoebe Avery and Olivia, the Duchess of Kelfield, standing near the grate, their auburn heads tipped together in deep conversation. Hmm... Her friends might have an idea about which gentleman owed Clayworth a debt. Phoebe and Cordie were sisters-in-law, and Olivia and Cordie had known each other since birth, after all. One or both of them might know the answer.

Lissy released her hold on Fin, but he snatched her hand back, holding on to it. "Oh, for heaven's sake, Fin! I'm just going to speak with Phoebe and Olivia." Then she yanked her hand back from him again and started across the floor toward her friends.

Upon seeing her, Phoebe frowned and reached out her hand to Lissy. "Why in the world did you run away from me last night?" she asked, concern shining in her blue eyes. "Didn't you hear me calling you?"

Mr. Heaton. The image of the man, whoever he was, from the previous night flashed once again in Lissy's mind and her stomach plummeted. Blast it all. She'd forgotten about him as soon as Bella had relayed her story about the Count of Hellsburg. "I—um—" She looked from Phoebe to Olivia and back. They were her friends. Two of her dearest friends, but she couldn't tell them the truth. They'd never understand. No one would. "Well, I didn't feel well, Phoeb. I am sorry."

The concern in Phoebe's eyes darkened a bit more. "But you're doing better now?"

Lissy's gaze darted around the drawing room. Mr. Heaton, or his double, was nowhere to be seen. So she smiled and nodded. "Much."

"Oh!" Olivia glanced toward the entrance. "Lord Carraway's here? That is a surprise. Don't know the last time I saw him."

Lissy's smile vanished. "He's decided I need a keeper, and he's been following me everywhere. Quite frustrating, actually."

"A keeper?" Olivia echoed.

"Uncle Fin?" Phoebe added, amusement now lining her voice.

Lissy rolled her eyes. "He's not my uncle."

"As I'm well aware," Phoebe replied, her amusement still in full force. "But you do delight in tormenting him with that moniker. Has he changed it around on you? If you insist like behaving like a wayward niece, then he'll be forced to behave like a concerned uncle? That sort of thing?"

There was probably more truth to that than Lissy would like to admit. She snorted in response, however. "I do not need a keeper, and most certainly not Phineas Granard."

"No?" Phoebe teased.

"He *is* handsome though," Olivia tossed in, unnecessarily, as though Fin's handsomeness was supposed to mean something.

"Who is handsome?" the Duke of Kelfield asked, appearing at his wife's back as though summoned there. Truthfully, the two were very rarely separated.

"Why my husband, of course." Olivia tipped her head to the side to better see the one-time dangerous duke.

A roguish grin settled on Kelfield's handsome face. "Flatterer."

Olivia giggled. "But I was speaking about Lord Carraway at the moment, Your Grace."

Kelfield shook his head. "Well, then I must be doing something wrong if *Carraway* has drawn your notice."

In an instant, Lissy's protective instinct nearly bubbled over in her chest. The scandalous Duke of Kelfield was the last fellow who should disparage Fin. "Well, his lordship is *quite* noticeable, Your Grace," she returned tartly.

She ignored the twin looks of surprise that Olivia and Phoebe exchanged. Just because she wouldn't let Kelfield mock Fin, didn't mean anything. They could save their meaningful glances for someone else.

"My apologies. I certainly didn't mean to offend, Lady Felicity," Kelfield said smoothly, his arm now draped across Olivia's shoulder.

Kelfield always meant to offend, it was part of his nature, part of his charm, if one asked Olivia. And while Lissy had once found

His Grace to be wildly attractive, that was a long time ago and she wasn't quite the same girl she'd been immediately after her return from Boston. In those early days, she would have gone down any road that made her forget what she'd just gone through. The more dangerous the man, the more scandalous the scheme, the better. But that dust had since settled and she had come more into the woman she was these days, a woman who truly didn't need a keeper. No matter how handsome Phineas Granard might or might not be.

Her eyes flashed across the room, landing on Fin, who was staring quite focusedly at her. Lissy narrowed her eyes on the viscount. Honestly, did he think she couldn't even be trusted to engage in a simple conversation with her friends?

"I saw Cordie today," Olivia said, drawing Lissy's attention back to her friends.

Lissy nodded. "I saw her as well."

Olivia smiled, her genuine sweetness twinkling in her hazel depths. "She told me. She was glad to see you."

Guilt washed over Lissy anew. "I should have visited before now. I'm a horrible friend."

Phoebe rolled her eyes. "You're a wonderful friend, and you know it. Where would I have been without your counsel?"

Olivia giggled. "Unhappily married to Russell Avery, instead of happily married to his brother?"

"Most likely." Phoebe shivered.

"Anyway," Olivia continued, "I am glad you saw her today. Whatever scheme the two of you are plotting has rejuvenated her spirits."

"You're plotting a scheme?" Phoebe's blue eyes focused on Lissy. "Do tell."

Lissy couldn't divulge the details about Bella's situation, not even to her dear friends. Everyone would need to believe Bella was truly betrothed to whomever Cordie had in mind. "It's not my scheme to reveal."

"Exactly what Cordie said," Olivia added. "And honestly, I don't care. I'm just glad to see the sparkle back in her eyes. So thank you for that."

Lissy breathed a slight sigh of relief. Even though she could have been a better friend to Cordie in the recent past, if her plan for Bella also helped Cordie get past a bit of her heartache, at least she'd done something good. She leaned a little closer to Olivia and Kelfield. "Have you ever heard talk of a gentleman who owes Clayworth a debt?"

"Which gentleman?" Olivia asked.

Lissy shook her head. "That's just it. I'm not sure who, if anyone. I thought you might have an idea."

"The man owes *me* a debt," Kelfield grumbled.

All eyes shot to the duke.

"Alex," Olivia warned under her breath. "That's not what she was asking."

What was all this about? Lissy looked from Olivia to her duke and back.

"She stayed with us some time ago when things were difficult for Clayworth," Olivia explained quietly. "Alex hasn't quite forgiven him for the turmoil Cordie went through during those days." Then she stood tall and said, "But everything has worked out, and there's no reason for any of us to hold a grudge."

"Of course not," her husband agreed, though he didn't sound as though he was in whole-hearted agreement.

<hr />

Damn the Duke of Kelfield straight to hell. Fin narrowed his eyes on the so-called reformed scapegrace. A man of his ilk could never be truly reformed, could he? Not that Fin thought Kelfield had designs on Lissy – by all accounts, the man was desperately in love with his own wife – but the duke was one of Haversham's closest friends. And that situation could not be considered good. If Lissy was engaging Kelfield's assistance with her little plan…

A hand clapped to Fin's back, and he turned his head to see the aged Earl of Rotherby at his side. "Evening, my boy."

"Good evening, sir."

The old man winced a bit. "I am glad you accepted our invitation tonight, Phineas. I was hoping to get the chance to talk with you in my study."

As the old earl had been a friend of Fin's late-father and a man he'd known most of his days, he could hardly refuse such a request. "Of course, sir." His eyes strayed back across the room to Lissy. If only she wasn't in Kelfield's company, he'd feel much better about escaping to Rotherby's study for a chat.

"Prestwick's pretty daughter will still be there when we get back," the old earl said with a chuckle.

Dear God. Was Fin truly that transparent? "I—Well, I'm just keeping an eye on her."

"Aye, I can see that." Rotherby gestured toward the entrance behind Fin. "But she's not going anywhere, and we won't be gone long." Then he hobbled, leaning heavily on his cane toward the corridor.

No, Lissy wasn't going anywhere; but that meant very little where she was concerned. She could get into quite a bit of trouble with just her words alone. He took one last glance back at the lady in question. She'd be all right for just the few minutes he'd be gone, wouldn't she? She would, or he'd have Kelfield's head.

As Rotherby was already disappearing from sight, Fin pushed through the crowd into the corridor to follow the old man. The earl turned right towards his study and then entered his private domain.

Fin followed suit, stepping over the threshold.

Rotherby cocked his head toward his sideboard. "If you want a drink, help yourself."

Though a bit of liquor might ease Fin's nerves, he rather thought he might need his wits about him, if he was truly to keep a watchful eye on Lissy that evening. "I'm fine, sir. Thank you."

"I wish I could say the same." Rotherby leaned his frail form against the edge of his desk.

"Sir?" Fin frowned at his father's old friend.

The man seemed to force a smile to his face. "I'm dying, Phineas."

The air whooshed out of Fin's lungs. He knew Rotherby wasn't in the best of health, but… "Dying?"

"And I haven't secured Eliza's future yet," Rotherby said quietly. "I had hoped my nephew might find her pleasing, that my passing wouldn't leave her vulnerable…"

"But?" Fin prodded when it seemed the old man wouldn't say anything else about his daughter, a young girl Fin had known all of her life.

"I haven't laid eyes on him in years, and no one has heard from Stephen in months." He heaved a sigh. "When he does return to England, I'll most likely be gone. I know I don't have a right to ask you, but…"

"What do you need, sir?" Fin asked. Whatever Rotherby needed, he'd do. The man had, after all, always been there for Fin.

"I just need to you to keep an eye on them. Make sure Helen is all right, that Eliza is taken care of. And when my nephew returns from wherever he's been, remind him that he'd promised to do his duty by Eliza."

What duty exactly? "Did he sign a marriage contract?" If so—

"I wish I could say yes to that." A sad laugh escaped Rotherby. "All I can hope for is that he is as honorable as his father was. And I'd like for you to ensure that he is."

Fin nodded, wishing he could do more. "Of course. What exactly did he promise to do, sir?"

"To marry her. My brother had just passed. We'd taken Stephen in. The boy was distraught at the time. Helen was past her childbearing years. I knew he was my heir, you see, and even then I needed to secure my daughter's future."

A sudden uneasiness washed over Fin. "He was a child?" Not much older than Edmund's current age if Fin remembered properly. Rotherby shouldn't have asked a parentless, grieving child such a thing. The boy probably thought the roof over his head was contingent upon his answer. Perhaps it had been.

"He was fourteen, hardly a child." Rotherby sighed. "We took him in, Fin, when he needed a home, and now I need him to do the same for Eliza. With the entailments to my estate, I don't have much choice in the matter."

Fin's uneasiness grew stronger. What an awful predicament.

"He'll get every last farthing." The earl wrung his hands. "If only she'd taken when she came out last year…"

But she had not. Eliza Ingram was a lanky bluestocking with skittish tendencies. She always had been. It was no wonder she hadn't taken. It was no wonder Rotherby had been concerned about her future when she was an odd child. Fin's brow furrowed as he said, "I'll make certain she is taken care of, my lord. Lady Rotherby too."

"Thank you, Phineas. You cannot know the weight you've lifted from my heart."

And placed squarely on Fin's shoulders. Oh, Fin was well aware of the weight. He nodded to the old man, said his farewell, and then made his way back to the drawing room. Music drifted down the corridor. Dancing must have begun in his absence.

As he stepped over the threshold, he scanned the room for Lissy. And there she was, in the middle of the floor waltzing with the Marquess of Haversham.

Fin's vision turned slightly red. Hadn't the man, that very day, promised to keep his distance from Lissy? Unscrupulous blackguard.

Nine

"Just what is it you couldn't say to me in front of my friends?" Lissy asked the disreputable Marquess of Haversham as he led her in a turn. She'd been more than surprised when the man showed up, once again uninvited, and swept her onto the dance floor.

Haversham's light blue eyes twinkled with mirth. "Carraway is like a rabid dog. I thought you should be aware."

Fin? "A rabid dog?" What a ridiculous thing to say. He could be priggishly annoying, but a rabid dog?

The marquess nodded. "Tracked me down at my club this afternoon to warn me away from you in no uncertain terms."

Lissy's mouth fell slightly open. What in the world had gotten into Fin?

"He was quite insistent. He refused to leave me to my play until I gave my word to keep my distance from you."

Lissy scoffed. "I see how well that turned out."

The marquess laughed. "One should never take the word of a scoundrel."

"Apparently," Lissy muttered softly, though her temper was rising. How dare Fin try to interfere in her life! The last fellow she wanted anything to do with was Lord Haverhsam, not that it was any of Fin's concern.

"But I thought you should know," he continued smoothly. "If someone was behaving that way in regards to *my* daughter someday, I would hope someone would tell her."

"And she's how old, your daughter?"

"Eight, I believe."

"You believe?" Lissy's brow lifted in judgment. No matter how uncaring her own father had been, Lissy was fairly certain the late Duke of Prestwick knew exactly how old his children were at any given time. Then again, one would have been foolish to question the old man about such things. Perhaps he hadn't had a clue and no one ever knew.

"Thereabouts. Somewhere between seven and nine."

"You might want to be certain before you see her next."

He chuckled. "I'll make certain to check my ledger before next I return to Yorkshire." His light blue eyes landed somewhere behind Lissy, and they twinkled with something akin to mirth. "And there's your shadow now," he drawled.

As they turned, Lissy glanced to where Haversham had indicated, and at once she spotted Fin. The overbearing saint. When she got her hands on him…

"Took me up on my advice, I see," the marquess interrupted her thoughts.

"I beg your pardon?" She drew her gaze from Fin back to Haversham.

"What did you do, Lady Felicity?" His wicked lips turned up to an all-knowing grin. "Did you smile a bit more, was that it?"

"What *are* you talking about?" She frowned. Honestly, did the man only talk in riddles?

"Well, you've done something to catch his notice. And now that you've got it, he doesn't seem inclined in the least to let go."

Lissy managed not to snort. Not that she needed to maintain a ladylike attitude around Haversham, but that was beside the point. "You are mistaken, my lord. I don't have his notice so much as his concern, his responsibility to my family."

"I hardly believe he sees you as an obligation."

"Then you don't know him very well, my lord. As though my sister was still alive, he seems to think that he's responsible for me, much the same way as a brother would."

Haversham smirked. "And I don't think you know him as well as you think you do, my lady."

The music came to a stop. The marquess released her and then offered her his arm. But before Lissy could accept or refuse him, Lord Haversham fell like a sack at her feet.

A gasp sounded across the room and in an instant, Lissy's gaze shot from the fallen marquess to the furious Phineas Granard, standing over the man, his hand still balled into a fist.

"Fin!" Lissy's hand fluttered to her lips. Heavens, he'd hit the marquess so fast, she hadn't even seen it. "Have you gone mad?"

But Fin paid her no attention, his eyes narrowed on Haversham at his feet. Through clenched teeth he growled, "You. Gave. Your. Word."

That was the outside of enough. Fin should never have spoken to Haversham about her as it was. She pushed Fin's arm until he lifted his gaze to her. "That is quite enough, my lord."

The intensity of Fin's dark eyes nearly scorched her soul. "Step away from him, Felicity."

⚜

Anger surged through Fin as he loomed over the Marquess of Haversham who, for some inexplicable reason, wore a blasted smirk.

"For God's sake, Marc," the Duke of Kelfield muttered under his breath.

Fin clenched his hand in a fist, but before he could do anything more, someone grabbed him from behind.

"Not here," a man said softly. Lieutenant Tristan Avery, if Fin wasn't mistaken.

But Fin wasn't finished with the malevolent marquess. "Let me go," he snapped, yanking his arm free of Avery's grasp. Haversham had given his word that very day to keep his distance from Lissy, and…

"I hate him as much as you do," Avery continued, "but this is hardly the place, Carraway."

The officer's words were like a splash of icy water, dousing a bit of Fin's fire. No, brawling in the middle of Lord Rotherby's drawing room wasn't the best idea. He glanced from Haversham's fallen form back to Lissy, who looked as furious as he'd ever seen her.

Let her be furious. Foolish chit. She was bound and determined to ruin herself and Lady Arabella right along with her. Someone had to save her from herself.

Lissy sucked in a breath, turned away from him, and then said to Avery's wife, "Phoebe, I would very much like to return home, but I didn't bring my carriage. Would you mind taking me?"

"Of course not," Mrs. Avery said softly, stepping closer to Lissy and sliding her arm around her friend's shoulders. "Come with me."

And before Fin could find the words, asking her not to go, asking for her to say something to him, she was gone.

The room was as still as a parish church at midnight. Fin glanced around the room to notice that everyone was staring at him. Well, of course they were. He'd downed one of London's most debauched blackguards right in the middle of a quaint soiree.

Haversham pushed back to his feet and dusted his hands on his trousers. "Not the first time I've been hit for dancing with a girl."

"Marc," Kelfield grumbled. "Please."

But the marquess paid his longtime compatriot no notice at all. He did flick his eyes towards the lieutenant however. "You could give Avery's mother a pointer on her upper cut."

"Do go somewhere else," Lieutenant Avery growled. "Don't you tire of making trouble everywhere you go?"

"We all have our talents, Avery." Haversham smirked. "Still, I should be going. A lady awaits me even now."

A *lady* wouldn't have a thing to do with the blackguard. Well, other than Lissy, which was more than unnerving. Determined not to give Haversham the satisfaction of any sort of reaction, Fin turned his back to the man and faced Lieutenant Avery instead.

"What in the world is wrong with the man?" Lissy complained as she settled beside Annie against the velvet squabs in the darkened Avery coach.

"I have never seen him like that," Phoebe agreed, which wasn't all that helpful. It was a vast understatement to say the least.

Lissy snorted in response. "Honestly, Phoeb, I think he may be losing his mind." And perhaps that was it. Perhaps Fin had finally lost all sense of reason and sanity. For heaven's sake, he'd actually *hit* the Marquess of Haversham in the middle of the Rotherbys' drawing room. Knocked the man to the floor!

The coach jostled forward, and Phoebe reached across the carriage and squeezed Lissy's hand. "Are you all right?"

She was shaken up. She was annoyed. She was beyond furious at Phineas Granard, but she was all right. "I'm fine, but what am I going to do about him? I can't have him trailing after me all season long, hovering over me, assaulting people. If Juliet was here, she'd —"

"What's changed?" Phoebe interrupted. "Why is he suddenly attending social gatherings now?"

Annie shrugged.

Lissy scoffed. "He's trying to protect me, as though I need it.

He thinks there's something between Lord Haversham and me, but—"

"Is there?" her friend asked.

Lissy's mouth fell open. Did Phoebe think so low of her? "Of course not! I know what sort of scoundrel he is."

"It's just unusual for Haversham to show up uninvited and—"

"Hardly unusual. He'd never go anywhere otherwise."

Phoebe sighed. "It *is* unusual for him to waltz with anyone, Lissy. He strode through the doors, spotted you, and swept you onto the floor without so much as a by your leave to anyone else, not even Kelfield."

Well, that was true, but inconsequential. Lissy shook her head. "He only came to tell me that Fin threatened him earlier in the day. He thought I should know."

"Threatened him?" Phoebe echoed as Annie sucked in a surprised breath.

True, it didn't sound like something Fin would do in the least. If he hadn't suddenly started behaving so strangely, Lissy would never have believed it, but… "What am I going to do, Phoeb? I've tried reasoning with him to no avail. I hardly recognize him anymore."

"You tried *reasoning* with him?" Phoebe's brow lifted in surprise.

"Yes." Lissy frowned. Just exactly what was her friend insinuating?

"I've seen you with him," Phoebe continued. "You thrust your chin out and demand to be treated like an adult."

"I *am* an adult." It was hardly an unreasonable thing to expect to be treated as one.

"Reason just isn't a word I would use in regards to your interactions. It's as though you're always trying to provoke him, to get him to acknowledge…something. I'm not even sure what. You poke him. You're argumentative. Stubborn."

Lissy blinked at her friend then turned her attention to Annie.

"Do you think that's true?"

With an uncomfortable expression, Annie shrugged.

"Don't put the poor girl on the spot." Phoebe sighed. "You know I love you, Lissy," she stressed. "I'm not trying to be unkind. I'm just pointing out that if you've approached him as you usually do, you might not be as reasonable as you think you are. Perhaps you should trying talking to him again, but without your back being up."

It appeared as though Lissy's maid was in agreement with Phoebe's assessment, but had the good sense not to say as much.

Lissy heaved a sigh. Perhaps she hadn't approached him as reasonably as she could have. But what did he expect? He wasn't her father or her brother. He had no say over her life. She didn't owe Phineas Granard anything. But...if he was going to shadow her all over London, she had to do something about the viscount.

"Perhaps," she finally muttered, not wanting to acknowledge that Phoebe might have a point.

Ten

"Thank you for offering to return me to my home," Lieutenant Avery said from across Fin's coach.

As though he could have done anything else. "Well, Felicity did abscond with your conveyance. Seemed the least I could do."

Even through the darkness, Fin could see the Army officer smirk. "You'll become a legend, you know?"

"A legend?" Fin echoed, thinking he must have misheard the man.

But the Lieutenant nodded quickly. "Do you know how many men have wanted to knock that bastard to the floor?" His smile widened. "I've been tempted to do so myself on more than one occasion. And though I'm fairly certain Clayworth once blackened the jackass' eye, there weren't any witnesses to the event."

Uneasiness washed over Fin. "I…Well, I shouldn't have done so. It was beyond the pale. He's a villain to be sure, but…"

"He had it coming. He's had it coming for years. If there's

something you want to pass through parliament, now would be the time, Carraway. I'm certain your celebrity could buy you any needed votes at the moment."

"Lucky only men can vote then, hmm?" Fin rubbed his brow. "Do you know, Avery, why women seem to find him charming? Harmless, even? It makes no sense to me."

"I have no idea." The lieutenant heaved a sigh. "One of life's great mysteries. My own sister, who is quite an intelligent woman, by the by, still has a soft spot for the blackguard." Then he snorted. "I think there are some women who find that sort of man a challenge. They know his reputation. They know he's dangerous, but they think that *they* can tame him, make him transform into a butterfly or some other such nonsense."

"They're fools," Fin grumbled.

"Indeed," Avery agreed. "Leopards and spots and all that. A man is who he is. No woman, no matter how wonderful, has the power to change the core of a man."

"Would you care to explain that to Felicity? Perhaps she'd listen to reason if I'm not the source."

The lieutenant shrugged. "I think she already knows that, Carraway, better than most women. The feeling I've always gotten from Lady Felicity is she doesn't trust *any* man, no matter his character."

Fin didn't think that was true. Lissy wasn't quite so cynical. On the contrary, if she trusted less, she'd find herself in fewer scrapes. "I think for the most part she trusts me."

"You're family," Avery replied. "You and Luke Beckford, she's different with the two of you. But the rest of the male of the species?" He shrugged once more. "Well, she keeps everyone else at arm's length. Has for as long as I've known her."

Lissy kept men at arm's length? If so, how had he never noticed? Fin scratched his head. It was true, Lissy hadn't seemed anxious to replace Pierce, but neither had he been so inclined to replace Georgie. He'd loved her too much to consider another woman.

"Phoebe says Lissy's marriage wasn't a happy one," Avery continued. "That probably explains her innate distrust."

An unhappy marriage? Fin had never heard Lissy utter one bad word against Captain Pierce. True, she rarely spoke of the man; but she *had* loved her husband, of that he was certain. Fin had seen the gushing letter she'd sent Georgie from Boston. Had she been unhappily married? He'd always just taken her at her word — that she simply didn't want to dwell on the past.

He'd never considered the possibility that she'd been unhappily married. It didn't even seen possible. She was always cheerful…Well, most of the time. She certainly wasn't happy with Fin at the moment.

"She told your wife she was unhappy in her marriage?"

"Not in so many words." The lieutenant shifted on his bench. "But she offered Phoebe sage advice when she needed it. Something along the lines of 'Short of death there's no escape from marrying the wrong man.' Something like that, anyway." He sighed. "Honestly, without Felicity, Phoebe might very well be unhappily married to my brother right now."

Short of death, there's no escape from marrying the wrong man? Fin's heart clenched. Dear God, Georgie might just as easily have muttered those words herself after her marriage to Teynham. The late marquess had treated his young bride abominably. And though Georgie's external bruises had healed, Fin wasn't certain her internal ones ever had. It was the reason she'd refused him over and over. Fear. He remembered how she'd trembled with fear the first time he'd kissed her.

Widowhood had freed Georgie from a terrible existence. It had taken years of him begging and pleading and showing her time and again that he wasn't like the old man before Georgie had finally agreed to marry him.

Was that what Lissy'd meant? Was this distrust of men from having witnessed Georgie's unhappy union, or had she experienced something awful herself? A pit formed in his stomach at the thought of anyone mistreating Lissy. The carefree, albeit flighty, creature had always been so trusting, so warm when she was younger. Was Avery right? Had someone taken that from her?

~c૯ЯԿ♪૨~

Marcus Gray, the Marquess of Haversham, tipped back his whisky glass, closed his eyes and let the raucous rumble of White's wash over him. So much more enjoyable than attending soirees.

Someone thumped him in the back of the head. Marc glanced over his shoulder to find his old friend Alexander Everett, the Duke of Kelfield, standing behind him.

"What the devil is wrong with you?" Alex asked as he navigated Marc's overstuffed leather chair and dropped into one of his own just a few feet away.

Marc quirked a grin at his old friend. "Where would you like for me to begin?"

"How about Felicity Pierce?" Alex's brow lifted expectantly. "Why don't you begin there?"

"What does it matter to you?" Marc took another sip of his whisky.

"She's a friend of Olivia's, one of her better ones, and at some point I'd like for my wife to actually tolerate you."

At that, Marc tossed back his head and laughed. He couldn't help it. The oh-so-prissy Duchess of Kelfield would never tolerate him. She'd made that more than clear over the years. "As though that was ever an actual possibility."

To his credit, Alex's lips upturned to a roguish smile. "Anything is possible, my friend."

"Just not probable, especially where a certain proper lady is concerned."

"Well, *Felicity Pierce* is a proper lady. And I know your aversion to the type. So what are you doing with the chit?" Alex pressed.

Marc shrugged. "Annoying Carraway."

At that, Alex shook his head. Then he rubbed his brow as though to stave off a headache. "And why are you poking Carraway, of all people?"

"Because the man is a sanctimonious prig. Is that reason enough?"

Alex shook his head once more. "No."

Of course Alex would want more than that. He'd become quite domesticated since his marriage. So Marc heaved a sigh and began to tell his friend the truth. "The jackass tracked me down...here." He gestured to the room at large, a place that should have been his sanctuary. "Of all the bloody places. A man ought to be able to enter his club to play cards without being set upon by bloody politicians."

"Better here than Madam Palmer's."

"If he'd tracked me down *there*, I'd have killed him where he stood." Marc scowled at his friend. "And then he had the gall to throw Callista at me."

"Callista?" Alex's eyes widened. "What did he say about your daughter?"

"Tried to use her existence to manipulate me. If some fool had done the same to you in regards to Poppy, you'd have made him pay a penance." Daughters were strictly off limits. Any dolt should know that, certainly one as politically savvy as Carraway.

"So that's what Rotherby's was about? Putting Carraway in his place?"

"I'm certainly not courting Lady Felicity, if that's what you're asking."

"Olivia will be relieved to hear it."

"Well, I'm so happy to set your wife's fears at rest."

Alex chuckled, looking almost like the rogue Marc had once wiled away many a night with. "I don't know that you'll ever do that, completely."

No, probably not. The prickly duchess *was* the cousin of a certain viscountess, after all. "How is Caroline?" he dared ask, but only because it was Alex and no one else was within earshot.

"Still happily married," his friend returned.

Though how she could be made no sense at all. "Staveley," Marc grumbled the man's name. "That humorless bore, he—"

"Is an old friend of mine," Alex finished. "I've known him longer than I've known you. So don't make me choose between my loyalties."

How Alex could stand to be bored by the man was a complete mystery. And then there was Caroline. It wasn't even possible Staveley took care of her as he ought. The man couldn't have a clue what to do with a lady like her. So vibrant, so delectable, so…

"Ah, Kelfield!" Simon Masters, the Earl of Thurlstone, interrupted Marc's thoughts as he ambled over to the pair. "Surprised to find you in Town this season."

Truly, it had been a while since Alex had braved London after the scandal his hasty marriage had caused. Though it wasn't terribly sporting of Thurlstone to say as much.

"Surprised they admitted *you* membership here." Marc lifted his whisky glass toward the disreputable earl in a mock toast.

Thurlstone lifted his own glass toward Marc. "Why not? They let you walk through the doors."

The earl did have him there. "Touché."

"Over here, Heaton!" Thurlstone called across the room, gesturing to some fellow Marc hadn't ever seen before. "American," the earl confided before his friend joined them. "Can't win at Hazard to save his life." Then he lifted his glass toward the American in greeting. "Do join us. John Heaton of Boston, this is Kelfield and Haversham." Then he chuckled to himself. "Actually, you're in very bad company, Heaton. Between the three of us, any scandal in London the last decade has had one or more of our names attached."

The American laughed as well. "Or very good company

depending on who you're asking."

Kelfield smirked. "I like him already."

"Might have been the source of a scandal or two myself back in Boston. In fact, one of my oldest compatriots is due in London within the week."

"We'll have to see what sort of trouble we can all get into together then," Thurlstone teased. "Well, except for Kelfield. His wife has him on the straight and narrow these days."

Kelfield settled back in his seat, a smug ducal expression upon his face. "I am quite happy with my path, gentlemen. And if you had a wife like mine, you'd be happy too."

If Marc had a wife like Olivia Kelfield, he'd never go home. A haughty harridan he could do without.

Eleven

Lissy flipped the pages of *La Belle Assemblée*, but she wasn't truly looking at the fashion plates, her mind was still awhirl about what to do with Fin. It was still difficult to believe that he'd actually hit the Marquess of Haversham, without so much as a warning.

Be reasonable, Phoebe's words echoed in her mind. But Lissy didn't know how to be reasonable with him. He was overbearing and controlling and most stubborn. Blast him! She shouldn't even have to try to figure out a plan to deal with him. He should simply just leave her in peace. He should simply trust her to make reasonable decisions of her own. He should...

"My lady." Crawford, her grey-haired and loyal butler, cleared his throat from the doorway, breaking Lissy from her musings.

She looked up from her periodical and nodded at the servant. "Yes, Crawford?"

The man stepped further into the pink parlor, a silver salver in his hand. "From Mr. Beckford, my lady." He presented the tray to her.

Luke? Lissy couldn't remember ever having received a letter from her brother-in-law. He was hardly the sort who penned letters. She snatched the note from the salver and broke the seal. Quickly, she scanned the contents.

Dearest Felicity,

I hate to interrupt your season, but I must beg you to return home at once. Juliet's delicate condition prevents her from writing to you herself.

She is in desperate need of your company. I am afraid this confinement has been more difficult than the last.

Please come home at your earliest convenience.

Lucas Beckford

Oh, good heavens! Lissy's heart twisted with pain. Was there a complication with Juliet's pregnancy? The memory of her own lost child, all the pain, agony and despair she'd suffered washed over her anew. She leapt from her seat. "Crawford, please have Annie pack my things."

"Is something amiss, Lady Felicity?" The old man's brow furrowed, and concern shone in his dark eyes.

She shrugged and started for the room, but she had nowhere to go, so she turned back around. "I hope not. Luke thinks Juliet would benefit from my company. Please have Donaldson ready the coach. I'd like to depart as soon as we are able."

"Depart for where?" came Fin's baritone voice from the threshold.

For a brief second, Lissy's heart stilled. Fin would make certain everything was all right. He always did. But then the memory of his unacceptable behavior from the previous night leapt to the forefront of her mind. "Who allowed you entrance?" she asked tartly.

"Monroe." Fin quirked her a smile. "As Crawford was busy attending you. Now what did you say? Where are you departing for?"

"I'm headed home to The Chase," she replied coolly. "Not that it's any of your concern."

"Oh." A look of relief flashed in his eyes, which only served to spark Lissy's ire once more. He needn't look so pleased about her imminent departure. Starched stickler, indeed.

"So you'll have to find some other lady to reprimand in my absence. Perhaps you could take up a daily regimen at Gentleman Jackson's so you can punch fellows whenever the whim should strike."

Fin turned his attention to Crawford. "Leave us, please."

"Of course, sir." The butler turned on his heel and strode back into the corridor.

Before Lissy could soundly reprimand *him* for dismissing her servant, Fin crossed the room and clutched her hands in his. "Sit, Lissy. You look like you might faint."

Did she? All she could do was stare up at him, unsure how to respond to that.

"Good God." He frowned, distorting his handsome features. "You're trembling." Fin dropped onto the nearby settee and tugged Lissy down beside him. "Tell me what's wrong. You're headed for The Chase. Is Juliet all right?"

"I-I don't know," she said, barely recognizing the scratchy sound of her own voice.

"Oh, sweetheart." Fin's dark eyes softened as he brushed a tear from Lissy's cheek.

Heavens, she was a ninny. She hadn't even known she was crying. "Sh-she has to be all right." And she did have to be all right. Edmund and Juliet were all Lissy had left in the world. The only people who truly mattered to her.

Fin drew her into his arms and held her, comforting her more than his words could have ever done. "Shh, Lissy. I'm right here."

He had always been right there. He'd always been a pillar of strength. He'd always made certain she was all right, that Edmund was all right. Her tears fell faster now, his jacket must be soaked through. "L-Luke said…"

"What did Luke say?" he asked, pulling back slightly from her. Fin's warm brown eyes soothed her, calming her from within, and she took a steadying breath.

Lissy pushed her brother-in-law's letter into Fin's hand. The viscount read the missive quickly then turned his attention back to Lissy.

"All he said was that this confinement has been more difficult than the last."

"I know," Lissy admitted, feeling a bit sheepish under his scrutiny. "But his tone was urgent, Fin. Jules must not be doing well at all, not if she couldn't even write her own letter." At that thought, panic seized her heart once more. "She can't even write her own letter! And if something happens to her…"

"Juliet is the strongest woman I know," Fin said softly. "She'll come through whatever this is."

"But the baby," Lissy began, then she bit her tongue to keep from telling him something she shouldn't tell anyone. She shook her head to keep from thinking of her own lost child and said instead, "Cordie miscarried a few months ago, you know. I don't want to think the same could happen to Juliet."

Fin tucked one of Lissy's curls behind her ear and said, "She's had one child successfully, I'm certain she'll be fine."

"Cordie has had a child as well, Fin. I don't think that necessarily guarantees success."

He took a long slow breath and squeezed her hand. "I hate to see you so upset, sweetheart. Why don't I escort you to Derbyshire?"

Somehow Lissy found herself nodding. She could use his strength, his even presence. But she didn't truly want to travel to Derbyshire with Fin, did she? Wasn't she still furious with him? He'd probably end up behaving like his usual controlling self, and she didn't want to suffer his condescension all the way to Prestwick Chase. "Well, I—"

"Very well." He kissed her brow. "We'll take my coach, if you don't mind. It's a bit faster, I think."

Faster *was* definitely a plus. Very well, she'd travel with Fin. Besides, his strength could be a blessing. Lissy nodded once more. "Speed would be best, all things considered."

"Then it's settled. We'll leave today."

Fin stepped over the threshold of his Charles Street home. He smiled at Ames, his butler, and requested the man have his carriage readied for travel, then he made his way to his study. Before they left for Derbyshire, he'd need to send the Prime Minister a note explaining his absence, and he'd need to send his regards to Caroline Staveley since he'd miss her soiree the following evening. But first, he'd need to get Lissy's panic-stricken expression out of his mind. But how to do that? The fear she wore this morning was worse than the fury she'd sported the night before, her beautiful face distorted with concern.

All night long, Lieutenant Avery's words had echoed in Fin's ears. Had Lissy truly been unhappily married? Was she truly distrustful of men? Well, aside from Beckford and himself? Had Captain Pierce harmed her somehow during the duration of their short marriage?

From the sideboard, Fin poured himself a generous glass of whisky.

Drink in hand, Fin dropped into the overstuffed leather chair behind his desk and took his first sip. The image of Georgie's tortured expression whenever the subject of Teynham arose flashed once more in his mind. Had Lissy endured a similar marriage? The mere thought of such a thing had him balling his hand into a fist.

For as long as he'd known Lissy, she was the sort who was forever giggling or dancing or enjoying some sort of merriment. Lighthearted. Carefree. Had the late Captain Pierce robbed her of that? And had Fin been blind to it all?

Seeing her so distressed this morning had torn at his heart. Just the suggestion that there could be complications with Juliet's pregnancy had been too much for Lissy. He'd never seen her look quite so distraught. He'd had the overwhelming urge to kiss her fears away and vow that all would be right with the world no matter what. And he had a feeling that were he to do so, were he to kiss Lissy, that he'd never want to stop, not for the remainder of his life.

Damn it all. He'd only ever felt that way about one woman in all of his life. And now he felt it again, though slightly different. Had he somehow fallen in love with Lissy? As the thought entered his mind, a bit of peace settled across him as though he'd arrived at the correct conclusion. That peace was swiftly followed by a wave of panic. God in heaven. He'd fallen in love with Felicity Pierce.

What the devil was he supposed to do about that? She was Georgie's sister, for God's sake.

A scratch sounded at his door, breaking him of his reverie. Fin glanced toward the sound, happy to focus on the interruption rather than on his plaguing thoughts. "Come," he called.

Ames pushed open the door. "Your coach is ready, sir."

Fin blinked at his butler. "Ready?" He'd barely had a chance to sit down, to try to put his thoughts in order. "So quickly?"

"Quickly?" Ames frowned a bit.

Fin realized in that moment that his study was bathed in a warmer light than it had been what seemed only moments ago, as though the sun had moved lower in the sky. "What time is it, Ames?"

"Just past three o'clock, milord."

Three o'clock? He'd left Prestwick House just before noon. What the devil was wrong with him? Fin looked down at the glass he still had clutched in his hand and realized he'd somehow downed the contents. Blast and damn! He still had those missives to write and he'd promised Lissy they'd leave today. "Thank you, Ames. I'll be ready to go shortly."

After he quickly penned a note to Lord Liverpool and was in the middle of his note to Lady Staveley, someone cleared his throat from the threshold. Fin glanced to the open doorway to find Sebastian lounged against the doorjamb, a self-satisfied expression on his cousin's face.

"Punched the man in the middle of Rotherby's drawing room, did you?"

Fin returned his attention to the note before him. "I'm headed out, Sebastian."

"Yes, Ames told me. Prestwick Chase, hmm?"

"What do you want?" Fin asked as he signed his name to Lady Staveley's note.

"Just to see how you're doing, cousin." Sebastian pushed away from the doorway and stepped further into the study. "Everyone is talking about you this morning. Well, you and Haversham."

"Let them talk." Fin looked up from his desk, spearing his cousin with a glare.

Sebastian chuckled as he dropped into a chair across from Fin's desk. "Shall I wager a guess? Was the marquess, by chance, chasing after Lady Felicity's skirts? And after you so nicely asked him not to?"

In truth, that was why he'd leveled Haversham, wasn't it? Not because the man had broken his tarnished word, but because he'd had his arms around Lissy. Fin's heart squeezed a bit. He'd thought he was being noble, but he'd been overcome with jealously, hadn't he? What a lowering thought.

Though, it didn't matter at this point. Fin and Lissy were headed to Derbyshire and by the time they returned, Haversham would have moved on to some other unsuspecting lady. At least Fin hoped that was the case. "It was on behalf of all of London's cuckolded gentlemen," he lied.

"So not because of Lady Felicity, then?" His cousin's brow lifted with mirth.

"Go to the devil, Sebastian." Damn it all. Was he so easy to see through?

"In good time, I'm sure." The jackanapes grinned. "And now you're headed to her family's estate? Probably easier to bed her there than with all of London's gossips watching you. Good thinking, cousin."

Fin clenched his teeth and ground out, "I am *not* bedding her." No matter how much he might want to. No matter how the suggestion would plague his every waking thought. Damn his cousin and his unsolicited suggestions.

Sebastian held up his hand as though in mock protest. "There's no reason to growl at me."

But while they were on the topic of the lady, perhaps Sebastian's insight could be helpful. Irritating as his cousin might be, at least the man was trustworthy. "Do you..." Fin heaved a sigh. Sebastian *was* trustworthy, but did he really want to give his cousin more ammunition in regards to the lady?

"Do I...?" Sebastian prodded.

Who else was he to ask? Sebastian *was* trustworthy. He'd poke fun at Fin, but at least he'd get a straight answer from the man. "Do you...Well, do you think Lady Felicity keeps men at arm's length?"

"Jealous of someone other than Haversham?" his cousin teased.

Fin narrowed his eyes on the man. "Stubble it and just answer the question, Sebastian. Lieutenant Avery said something to that affect, but I think I might be too close to her to see it."

Sebastian leaned back in his seat, frowning just a bit. "She has a cool air about her, but then she is Juliet Beckford's sister."

Cool. That was not a word Fin would have ever used to describe Lissy. Warm, vibrant, cheerful. But not cool. She was a spitfire, most days. "Just with men or with everyone?"

Sebastian's frown deepened as though he was in serious thought. "Men, mostly." Then he shook his head. "I suppose she could be so with so with women too, but I've never noticed it. I never really thought about it one way or the other before now, honestly. She does have a collection of friends, doesn't she?"

She did. She had many, many friends. Many *female* friends. Perhaps Avery had been on to something.

"What are you trying to sort out?" Sebastian asked, his oh-so-intelligent eyes focused on Fin.

"I'm not sure," he replied. And he wasn't, not really. But even if he was more certain, and no matter how trustworthy his cousin was, Fin wasn't all that anxious to divulge the inner workings of his thoughts to the man anyway. "Just interested in your take on things."

Sebastian's smirk was once again firmly in place as he chuckled. "She has you wrapped so neatly around her little finger. You don't even know it."

But Fin was beginning to suspect it, not that he would ever admit as much to his cousin. "For a man who spends little time around proper girls, you do have an opinion on most everything involving them."

His cousin shrugged. "Proper girls, improper ones. They all have the ability to tie a man up in knots. My suggestion is the same as it was yesterday."

Fin barely kept the growl from his voice as he said, "If you mutter those words again, Sebastian, I'll crash my fist into your jaw just like I did Haversham last night."

"There's no need for me to say it. You're thinking about it anyway, I can see it on your face." Sebastian lifted both hands in the air as though to surrender. "Do have a lovely time in Derbyshire."

Twelve

Lissy ambled down the steps of Prestwick House, her maid Annie quick on her heels. They were getting a later start than she'd hope for, but Fin's coach was now loaded down with her belongings, and she breathed slightly easier when the viscount rounded the carriage, stopping before her on the steps. He reached a hand out to her, and Lissy gladly accepted his assistance.

"You don't have to go with me, Fin. I'm certain I can manage on my own," she said because it was expected. But the truth was, the longer she'd thought about traveling with him to Derbyshire, the safer she felt.

Fin smiled that reassuring smile he'd always seemed to save for her. "I'm certain you can, but I'm happy to go all the same." He guided her to the door of his coach and opened it for her.

Lissy stepped inside the conveyance and claimed a spot on the forward facing bench. Annie followed her, taking the space opposite Lissy.

Fin glanced back at Crawford on the stoop and said, "We'll send word about her ladyship once we reach Prestwick Chase."

"Thank you, my lord," Crawford returned. "And please let Lady Juliet know we are all thinking about her."

Then Fin climbed inside the carriage and assumed the spot beside Lissy. He rested his arm on the back of the squabs, and she leaned against him, the same way she had when she'd learned of her father's passing all those years ago. Fin squeezed her shoulder and said, "Everything will be fine. I'll see to that, sweetheart."

And though he was the furthest thing from a doctor, Lissy believed him. Fin always did what he said. She nodded and then closed her eyes, wishing the trip to Derbyshire would take only a few moments instead of a few days. She breathed in Fin's sandalwood scent and steeled herself for the journey to come as his coach lurched forward.

Jonathan Heaton couldn't quite believe his eyes. It wasn't, after all, terribly often that one saw a ghost. He shook his head, trying to make sense of what his eyes had seen. If he'd been a betting man, he'd have wagered every last dollar he possessed that Mrs. Felicity Pierce had just climbed inside some fellow's carriage. But Mrs. Pierce was dead. Her body hadn't been discovered, of course, even after the hours and hours John had spent searching the bay; but it was inconceivable that she was alive. No one could have lost as much blood as Mrs. Pierce had done and survived her injuries. She'd left that despondent note and he'd searched the bay himself for her body until he couldn't see straight...

John's eyes flashed back towards the now disappearing coach. Perhaps the woman was Mrs. Pierce's sister or perhaps a cousin. The likeness between the two was simply uncanny. Of course, it had been three years or so since he'd laid eyes on Aaron's English wife. Perhaps the sunlight, so rare here in London the few days he'd been here, was playing tricks with his eyes. That could be the case. In fact, it was most likely the case. So very strange though. Seeing the woman, whoever she was, had made the hair on the back of his neck stand at attention and a shiver raced down his spine. Though ghosts, John supposed, had a way of doing that.

It was too bad Aaron wasn't in Town yet. He'd have put John's concerns at rest. He shook his head to clear his muddled thoughts. Truly, the woman couldn't be Felicity Pierce. She couldn't be. That simply wouldn't make any sense at all.

Fin was most certainly going to hell. While Lissy was snuggled against his side, worried for her sister, all he could think about was the softness of her breasts pressed against his arm. Thank God Annie was sitting across the coach from them. Her presence would keep him from doing something he shouldn't, something that couldn't be undone.

He glanced down at Lissy's blonde head, resting against his shoulder, and he sighed. She could be maddening at times, but her heart was always in the right place. She was a loyal friend to those lucky enough to call her such. She was a loving sister, even if she did come up with featherbrained schemes that involved fake betrothals of her twelve-year-old brother. And she was lovely, inside and out. Lovely? She was gorgeous, her image dancing about his mind day and night, tempting him like an ethereal seductress. She was vivacious, energetic, full of life. She was…perfect. Or she would be if she wasn't Lissy.

But she was Lissy. The Lissy he'd known all her life. Georgie's little sister. Georgie. What must she be thinking of this situation? He glanced upwards as though he could spot her peering down at him from the heavens, but all he saw was the top of the carriage. Would Georgie hate him if she knew the thoughts that plagued him? Or would she give him her blessing? Georgie, better than anyone, knew Fin would never hurt Lissy. And she did love her sister, had always wanted the best for her. But…Damn it all, disloyal thoughts such as these would certainly be reason enough for Georgie to curse him to the devil.

"Fin?" Lissy lifted her head to spear him with her azure gaze. "Are you all right?"

He blinked at her. "Beg your pardon?"

She shrugged slightly. "You just seem a bit...tortured. Is everything all right?"

Certainly, she couldn't hear his thoughts. "Of course. Of course. I'm simply woolgathering."

Her pretty pink lips tilted downward in a frown. "You must have things you've left undone to accompany me. I am sorry. I shouldn't have asked—"

Fin placed his finger over her lips, halting her from speaking another word. "You didn't ask, Lissy. I offered. And there's no where else in the world I'd rather be." Even if thoughts of her did plague him and even if her mere existence did tempt him beyond measure. He brushed his hand across her soft cheek and added, "So don't worry about me. All right?"

Her eyes fluttered shut at his caress as though she was starved for affection, and Fin's heart squeezed. Lieutenant Avery's words from the night before echoed once more in his ears. Lissy had endured an unhappy marriage. But had she endured more than just unhappiness? How he would love to know the answer to that question. Broaching the topic of Captain Pierce had never ended well for him, however. She was beyond evasive whenever his name arose. How would he ever find out the truth?

A soft snore sounded across the carriage, and Fin's gaze shot to Annie on the opposite bench. The maid's head rested against the side of the coach and she looked rather peaceful, sleeping so soundly. Damn her. Couldn't she be counted on to stay awake longer than five minutes?

Lissy giggled softly. "I should have warned you that Annie snores."

Some chaperone Annie was turning out to be...Then again, perhaps Fin might encourage Lissy to talk to him if her maid wasn't listening in. "Felicity," he began.

When Lissy's blue eyes stared up into his, Fin's mouth went slightly dry. Damn it all, it was almost as though she could stare straight into his soul. When had she started looking at him like that?

Fin shook his head, trying to regain his composure. "Lissy, I…"

"What is it, Fin?" she asked.

Tell me Captain Pierce treated you well, he wanted to say; but, "I saw Edmund," flew out of his mouth instead.

"You did?"

Well, he *had*. So Fin nodded. "A few weeks ago, I visited him at Eton."

"And?" she asked.

And nothing. It was just a usual visit. Fin generally saw his nephew every couple of weeks, ensuring the boy took his studies seriously, making certain he behaved in a ducal manner. But he had started this conversation. He had to say something, especially since she was frowning at him. "He was doing well," he finally said.

"Is that all?"

Fin nodded, as there really wasn't anything else to add. Edmund had been perfectly happy, after all.

"Glad to hear it," she said, though her frown deepened as though she was trying to sort him out. "You don't think Luke sent a note to Edmund, do you? I'd hate for him to worry. There's nothing he could do."

Perfect. Mentioning her brother had only made her think of her sister, which was the last thing Fin wanted to remind her of. He was a damned idiot. Well, there was one topic that wouldn't lead back to Juliet. "I—um—Well, I owe you an apology, Lissy."

At that her brow rose in surprise? "You?" she laughed softly. "Phineas Granard, I don't recall ever hearing you apologize to anyone. Pray tell, what are you apologizing for?"

Fin heaved a sigh. He did owe her an apology, he supposed,

even if he wasn't sorry for his actions. Under the same circumstances, he might very well do the same thing again, but she wouldn't want to hear that. So instead he said, "I shouldn't have punched Haversham last night."

"No, you shouldn't have," she agreed. "You made quite the fool of me. I'm certain I'm the talk of the Town this morning."

"He's a dangerous man, Lissy. I don't want to see you get hurt." And the man had given his word that very afternoon to stay away from her. Disingenuous blackguard. He deserved to be leveled again, honestly.

"And you don't think I can sort out a dangerous man from a benign one?"

After listening to Lieutenant Avery the night before, Fin wasn't certain what to think. "Can you?" he asked softly, wanting more than anything to know the answer to that question.

"I beg your pardon?" Her back straightened a bit, almost as though he'd affronted her.

But he pressed on, needing the truth once and for all. "I rarely see you interact with men, and that is my fault as I've stayed so far away from society. But it's true nonetheless. I don't know how well you can size up a man. I don't know the first thing about Captain Pierce, since you never speak of him. Was he a dangerous man, or a benign one, as you put it?"

A bit of panic flashed in her eyes, and at once she reminded him of a skittish mare. If they hadn't been inside a coach, he wouldn't have been surprised to see her bolt from him as fast as her legs would carry her. "I can't even imagine what would make you ask me such a thing," she evaded.

But it didn't matter what she said. He could see the truth in her haunted expression, it mirrored the one Georgie had worn all those years ago whenever Teynham's name was mentioned. Damn it all, how had Fin not noticed it earlier? Because he wasn't looking for it? Because he didn't want to know? Because he'd been too focused on his own heartache to notice much else? But he noticed it now and he would never forget it. "It's a very good thing he's dead," he muttered under his breath, balling his hand into a fist.

The quick intake of air from Lissy made it quite clear, however, that she'd heard him. "Fin!"

He grasped her hands in his and said, "Death has been kinder to him than I would ever be."

Lissy could only blink at Fin. Panic seized her heart and she tried desperately to calm it. Could he see through her? Did he know everything? No. No, he didn't...he couldn't know everything.

He *thought* Aaron was dead. He just said that very thing, hadn't he? There was nothing for her to worry about, not really. Fin didn't know anything. He just thought he did for some reason. Though why he should suddenly take an interest in such a thing made no sense at all.

"Phineas Granard," she finally said, "I have no idea what has gotten into you."

His dark eyes bore into hers, and for a moment, she thought it quite likely he did know everything. The intensity of his gaze, the anguish across his brow, the sincerity splashed across his face. "You know I would do anything for you, Lissy?"

He would try, she had no doubt. It was in his nature, his upstanding, honorable, honest nature. Fin would have made the perfect knight in shinning armor during an earlier age. Courtly and noble to a fault. But there was nothing he could do about her present situation. He couldn't dissolve her marriage. He couldn't erase the past or her poor decisions. So it was better just to leave things as they were. Sleeping dogs and all that. "I know," she said, because there was nothing else she could say.

He stared at her for the longest while, an enigmatic expression in his eyes that made something reverberate within her.

Tingles rippled across Lissy's skin and for the first time in her life she was quite jealous of Georgie. Staid, even, boring Georgie who never did anything wrong, who never did anything exciting, who never had any fun at all. But Georgie'd had *this* man's love, she still did, and that was more than Lissy could ever hope for. What would it be like to have an honest, kind, gentle man love her? What would it be like to have *Phineas Granard's* love and undying devotion? It must be the most wonderful thing in all the world, but she would never know that for certain. Her own foolishness, her own recklessness had decided her fate long ago. And there was nothing for it now. What was done was done.

Sadness gripped her, and Lissy turned away from the intensity of Fin's gaze. "If you don't mind," she said with more cheer in her voice then she felt, "I'd like to try and finish my novel." And she reached for the traveling valise at her feet, hoping Annie had packed a book for the journey.

"Of course," he replied, his voice so smooth it was almost a caress. "Whatever you want, Lissy."

But she could never have what it was she truly wanted. And she had no one to blame but herself. Her fingers touched a leather binding and she breathed a sigh of relief. At least she would have something to distract her from Fin.

Thirteen

After two days of traveling, focusing on the second volume of *Emma* was rather difficult. Probably because Lissy could relate to Emma Woodhouse's desire to see her friend Harriett properly situated, much in the same way Lissy had wanted to help Bella. Hopefully her friend was fairing well under Cordie's guidance. Emma could have used a Cordie. Of course, Lissy's opinions on marriage differed to that of Emma Woodhouse's. Marriage was not the answer to a woman's problems, sometimes it *was* the problem. None of that was neither here nor there, however, and not the true reason focusing on the book was more than difficult. Mainly, Lissy's distraction stemmed from the fact that the longer she sat beside Fin on this journey, the more she realized that he reminded her a bit of Mr. Knightley and the way he scolded Emma time and time again that reverberated though Lissy's soul. It was difficult trying to put Fin from her mind when Mr. Knightley embodied him so well. And having Fin at her side, while she read about Mr. Knightley, was a bit surreal, to be honest.

She cast him a sidelong glance to find him—

"Agh!" Lissy cried out as the carriage suddenly lurched in the air and then landed back on the road with a thud. The book flew from her grasp and she would have fallen from the bench, but Fin's hand caught her about the waist and tugged her onto his lap, holding her securely against him.

"Are you all right?" he rasped against her ear.

She thought she was and she nodded, but then the carriage listed forward and she nearly slid from his lap to the floor.

The carriage jerked to a stop. Across the coach, Annie woke with a scream; and from his box, the coachman cursed loudly.

"Good God," Fin complained. He squeezed Lissy's waist tightly in his hands. "Still good, sweetheart?"

She nodded once more.

"Good." Fin slid her from his lap and reached for the door. "Stay here," he said, as he pushed the door open and climbed out of the coach. "You all right, Chivers?" he called to his driver.

Annie patted the spot on the opposite bench beside her. "Easier to sit here, my lady."

That was probably true. She wouldn't have to struggle to stay upright next to Annie since the coach was listing to that side. Lissy slid forward on the coach floor and then settled onto the bench beside her maid.

At once, her heart clenched as she looked at her servant. "Annie," she whispered, "you're bleeding."

"I am?" The servant girl's eyes rounded in surprise.

Lissy nodded. "Your head," she said, riffling through her traveling valise at her feet for a handkerchief. Finding it quickly, she pressed the linen against Annie's temple. "You must have fallen against the wall when we hit that bump."

Annie held the handkerchief in place. "Are you all right, my lady?"

"Yes." She smiled reassuringly. "I'm just going to check on Lord Carraway." What if Fin needed help? He'd be too stubborn to ask for it.

"But," Annie began as Lissy reached for the coach door, "he said to stay here."

"Heaven's sake," Lissy returned. "We hit a root in the road or something. There isn't a band of highwaymen out there." At least she hoped not, but even if there were villains about, sitting inside a downed carriage was hardly the safest place to hide from such men.

She opened the door, crawled past her maid and stepped out onto the road. The pink and orange sky above cast a warm glow upon the outside world. Blast it all, it would be dark soon. And then the threat of highwaymen would be quite real.

On the side of the road, not far away, Fin's coachman rested against a tree, pain etched across his face and what looked like a bone sticking out of his calf. Heavens!

"We'll use this," Fin called to the man, tugging at his own cravat. She must have made some sort of sound, because he glanced back over his shoulder and frowned. "Didn't I tell you to stay put?"

Lissy shrugged, closing the distance between the lopsided carriage and injured driver. "And I believe I've told you on more than one occasion that I don't answer to you." She reached Fin's side, standing over the driver and frowned herself. The poor man's leg did look bad. Blood pooled on the ground beneath him. He was shaking just a bit, and his face was ghostly white. She glanced up at Fin at her side and said softly, "If you're trying to bind his leg, Fin, you'll need more than your cravat. But go ahead and press it to the wound to stop the bleeding. I'll get something better to wrap it up."

Fin gaped at her as though she was some sort of foreign species he'd never encountered before. "You shouldn't have to see this, Lissy."

Heavens. She'd seen worse than Chiver's leg before. She'd *suffered* worse than Chiver's leg before. She waved her hand in the air as she turned back to the coach and called, "Worry about him, not me." Then she opened the coach door and smiled at Annie. "Doing all right?"

Annie shrugged. "Is the coachman hurt?"

Lissy nodded. "Looks like he was thrown and broke his leg. Will you please hand me my valise?"

"Broken leg?" Annie winced as she slid the valise on the coach floor towards Lissy.

"Oh! Oh! Ohhhh!" Chivers cried out in pain.

Annie's eyes widened in horror. "And the coach is broken," she whispered loud enough for only Lissy to hear.

Lissy hadn't even thought about the coach, not after she'd seen Chiver's leg. She stepped back from the conveyance and damage was quite visible. "We'll need another wheel, it looks like." The she gestured to the copse of trees where Fin and his driver were located and said, "You might rather sit outside, Annie. It's going to be a long night."

Without waiting for her maid to answer, Lissy stepped away from the coach, placed her valise on the ground and opened it up, hoping for something that could be of some use. An apple, the third volume of Emma, a brush, some soap and her silk nightrail. The nightrail it would have to be.

"Fin!" she called. "Do you have a knife?"

Bent on the ground over his driver's leg, Fin turned his attention to Lissy. "Chivers keeps one in his box." Then he rose from his spot and crossed the road until he was standing beside her. "Your nightrail?" he asked softly.

"Have you any better ideas?" she asked.

He shook his head, his dark eyes boring into hers. "I'll get the knife." He quickly climbed up into the coachman's box and returned a moment later, brandishing the weapon.

Lissy took the blade from him and sliced across the hem of her nightrail. Then she began cutting the silk in a way to make it to one long strip. "We're going to have to walk for help, Fin. The wheel is broken, we can't drive it another inch."

He nodded in agreement. "Chivers said there was an inn about a mile and a half back. Once we wrap his leg, I'll start for it."

Lissy made quick work with her nightrail and when she was done, she knelt beside Chivers. "You'll be just fine," she assured him with a smile. Then she gently slid one end of the silk under his broken leg.

Fin watched Lissy in awe as she wrapped the driver's leg. She was gentle but thorough in her work. He would have never imagined she could be such a skilled nursemaid. He helped, of course, lifting Chivers' leg since the coachman was unable to do so, but all the while he couldn't keep his eyes off Lissy. She was amazing in every way, amazing in ways he hadn't even realized until now.

When she finished wrapping the driver's leg, Lissy glanced up at Fin, and he felt it all the way in the marrow of his bones. Damn it all, he was lost to her. He knew it in that instant as well as he knew his own name.

"Now we walk to the inn?" Lissy asked, dusting her hands on her traveling gown.

We. Fin heaved a sigh. Any girl with sense would stay safely put with her maid and the driver. Any girl with sense would realize walking a mile and a half in her kid slippers upon the bumpy road wasn't the best idea. And any girl with sense wouldn't spend the remaining light they did have arguing the point. But as he would be arguing with Lissy and wasting the remaining light they had, Fin decided against doing so.

He climbed back up into the coachman's box and retrieved the pair of pistols his driver kept there for safety.

"Pistols?" Lissy asked after he dropped back down to the road.

"No idea who inhabits these woods after dark." Fin then

returned to Chivers and Annie, offering one of the pistols to the pair. "Just in case," he said.

His coachman took the pistol and laid it across his lap. "I am sorry, my lord."

Sorry for hitting a hole that couldn't be avoided and for breaking his leg? It was Fin's fault for getting such a late start that first day. They'd been trying to make up time ever since. In fact, they probably should have stopped a few miles back while they still had good light instead of trying to make it to the Chase this evening. He shook his head. "Hardly your fault. Just stay together, and we'll be back as soon as we can with help."

He shoved the pistol he held beneath the waistband of his trousers, turned around to assess the road he was about to travel, but his eyes landed on Lissy instead. His heart pulsed a bit faster and he couldn't help but wonder about what a fool he'd been for so long. He lifted his hand out to her and said, "My lady."

Lissy smiled softy and then slid her arm around Fin's elbow. "This is hardly a walk down Rotten Row, you know?" she teased once they were out of earshot of their servants.

This was better than a walk down Rotten Row with hundreds of sets of eyes on them. This, in the waning light along the country road, was just the two of them. "Indeed, you always wear better walking shoes in Hyde Park," he said instead.

"Well, I like to be comfortable when traveling," Lissy giggled. "I'm surprised you didn't put up a fight about my shoes, about me coming with you."

"Would it have done any good?" He cast her a sidelong glance.

She shook her head, making her flaxen curls bounce about her delectable shoulders. "But that's never stopped you before."

"We didn't have time to argue, not with the light almost gone."

She nodded in agreement. "Always so reasonable, Fin."

Reasonable. He felt the very furthest thing from reasonable. Sebastian's assertions echoed in Fin's ears. His cousin seemed to believe that Fin thrived on the madness that swirled about Lissy.

A reasonable man wouldn't thrive on such things, would he? A reasonable man wouldn't fall in love with a woman who drove him half-mad all the time, would he?

So bed her and get it over with, his cousin had suggested. More than once, actually. Fin had hardly been able to think of anything else ever since hearing Sebastian's unsolicited advice all those many days ago. He'd lain awake each night along this journey, knowing *she* was in the room next door.

A reasonable man in Fin's position, walking along the darkened road to get assistance, would be thinking about how to go about getting their carriage wheel fixed, hoping the small village a mile back had a doctor who could attend Chivers' broken leg, wondering if the inn had enough rooms to accommodate them. "You gave up your nightrail," he said instead. "What will you sleep in tonight?"

Because that thought had flitted about his mind ever since she'd removed her silk nightrail from her valise. The idea of her lying in bed without a stitch on her would keep him up one more night.

She looked up at him as though he was half-mad. "I'll manage. Besides, poor Chivers needed it more urgently than I did."

"I hate to think of you being cold," he replied. All she had to do was stay in his room that night and he'd make sure she was warm. Fin gritted his teeth together, willing one inappropriate thought after another from his mind. What in damnation *had* come over him? He'd known her nearly all her life, but now...

"I'm certain they'll have blankets at—" Lissy stumbled forward and dropped to the ground. The hem of her traveling dress was up around her knees at the fall, and Fin couldn't help but be mesmerized. She did have pretty knees, and he'd wager her thighs and—

"Ack! Blasted stone," she complained, interrupting the most inappropriate of his musings.

"More like blasted foolish slippers, I'd wager," Fin said as he arched one brow at her, attempting to rein in his depraved thoughts. Then he sighed and lifted his hand down to her. "Are you all right?"

"Am I all right?" She snorted. "One would think a concerned gentleman would ask that question *before* mentioning my foolish slippers."

He couldn't help but laugh as he wiggled his fingers in her direction, urging her to take his assistance in finding her feet once more. "Come on, Lissy, let me help you."

She smiled sweetly, which should have been his first clue that something devious was going on in her mind, but that thought came a moment too late as she reached for his hand and tugged him down onto the ground beside her. "A shame you tumbled, Fin," she teased, turning towards him, giving him a rather nice view of her charms. "You might want to wear better *boots* next time."

"Or choose my traveling companions better." He brushed his thumb across her cheek as he couldn't help but touch her, not after he'd thought of little else with her pressed against his side in the coach for days, not after he'd thought of little else for quite some time.

Lissy's pretty blue eyes rounded in surprise at his caress. "Fin," she began, her voice a mere whisper.

Before she could say anything else, before she could protest and break the spell swirling around them, he cupped her jaw with his hand and pressed his lips to hers.

Fourteen

Dear God, kissing Lissy was better than Fin had imagined. Tingles rippled across his skin and a soft moan escaped her lips, the sound of which brought his cock to full attention.

Lissy's lips opened for him, the most delicious of invitations. Fin swept inside the haven of her mouth, touching his tongue to hers. She tasted like heaven, like the sweetest, purest heaven he'd ever experienced.

Kissing her seemed the most natural, most *right* thing he'd ever done in his life. But she began to tremble slightly, so Fin pulled her closer to him with his free arm, wanting to soothe her, to reassure her that everything was all right, that everything was exactly how it should be.

She clutched his jacket in her hands, pulling him even closer. She kissed him back, just as passionately as he was kissing her. And for the first time in what felt like a lifetime, Fin's heart lifted. "Dear God, Lissy," he rasped. Then he kissed his way across her jaw.

He would have kissed her neck and the tops of her creamy breasts, if the sound of an approaching carriage hadn't hit his ears. But as the sound *had* hit his ears, Fin pulled slightly back from Lissy to look down upon her.

Damn it all, was there a lovelier sight in the world? Fin didn't think so. With her pretty blue eyes gazing upon him and her slightly swollen lips begging him to kiss her again, Fin couldn't believe his amazing good fortune. "Someone's coming," he said, gesturing in the direction they'd been traveling. Then he gently brushed his thumb across her soft lips. "We'll continue this soon, sweetheart."

Soon? Lissy gulped, not certain at all what to say to him, not certain at all what had just happened between them, but she was certainly light-headed.

Fin pushed back to his feet and reached his hand down to help her. Still slightly in a daze, Lissy grasped his fingers, ignoring the warmth that filled her at his touch. She shouldn't feel warmth at his touch. He was *Fin*. Georgie's Fin. No matter that she'd urged him time and time again to get on with his life, she never imagined…

Fin's hand slid around her back and he grasped her waist, pulling her closer to him as though she belonged at his side. With his free hand, he waved at an approaching carriage. "Do stop, please!" he called.

The driver waved back and the coach slowed to a stop. Lissy didn't recognize the crest on the side of the door. The words *Creag an Turic* in an arc above a black lion wearing a golden crown, but it appeared quite the fancy traveling carriage.

"Ericht," Fin muttered under his breath. "Scoundrel. Hasn't taken up his seat in several years."

That was what made a man a scoundrel? Lissy scoffed as she glanced up at the very noble viscount beside her. The moniker

Saint Fin was hardly an exaggeration. She could never be as perfect as him, not if she made it her life's mission. Honestly, she doubted anyone could.

He must have interpreted her look correctly because he hastened to explain in *sotto voce*. "Spends every night in one gaming hell or another. More concerned with lining his own pockets than with the well-being of England."

In other words, Lord Ericht was like most men of Lissy's acquaintance, not that she said as much. Besides, she didn't have the time to do so as the carriage rambled to a stop before them.

"Hoping you can be of assistance," Fin called. "Our coach hit a hole up ahead. Threw my driver, broke our wheel. There's an inn not too far down the road, I understand."

The carriage door opened and the Earl of Ericht, strapping Highland Scot with black hair that he was, alighted from the coach. "Carraway?"

"We are lucky you happened upon us," Fin said. "I'm afraid Lady Felicity's slippers are hardly conducive to the walk."

Lissy squeaked in protest. What a thing for him to say!

"Ye hit a hole up ahead?" The Scot looked off in the distance. "It *is* getting dark." Then he poked his head back inside the coach. "Make room, Ellie."

"Thank you." Fin nodded.

"Of course, of course," Ericht replied. "It's too late for us to carry on any further anyway, especially if the road is as bad as ye say." Then he stepped aside and gestured for Lissy to enter his carriage. "My lady."

She started for the conveyance with Fin right on her heels, his hand on the small of her back. "Thank you, my lord." She ducked her head and climbed inside the coach. At once, she spotted Lady Elspeth MacLaren, the earl's pretty blonde sister, sitting on the backwards-facing bench. Lissy smiled at the Scottish girl, glad she was there. "Lady Elspeth, so kind of you to stop," she said, sliding onto the bench beside the blonde, relieved to have some distance from Fin, if only for a moment. But her mind was awhirl, and she needed time and little bit of space for her thoughts to unjumble themselves.

"Is the road terribly bad?" the Scottish girl asked, a bit of panic in her voice.

"It's a bit bumpy," Lissy replied. "With more light, I'm sure it's safe enough."

Lady Elspeth nodded quickly. "Just in a hurry to get home," she said as Fin climbed inside the coach and Lord Ericht called out instructions to his driver.

The look Fin cast Lissy as he dropped onto the opposite bench heated her skin, and she wished she had a fan on her person at the moment. Heavens, what had she gotten herself into now? She turned her attention back to Lady Elspeth and said, "I am too, in a hurry to get home, that is." And they'd been quite close in reaching that goal. Prestwick Chase was just a few hours away. They'd almost made it tonight.

"Juliet will be fine." Fin's voice washed over her and Lissy struggled not to shiver.

Good heavens, what was she going to do about him? Part of her wanted to throw her arms around his neck, hold him close and throw caution to the wind. That kiss, that soul-searing kiss had been like nothing she'd ever experienced before. And Fin was…Well, Saint Fin was the only truly perfect man she'd ever known. In another life perhaps…

Lissy tried to put those thoughts from her mind. She couldn't throw her arms around Fin's neck. She couldn't hold him close or throw caution to the wind. Doing so was reckless, to both him and to her. And she'd been quite reckless enough in her life.

Lord Ericht climbed inside the coach, settling on the bench beside Fin. "Lucky we happened upon ye, Carraway."

Lissy met Fin's gaze and the smile he bestowed upon her said better than words could ever have done that he'd have been quite happy if they hadn't been stumbled upon at all. "Lucky indeed," he agreed.

"Ian," Lady Elspeth began as the coach lurched into a turn, "we *have* to leave at morning's light. Promise me."

"Aye." Her brother sighed. "We'll get home as soon as we can, Ellie. But I'm not going to kill myself getting there."

Lady Elspeth sat back with a huff, folding her arms across her chest, silently shooting daggers in her brother's direction.

"Everything all right?" Fin asked.

Lord Ericht shrugged. "Everything's fine. She just hasn't been home in a very long time and recently realized she missed the place. Or something like that."

Lissy never missed home. If it hadn't been for Luke's summons, she wouldn't be headed there now. She might not ever go there again if she could avoid it. The halls of Prestwick Chase offered nothing but haunting memories and a lifetime of unfortunate events. "I hope you'll find your home in good spirits," she said because someone had to say something.

Lady Elspeth unfolded her arms, worrying her skirts between her fingers as though sitting still might be the death of her. "Thank ye."

Whatever was going on with the girl, it wasn't a sudden desire to see her home, no matter what the earl said. Had something happened to Lady Elspeth in London? Was she escaping something by fleeing back to Scotland? Normally, Lissy would ponder about the girl's obvious anxiety, her brother's cryptic comment. Normally, she would inquire about it even. But not now, not with Fin sitting across from her, not with his gaze still heating her skin, not with the memory of his kiss so fresh in her mind.

"We can leave the ladies at the inn," Lord Ericht said. "Then we can go back for yer driver and carriage."

"That's very kind of you," Fin replied. "We do appreciate it."

"Not a problem at all. Glad to be of assistance."

Lady Elspeth muttered something under her breath and Fin

and Lord Ericht exchanged more pleasantries; but Lissy couldn't focus on any of it. Her mind kept returning to Fin's kiss, the softness of his hand on her cheek and the warmth and strength of his body, pressed against hers. Oh, she was in trouble, and she didn't have a clue what to do about it.

When the coach finally came to a stop, Lissy was a bundle of nerves and she couldn't wait to escape the confines of the carriage and the swarming thoughts in her head. Lord Ericht opened the door and lifted his hand to Lissy, helping her alight from the coach, and Lady Elspeth was right behind her.

"We'll get our rooms and then head back for Carraway's coach," the Scotsman said to his sister.

Her back to the coach, Lissy stared up at the Tudor-era inn before them. She'd escaped the carriage, but her thoughts about Fin still plagued her. There would be no escaping that, probably not ever.

A warm hand squeezed her shoulder and she knew it was him. The gentle pressure of his grasp, the soft scent of sandalwood, the heat that shot straight to her core.

"Lissy." His voice rumbled and his warm breath against her neck made her shiver from want.

She closed her eyes. What a mess she'd made of her life. She'd like nothing better than throw her arms around his neck and beg him to kiss her once again, to make her feel as carefree as she'd felt in the middle of the road when it was just the two of them. But her life *was* a mess and she couldn't travel down that particular path, and certainly not with him. He deserved better.

Lissy stepped away from Fin, not able to look at him for fear that her resolve would melt away. "Please do hurry, Uncle Fin," she said. "Poor Annie is probably terrified." Then she started for the taproom entrance without so much as a glance back over her shoulder.

Fifteen

Uncle Fin. Why the devil had she called him that? To torture him? To vex him to no end? To put some distance between them? Fin was most concerned it was that last one. Damn it all, he didn't want there to be distance between them. The first time he'd felt right with the world in a very long time had been with her in his arms, alongside the road. He didn't want to go back to how things had been before. He wanted to pull her into his arms and make the world feel right once more. He wanted to kiss every inch of her skin. He wanted her in his bed, waiting for him. He wanted…

"…that interesting, am I?" Lord Ericht's voice broke Fin from his reverie.

He glanced up at the Scot across the carriage from him and said, "I beg your pardon."

"I don't think ye've heard one thing I said since we left the inn."

The man would be most certainly correct about that. "I—uh—

I'm…" He sighed. "I do apologize, Ericht. Just concerned about Lady Juliet's condition, is all," he lied. "I'm afraid I've been lost in my thoughts."

"And I'm the Loch Ericht Kelpie." The earl snorted. "It's none of my concern, Carraway. And ye can tell me to go hang, but that look ye're sporting, I'd wager my blunt that the reason for yer expression is that pretty blonde back at the inn with my sister."

The last person Fin was about to bare his soul for was the Earl of Ericht, gambling scoundrel that he was. "You *can* go hang," he said, though there was no heat in his voice. The Scot was, after all, helping him retrieve his coach, driver and Lissy's maid.

"Fair enough." Ericht laughed, a warm sound that made Fin feel the slightest bit guilty for his uncomplimentary thoughts about the man. "It's just that I've seen that very expression on the face my oldest friend this last month. And if ye're as tortured as he's been, then I'm quite sorry for ye."

Perhaps Fin had been harsh in his judgment about the earl. He shrugged a bit and said, "Tortured might be a slight exaggeration."

Ericht nodded. "Aye, my friend would say the same, I'm sure. God keep me from falling under whatever spell that bit the two of ye. I'm rather happy keeping my own hours and my own council."

A fortnight ago, Fin would have said the same. But that was before everything changed. Before his life stopped making sense. Before he truly saw Felicity Pierce for who she was, heart and soul. Before he realized she beckoned to him, that he loved her. Before that kiss…

Lissy. Lissy. Lissy.

Had Fin moved too quickly for her with that kiss? Was she truly as terrified of men as Lieutenant Avery had suggested? Or was he reading too much into her response back at the inn? Was she simply trying to vex him? Uncle Fin, indeed. If she ever called him that again…

The coach slowed to a stop and out the window, Fin spotted Annie and Chivers, the coachman's leg propped up atop one of Lissy's portmanteaus, sitting along the side of the darkened road. He'd focus on Lissy just as soon as he got back to the inn, but now he had other tasks that demanded his attention.

A knock sounded at Lissy's door and she frowned towards the threshold, wishing she could see through the dratted door. It couldn't be Fin on the other side, could it? The knock hadn't sounded quite as determined as his usually did. Then again her world had just been turned upside down. She might not be the best judge of usual things.

The knock came again, a little louder this time.

Blast it all. There was only one way to find out. "Yes?" she called from her spot in the middle of her rented bed.

"Ye *are* there." Lady Elspeth's voice filtered into the room. "I thought ye might like a bit of company."

The Scottish girl had thought most wrongly, not that Lissy could say as much. She'd have to play the role of pleasant host, even if it was the last thing she wanted to do. "Door's open," she called more brightly than she felt. Much more brightly.

A second later, Lady Elspeth poked her flaxen curled head inside Lissy's room. "I hope ye don't mind me barging in on ye. Being alone, I find I'm nearly climbing the walls."

"Not at all," Lissy lied, though she did pat a space on the bed beside her for the Scottish girl to join her.

Lady Elspeth hardly needed the invitation, however, as she dropped onto the bed, facing Lissy, a most anxious expression upon her face. "Have ye ever felt so incredibly helpless that ye didn't know what to do with yerself?"

The first few months of her marriage, Lissy felt nothing but helplessness, but she wasn't about to admit as much. "Are you all right?" she asked instead.

Lady Elspeth shook her head, making her blonde curls bounce

about her shoulders. "That's just it. I don't know. And I won't know, not until I reach Loch Ericht. And I can't get there any faster than we're going. I think I'll be half-mad by the time I do get home."

"What is the hurry?" Lissy couldn't help but ask, though she had a fairly good idea it had something to do with a gentleman. Lady Elspeth had that lovesick look about herself. A look Lissy desperately hoped she didn't sport herself. She'd have to examine herself in the mirror once the Scottish girl left to see if any telltale signs were obvious upon her countenance.

Lady Elspeth sighed. "I'm afraid I've been blind and kept in the dark about something rather important. And if I don't get home before he leaves for parts unknown..."

It *was* a he. Lissy'd been right about that, not that the fact made her terribly happy. One more naive girl, thinking the sun rose and set because of some man. "I'm sure all will be fine. If the gentleman is worth his salt..."

"He's worth everything," Lady Elspeth insisted. "He's prefect."

Perfect. No man was perfect. Well, no man other than Phineas Granard, but Lissy pushed that thought from her mind. "And does he think you're perfect, Lady Elspeth? I find that would be the true test of the man."

"Probably not." The Scottish girl frowned. "But I've bungled everything. Ian says a blind simpleton sees things more clearly than I do." She shook her head quite despondently. "And, in this, I'm afraid he might be right, which is rather frustrating, to be honest."

At that, a laugh escaped Lissy. "Oh, I know that feeling better than most. There was never anything more frustrating than when my sister Georgie was correct about something. The look she'd wear, always so filled with the most acute disappointment, was something to be avoided at all costs. No matter what."

Lady Elspeth laughed as well. "Fortunately, Ian's not right most of the time."

"Then you are more fortunate than me." Lissy squeezed the Scottish girl's hand. "My sister was always right about everything, which was quite maddening, let me assure you."

"I didn't know her." Lady Elspeth smiled sadly.

Lissy returned the gesture. "She was the most wonderful lady. I could try all of my days, but I would never match her grace or wisdom."

"I'm sure—" the Scottish girl began, but stopped when a firm knock sounded at the door.

That was a knock that had a familiar determination to it and Lissy gulped. She glanced towards the door. How she'd love to clamp her lips shut and not utter a sound, simply wait for Fin to tire of standing at her door; but with Lady Elspeth sitting just a few feet away, her eyes boring into Lissy, that was most definitely not an option.

"Yes?" she called, since she didn't have a choice.

"Lissy?" Fin's voice hit her ears. "Annie and Chivers are settling into their rooms and the innkeeper's sent for a doctor."

Lissy scrambled off the bed, Lady Elspeth quick on her heels. She opened the door and her gaze locked with Fin's. Heavens! The intensity of his brown eyes, focused on her, made Lissy's breath catch in her throat. Never in a million years had she ever imagined having Fin look at her like *that*.

Sixteen

"Well," Lady Elspeth said rather awkwardly, as no one else was saying anything. "I suppose I should find Ian. Do excuse me." Then she quickly brushed past the two of them, though neither Lissy nor Fin gave her the least bit of attention.

After a moment, Lissy cleared her throat. "I should check on Annie."

But Fin shook his head. "Annie's fine," he said, stepping over the threshold into the small room, which seemed quite a bit smaller now with him taking up most of the space with his large frame. "But we should talk." He kicked the door closed behind him.

Heavens! The last thing Lissy wanted to do was talk. What was there to say? Couldn't they just forget about everything? Pretend that kiss along the side of the road hadn't happened? "I don't think there's anything to say," she began.

But he gently cupped the side of her jaw before she could say

44

more. "Then let's not say anything." And a second later, he pressed his lips against hers. That delicious swirling feeling that encompassed her earlier that evening washed across her once more, and Lissy had to grasp the lapel of his jacket to keep from melting to the floor in a heap.

She knew she shouldn't kiss him back, but...Well, she couldn't help it. Kissing Fin, being held by him, was like nothing she'd ever experienced and wasn't likely to ever experience again.

Her tongue tangled with his, sending desire racing to her core. One of Fin's arms snaked around her back and secured her against the wall of his chest, and Lissy nearly sighed. She'd never felt so desired, so loved, so...safe. She was safe. She was always safe with Fin.

He growled slightly across her lips as his hand on her back drifted lower and lower. When he squeezed her bottom, Lissy gasped in surprise and she reared back just a bit.

Oh, they shouldn't be doing this. What were they thinking? "Fin," she began, trying to catch her breath and think clearly all at the same time, which was more than difficult.

His warm, passion-filled eyes peered down at her, and he shook his head. "Don't, Lissy. Whatever you're about to say, don't say it."

So she said nothing. She just blinked up at him, wondering what in the world had changed between them. Never in a million years would she have ever thought Phineas Granard, the starched and proper Viscount Carraway, would have inserted himself into her chambers and kissed her for all he was worth. Never in a million years would she have imagined that kissing him would shake her to her very core. And never in a million years would she have ever thought that she'd do just about anything for him to kiss her again, but they couldn't.

"You shouldn't be in here, Fin."

"I probably shouldn't," he agreed, smiling rakishly in return. Heavens! Who would have ever guessed that Fin knew how to smile that way? "And I shouldn't—" his fingers trailed from her jaw, down her neck, stopping right above her *décolletage* "—do this either." His hand slipped beneath her bodice and chemise until he held the weight of one of her breasts in his palm.

Lissy sucked in a breath. It felt so wonderful, his touch, like nothing she'd ever experienced before. She closed her eyes, trying to recompose her thoughts, trying to block out the sensation of Fin's gentle fingers caressing her flesh, hoping to—

"Or this." He rolled her straining nipple between his thumb and forefinger and every semblance of rational thought fled her mind.

Her eyes flew open. Fin pinched her just a little bit harder and she nearly leapt into his arms right there.

As though he was a master seducer, one confident brow lifted, silently challenging her to beg him to stop...or maybe to never stop, she wasn't certain which. With his free hand, he tugged the edge of her bodice lower until he freed both of her breasts from their confines. Then he caressed her most reverently as his gaze dropped to her exposed flesh. "So beautiful, Lissy," he said, his voice a mere whisper.

Then he dipped his head down and captured one peaked nipple in his mouth. Heavens, she had to grasp his shoulders to remain upright. Even still it was difficult. He suckled her so sweetly, his tongue flicking across her sensitive flesh, his teeth tugging ever so slightly, and Lissy wasn't certain how long she could stand there before her weak knees buckled beneath her.

He moaned against her skin and Lissy clutched his shoulders even tighter, willing herself not to fall. Fin must have noticed because he slowly released her nipple from his lips and rose back to his full height before scooping her up in his arms and carrying her the very short distance to her bed.

He deposited her in the middle of the bed and began pulling at his cravat until the knot came undone and he let the silk flutter to the floor somewhere behind him. Lissy couldn't move. She could only stare up at him as he ripped his jacket and waistcoat off, then yanked his shirt over his head.

She gulped at the sight of a half-naked Fin. Heavens, he was a sight. All muscled and handsome with a light smattering of dark hair across his chest. At once, however, terror reached up and grasped her heart. She'd once thought Aaron to be quite the Adonis, though not after their wedding night and never again.

She tried to shake the terrible memories of that first night from her mind. Fin wasn't like Aaron in the least. He'd already taken much more care with her than Aaron ever had.

"Are you all right?" he asked softly, and Lissy almost burst into tears.

Was she all right? She had no idea how to answer that, not with the awful memories swirling about her mind, not with the sudden confusion about her feelings for Fin.

"Lissy." He dropped onto the bed beside her. "I want you most desperately, but—" his warm, brown eyes locked with hers "—are you all right?"

And with those words, she knew she'd be all right with him. Though, honestly, she'd known that before he'd spoken. But his words were just what she needed to hear, a reassurance that he cared for her, that her well-being was important to him.

Her heart expanded in her chest and she nodded quickly. "I'm all right."

A relived smile spread across his face, then he pressed her back against the pillows and settled right beside her. Fin kissed her once more, kneading her breast with one hand and sending frissons of desire and anticipation racing to her core.

Dear God, she was so soft to the touch, softer than he'd imagined. He could kiss her, run his hands over her naked flesh all day, and never tire of it. But right now, with his cock straining against his trousers, what he wanted more than anything in the world, was to sink into her, to become one with her for now and always.

He deepened his kiss, relishing in the slight mew that escaped her. He moved his hand to her belly and began tugging her dress northward until the hem reached his fingers. Then he smoothed his hand across the tie of her drawers. So close. He was so close to having everything he wanted.

Fin slid his fingers beneath her drawers and through her springy curls, and then…Then he found her slickness and the urgency to have her heightened even more. He growled across her lips and tweaked her little nub, which made her jerk away from him.

Lissy's pretty blue eyes rounded in surprise. "What did you do?" she said as she tried to catch her breath.

What had he done? Fin brushed his fingers across her nub once more, eliciting a very wanton moan from her. "This?" he asked.

She nodded quickly.

Dear God, had her husband never caressed her there? Fin pushed the thought away as quickly as it entered his mind. This night was about them, not anyone else. "Here," he said. "Give me your hand."

Tentatively, she offered her hand to him.

Fin shook his head. "Down where my hand is, sweetheart." He encircled her nub with his finger. "Right here."

"Oh," she said with a shaky voice. Then she slid her hand inside her drawers and speared him with the most innocent of gazes.

"There." Fin took her hand in his and guided her fingers across her most sensitive flesh. "Just like that, Lissy. Just keeping doing that." He watched her for a moment, the expressions of surprise and desire play across her face at her own touch. She seemed so innocent all of a sudden, not at all practiced in the art of lovemaking.

It had been quite some time for Fin, but it seemed like…Well, it seemed like Lissy's first time. But it couldn't be. She was a widow, there was no possible way she was a virgin, was there? It wasn't something he could ask, not without spoiling the mood, which was the very last thing in the world that he wanted. There would be time for answers later. Right now, he wanted her. He wanted her more than he may have ever wanted anything in his life.

To that end, Fin quickly retrieved his hand from under her drawers and made quick work with the ribbon at her waist. "Take these off," he said, as he sat up and yanked the boots from his feet, letting them fall to the floor with a thud.

Her eyes on him, Lissy did as he bade, first tossing her dress aside and then sliding her drawers down her slender legs until she was bared completely for him. Dear God, she was a pretty sight, all pink and glistening and welcoming and…

Fin worked the buttons on his trousers, freeing his straining cock. Then he pushed to his knees and settled in the space between her thighs. "My sweetest Felicity," he said as he leaned forward, pressing the tip of him at her entrance. "You do drive me to brink of madness."

"Just to the brink?" She smiled rather cheekily, much more like she usually did. "I'll have to do better."

"You do just fine." He smiled in return. Then he thrust forward, sheathing himself completely in her warm wetness.

A pleasured moan escaped her as her eyes fluttered closed. Fin couldn't help but stare at the beauty of her, right before him. A prettier sight he'd never seen.

He leaned over her, his weight pressing her further into the feather mattress beneath them, and her arms settled around his neck. Fin kissed her, then. Softly, slowly, reveling in her gasps and the taste of her sweetness.

He pulled slightly from her and then slowly filled her once more. The tips of her nipples pressed against his chest and the sensation rippled across him, nearly unmanning him right then. But he wasn't through with her yet. It seemed as though he'd been waiting for her forever and he wanted to enjoy every second of her in his arms.

❦

Lissy was in heaven. Pure heaven, not that she could form coherent thoughts, not with Fin atop her, inside her, filling her so fully; but it was heaven none-the-less. She had no idea sharing a man's bed could be so…wonderful, so liberating.

Fin retreated slightly and then filled her again, finding a nice slow rhythm that heightened every nerve in her body.

His kiss deepened and she held him tighter, loving the weight of him pressed against her. He groaned against her lips and his thrusts became a little faster, a bit more urgent.

Something began to build, deep in her belly, a need. A need she'd never felt before, almost as though she was about to reach the tip of the highest mountain and…

Fin thrust harder, faster as though he too was a reaching for that same point and then…

"Fin!" she cried out, as the most pleasurable release washed over her. Wave after joyous wave.

He growled low, pressing himself more urgently inside her until he too cried out in ecstasy. He buried his face beside her neck, kissing her oh-so-gently. "Dear God, I love you, Lissy."

He loved her? A flood of hopes and dreams rushed to her mind but were instantly pushed away as the truth and unpleasant memories washed over Lissy. He couldn't love her. He *shouldn't* love her.

Heavens, what had she done?

Fin rolled to the spot beside her and cradled her against his chest, his strong arm draped across her back, his gentle fingers caressing her skin.

Lissy blinked back tears, refusing to cry. Crying wouldn't do her any good. Crying would do *him* any good. It was a useless, worthless activity. Even so, a few traitorous tears spilled against his chest anyway. Luckily, he seemed too lost in his own bliss to notice the dampness.

Blast it all! What in the world had she done?

She'd made love to Phineas Granard, that was what. The sweetest, most tender love she'd ever experienced. But she shouldn't have done so. It wasn't fair to him. It wasn't fair to her. How could she go on alone the rest of her life and know that such passion existed? She'd be tortured the rest of her days.

"I told Ericht that we'd dine with his sister and him this evening," Fin said rather groggily, completely unaware of her inner turmoil.

Heavens. Now she had to look Lord Ericht and his sister in the face? "Why did you do that?" she complained.

A laugh escaped him. "Because at the time I had no idea that I'd find myself in your bed or that I'd never have the desire to leave it."

She didn't want to leave it either. Right now, the consequences of her actions weren't staring her in the face. They would very soon, but not now, not while she was still in his arms and her body still hummed from the passion they'd shared. "Can't we send our regards?" And just spend a moment or two more in a make-believe world where they could live happily ever after together?

"We can do whatever you want, Lissy." He yawned. "But I think our absence would seem curious."

He was right about that. It would be best to have dinner with Lord Ericht and Lady Elspeth. Hopefully the pair wouldn't have a clue about what had transpired between Fin and Lissy. But if they didn't go to dinner, the two might very well speculate as to the why. Lady Elspeth had, after all, seen the way Fin had looked at Lissy. It wouldn't take a genius to put two and two together.

"I suppose we should go then," she agreed. Fanciful thoughts about a life with Fin wouldn't do her any good in the end anyway. She started to push up to her arms.

"Don't leave just yet, sweetheart." He clutched her tighter to him and kissed the top of her head.

Lissy sagged against him. She should enjoy every second in his arms because once they left this bed, the real world would come crashing down about them soon enough. But she should explain…not everything, of course. He'd never understand everything, but in his very docile state, she could hopefully get him to see a few things.

She brushed her fingers through the dusting of dark hair across his chest, trying to figure out what she could tell him, what wouldn't lead to questions she didn't want to answer.

"Lissy," he began before she'd even come close to finding the right words.

"Hmm?"

"When we get to Prestwick Chase, I think we should start the banns, don't you?"

The banns! She jerked away from him as though she'd been scorched. "I beg your pardon?"

He pushed up to his elbows, a frown marring his handsome face. "I never was the most romantic fellow. I am sorry." He heaved a sigh, then smiled rather boyishly and quite charmingly. "Let me try again. I love you, Felicity. I love you with all my heart and I want to share the rest of my life with you."

Her heart fluttered at his confession and then it very clearly broke in two for the both of them. "Fin," she whispered, not sure how she could even respond.

"Will you marry me, Lissy? Please."

Lissy didn't think her heart could ever hurt as badly as it did in that moment. Things would be so different in another life, another time…But she was in this life at this time. "I can't."

Confusion clouded his eyes and his brow furrowed once more. "But…"

"I really should check on Annie," she said, not wanting to hear whatever else he meant to say. There was nothing he could say that would change the situation, and listening to it would only hurt more.

She snatched her dress up from the floor and turned her back to him. Drat! It would have been much easier to flee the room if she'd already been clothed.

He was at her back, his hand on her shoulder. "I know you feel something for me, Lissy," he said softly. "We were both in that bed. I know you felt it too."

She'd felt it. She'd never forget it. But that didn't change her circumstances. "Please, Fin. I need to check on Annie."

He released her shoulder and took a slight step away from her, but she could still feel his eyes on her. Luckily, the dress was easy to toss over her head and she could make a quick escape sans her chemise or drawers. There wasn't time for unmentionables, not when every second spent in those chambers threatened to suffocate her.

She stepped into her slippers and started for the doorway and turned the handle.

"I don't know what he did you," Fin said softly from somewhere behind her, halting her in her step. "But I'm not him, Felicity."

Truer words were never spoken. A sob lodged in the middle of her throat. "I know," she whispered, not sure if he even heard her before she escaped to safety of the inn corridor.

Seventeen

One more. If just one more fellow smirked in Marcus Gray's direction, he'd pound the smirker right into the ground, which would pale in comparison to what he would do to Carraway, should that particular jackass cross his path again. He climbed the steps of Whites, relieved the footman nodded in greeting without a damned smirk on his face. The fellow had no idea how lucky he was.

Perhaps the tittle-tattle had died down a bit the last few days. He handed his beaver hat to the man and then stepped into the front room.

"Ah, Haversham! There you are," the Earl of Thurlstone called from his spot at the far edge of the room. "Wondered when you'd show your face again."

There was no need to point out the fact that Marc had been avoiding society, even the rougher edges of it since that damned night at Rotherby's. Over the years, he'd cultivated a rather nice reputation for himself, at least he thought it was rather nice. And one punch to the jaw from that sanctimonious prig Carraway, and Marc had been reduced to a laughingstock.

At the moment, Marc would have been quite happy to punch *Thurlstone* in the jaw for alluding to the encounter, but opted to cross the room towards his old friend and the group of men he was with instead. There was no need to start a row as soon as he entered the club, not when a nice, strong warning would do just as well, at least not yet.

Thurlstone lifted up a glass of whisky in welcome as Marc approached the small gathering of men. "No bruising at all, that I can see." The reprobate *smirked*.

Marc balled his hand into a fist. "One more word, Simon, and you won't recognize yourself in the mirror tomorrow."

Thurlstone laughed, as he'd always been the jovial sort and said, "Oh, it's all in good fun." Then he gestured to an open spot across from him. "Come now, Marc. Stop scowling and join us, will you?"

Marc glanced at Thurlstone's companions and immediately recognized the American from the other night as well as some fellow he'd never met before. As the pair were fairly unfamiliar, odds were neither of them would mention Carraway or Lord Rotherby's ballroom.

"Good to see you again," Mr. Heaton remarked.

"And you," Marc grumbled as he dropped into the overstuffed chair Thurlstone had indicated a moment before. Then he nodded in the stranger's direction. "Haversham," he said in greeting.

"Aaron Pierce," the man returned. Another American from his accent. What was it with Thurlstone and his sudden affinity for Americans? Very odd, that. The earl hadn't even traveled as far north as Yorkshire, at least not to Marc's knowledge anyway.

"I had no idea there were so many Americans in Town this Season."

Heaton chuckled. "Just here on business."

Business. How very tedious and boring. Marc somehow managed to keep from yawning in response.

"Aye," Thurlstone added, his chest puffed out a bit proudly. "You are looking at Heaton, Pierce and *Masters* Shipping. Feel free to find yourself in awe."

That answered it. Though why Thurlston had joined a shipping company didn't make a ton of sense. "Entering trade, are you?" Marc lifted one brow in amusement. "How very bourgeois."

"Hardly," Thurlstone replied, not appearing insulted in the least. "It'll be a grand adventure, I think. America, the Caribbean, India, China."

A grand adventure for a man who hadn't even made it to Scotland. Marc snorted. "A wonder you're not calling it Heaton, Pierce and Thurlstone."

At that, the earl tossed back his head and laughed once more. "Oh, for God's sake, my father would roll over in his grave."

"With good reason," Marc muttered under his breath, but his old friend heard him just the same.

The earl shook his head and said to the Americans, "You'll have to forgive him. He's been in a rotten mood ever since Lord Carraway crashed his fist into his jaw in the middle of a ballroom the other night."

Marc narrowed his eyes on the loose-lipped earl. "Next time I'll do more than just dance with Felicity Pierce and see how the fool likes that."

Both Americans sucked in surprised breaths, then the two exchanged a pair of rather worrisome expressions. "Honestly, Aaron," Heaton began, "I could have sworn I saw her the other afternoon. But I thought—" his frown deepened "—Well, I *thought* she was just a figment of my imagination."

"You *saw* her?" Pierce's face took on a quite frightening visage. "*Lissy?*"

"I do feel like I'm missing something of a sudden," Thurlstone said, sliding to the edge of his seat.

Aaron *Pierce*, Felicity *Pierce*. It wasn't a terribly uncommon name, but clearly there was some connection. Who was the fellow? Some relative of Lady Felicity's late-husband or something? "Am I to take it you know the lady in question?" Marc asked. "I understand she did live in Boston for a time."

"How the Hell…" Pierce's voice trailed off, though he refocused on his friend. "You saw her with your own eyes?"

Heaton shrugged. "I thought perhaps she was a sister or cousin of some sort. Felicity did have family here, after all."

"Felicity Pierce?" Thurlstone seemed to finally catch on. "The Duke of Prestwick's youngest daughter?"

The two Americans shared another fairly disconcerting look. "She's alive?" Heaton breathed out as though he truly didn't even believe his own words. "How could she be?"

Aaron Pierce's hand balled into a much more frightening fist than Marc's had been. "My wife is *alive*?" he asked incredulously, his gaze flicking to Thurlstone. "You know her?"

The earl shrugged a bit. "The Felicity Pierce I know is a widow, though I don't know her all that well. Clearly, Haversham knows her better than I do."

Suddenly, all three men's eyes were on Marc. "Widowed three years," he said because he had to say something.

"And just how well do you *know* her?" Pierce demanded.

"Her sister is married to friend of mine," Marc replied evenly, hoping to diffuse the situation just a bit as he certainly didn't like the look in Pierce's eye. The man appeared quite fearsome, to be honest. Probably any man would be upset if he found out his dead wife was alive, which was what had clearly happened just a moment before. God knew Marc would hole himself up inside his study and wish himself dead with a full decanter of whisky if *his* wife suddenly emerged from the grave. But Marc doubted he'd look as murderous as Pierce did just now. A bit of dread settled in his belly. Something was most definitely wrong.

"Friend?" Pierce barked.

"Lucas Beckford," Thurlstone supplied. "He's an all right sort. Is she really your wife?"

"She really will be my late-wife when I get my hands on her." Pierce rose from his seat, paced a few steps away and then turned back, spearing Heaton with a dangerous look. "Where the Hell is she?"

Probably at the most fashionable event that evening, wherever it happened to be. But if Aaron Pierce went in search of the lady in his present condition, it wouldn't bode well for anyone. "She could be anywhere this evening," Marc said quickly, though he wasn't certain why he was interfering in something that was none of his concern. "Truly, anywhere. Probably best to call on the lady in the morning at her home, I would think." Which would allow time for the man cool off just a bit, though that was probably wishful thinking on Marc's part.

"I can take you there in the morning," Thurlstone offered. "I'm certain there's a reasonable explanation."

Then the earl was the only one of the assembled men who thought so, but Marc didn't say as much out loud. Felicity Pierce had never been one to think her actions through clearly, but this…whatever this was, was something of a most grandiose nature. And with as angry as Aaron Pierce seemed to be, it was probably in the lady's best interest to find out her husband was in Town before the man found her. A little warning was most definitely in order.

Marc would rather not have Pierce know of his plans, however, so he ordered a glass of whisky from a passing footman and tried to appear as nonchalant as he possibly could. He kicked his feet out in front of him and teased Thurlstone mercilessly for a time about being in trade, even though the two Americans paid very little attention to anything other than a few hushed words between the pair of them. After a bit of time had passed, Marc declared himself off to Madam Palmer's for a quick tumble and then said his leave.

As he retrieved his beaver hat from the footman at the door, Marc asked quietly, "Do you happen to know which is the most fashionable event this evening, my good man?"

The footman thought for a second and then said, "I've heard several men discussing Lady Carteret's soiree, my lord."

Carteret House. Felicity Pierce might very well be there as it was someplace Marc would not be greeted warmly. Lord Carteret was, after all, one of Lord Staveley's oldest friends. He might not even be allowed over the threshold. Best to try Prestwick House first and see if the lady's butler could be persuaded to divulge his mistress' destination for the evening.

***

Derbyshire. Of all the damned places Felicity Pierce could have gone…Well, that wasn't such a bad place, all things considered, as it was a few days drive away. Still, it wouldn't be terribly easy to get word to her at her family seat either. But Caroline Staveley could, at least that was what Marc told himself as he stepped over the threshold of Lady Carteret's ballroom.

The truth, however, was that as soon as her name had popped to his mind, Marc needed to see her again. Even if she railed at him, even if she cursed his existence, even if she looked at him as though he was the scourge of the Earth, at least she would be looking at him.

He spotted her instantly through the crush, but he always spotted her instantly. Such was his curse for falling in love with another man's wife. Laughing with a tall blonde who was of no consequence, Caroline stood at the far end of the room, the chandeliers above head making her dark curls look a bit reddish under their glow. Marc's mouth went dry at the sight of her. Charming, delectable, utterly gorgeous. She was most definitely wasted on that oaf Staveley. Life was the furthest thing from fair.

She must have felt his eyes on her because she glanced across the room and met his gaze. A second later, her jaw took on a most stubborn jut and she averted her eyes quickly from him. But it was no matter. She'd see him tonight. She'd talk to him. With a little luck, he'd get more than that from her.

Marc pushed his way through the crowd, ignoring the whispers in his wake. Whether they were discussing Carraway's infamous punch or the fact that Marc made a direct path to society's darling, Caroline Staveley, made no difference at all to him, not with her this close and him having a reason that she would finally speak to him.

He stopped right before her, ignoring the woman to her side. "My lady," he said, noting the gravely tone in his own voice. "A dance, if you please."

Caroline heaved a rather unhappy sigh as she lifted her gaze to his once more. "I think I've made myself rather clear, Lord Haversham. But in case you weren't paying attention, what would please me immensely is to never lay eyes on *you* for the rest of my days. Please do go bother someone else."

He'd hardly let that deter him. Marc nodded once. "You have made that quite clear, my dear, but I fear that a mutual friend of ours is in a bit of trouble and needs your help."

That ought to be enigmatic enough to spark her curiosity. If there was one thing Caroline Staveley was, it was curious. And meddlesome. Both were qualities he admired in her, and they'd be her undoing in the end.

Caroline's pretty brow furrowed and she seemed to assess his face for signs of deception. Then she glanced to her left and said, "Hannah, I'm just going to take in a bit of air on the veranda, in case anyone needs me." Then she turned on her heel and started towards the pair of large glass doors at the end of the ballroom without even a glance back over her shoulder.

There was, of course, no need to worry that he wouldn't follow her. Marc would follow her to the ends of the Earth as long as there was breath in his lungs. He stepped out through the doors and the cool wind on the veranda whipped about his hair, but he wasn't chilly in the least, not with Caroline within an arm's reach.

She turned around to face him, her arms folded across her chest, which only served to lift those tempting mounds of hers a bit higher for his gaze. Damn it all, what he wouldn't give just to touch one of them...

"I do hope you're not lying to me," she said rather waspishly. "My husband is just inside Carteret's study."

As though Staveley's presence meant anything to him. Unfortunately, the oaf's presence meant something to her. Marc shook his head. "I don't believe I have ever lied to you, Caroline."

She narrowed her eyes on him at the use of her Christian name. "I'm not about to argue that fact, my lord. So simply tell me, what do you want?"

You, he wanted to say; but that was not why he'd come, not really. "I think Felicity Pierce is in trouble."

"Lissy?" She scoffed. "The only trouble she has is you chasing after her skirts."

"Jealous?" he asked before he could stop himself.

She pursed her lips, which only made him want to taste them again. Then she said, "That is the last time I listen to you and your tales of friends in trouble, Lord Haversham," as she started to brush past him.

But Marc grasped her elbow and refused to let her take another step away from him. "Her husband isn't dead," he said softly. "He is here. In London. And tomorrow he'll head over to Prestwick House as I did tonight and learn that she and Carraway have set off for Derbyshire to attend Lady Juliet. I don't like the look of the man, Caroline. I think the girl needs to be warned."

"I beg your pardon?" She blinked up at him, her hazel eyes clouded with confusion. "Her husband isn't dead?"

"Alive, well, and not a terribly charming fellow."

"She is a *widow*," Caroline stressed as though she didn't truly believe him.

"I met the man this evening at Whites. Aaron Pierce. He's gone into business with Thurlstone and until tonight was under the impression that his wife was dead. He didn't appear pleased to learn otherwise."

She shook her head as though he made less sense the more he talked. "They each thought the other was dead?"

"I can't truly answer to that, and I'm not certain at all about what is going on; but I can tell you that the man seemed rather murderous. I think you should send word to your brother, warn him that Pierce will be headed to Prestwick Chase, just to be safe."

"Oh, heavens." She touched a hand to her heart. "Luke's been so distracted as Juliet hasn't been faring well of late." She sighed as though trying to sort out the best plan of attack. "A note might not reach there in time. You'll have to go after them."

"Me?" Marc scoffed. "I most certainly do not. It's your family. I've warned you. My duty here is done."

She grasped his waistcoat in her hands and gazed up at him. Heat coursed through his veins and it was all he could do not to pull her into his arms.

"Please, Marc," she whispered.

Oh God. She knew just how to twist him around her finger. But it wasn't her finger that he wanted. "Kiss me, Caroline. Kiss me and I'll do whatever you wish."

From the entrance to the ballroom, someone cleared their throat, and she took a step backwards, away from Marc. Then she gulped and seemed to force a smile to her face. "David darling," she said. "There you are."

Of all the Goddamned people to interrupt them. Marc heaved a sigh and glanced over his shoulder to find the very studious Viscount Staveley standing just a few feet away. "Staveley," he grumbled.

"Bethany Carteret said you'd come to get a breath of fresh air," the man said to his wife, not acknowledging Marc's presence in the least.

Caroline nodded quickly. "I think Felicity is in trouble and she's headed to Prestwick Chase." Then she turned her attention once more to Marc. "Please. If Captain Pierce truly worries you, Lord Haversham, please go after them. I beg you."

Before Marc could reply, however, Staveley said, "Love, *I* can head to Prestwick Chase. There's no need to impose upon Lord Haversham for help."

"You?" She blinked at her husband in surprise.

Honestly, Marc was surprised too. The man rarely left his library. He certainly wouldn't be anyone's first choice as far as champions went.

"Of course," the viscount replied, pushing his spectacles up the bridge of his nose. "I'm just as capable as anyone else. And I'd hate for us to be beholden to Lord Haversham."

Meaning the man had heard every word Marc had said to his wife. An honorable man would be ashamed, Marc supposed, but he'd never been accused of being honorable. So he turned slightly and flashed the viscount an uncharitable grin. "Godspeed, then, Staveley. About time you played Sir Galahad for her." Then he tipped his head in farewell to Caroline and said, "Evening, my dear," before brushing past Staveley and back inside the Carteret ballroom.

Eighteen

Fin wrapped on Lissy's door. Ericht and his sister were already in the private dinning room, waiting for them. "Lissy, dinner," he called. But there was no sound on the other side. Clearly, she was still avoiding him.

What the devil was he going to do about her? About them? Things had been perfect between them, better than perfect. Making love to her had felt like the most right thing he'd ever done, and she'd been just as swept away as he was, he'd have bet every last farthing he possessed. He'd simply declared himself too quickly was all and frightened her, damned idiot that he was.

He had, after all, heard Lieutenant Avery's words that night in the carriage. Captain Pierce obviously hadn't treated Lissy well. The very idea of marriage had to frighten her to her core just like…Well, just like Georgie had been.

Oh, Georgie and Lissy were night and day. No matter that they were sisters, two more different women didn't exist. And yet they'd both been mistreated by their husbands. The mere mention of marriage could make Georgie scurry from a room as though the devil himself was chasing after her. She'd relished the freedom her widowhood had given her, the freedom to not be under an abusive husband's thumb. And Lissy was the same in that; it was quite obvious now that he knew what to look for.

Fin scoffed. She had literally run from the room with nothing more than the dress on her back and the slippers on her feet. Damn it all, what *had* Pierce done to her? And how could Fin convince her that he would never do the same? It had taken forever to wear Georgie's defenses down, for her to finally agree to marry him. Was he in for an equally long battle with Lissy's demons?

Damn, he hoped not. He truly did love her, he truly did want to marry her. But how to convince her? That was the question that had plagued him the rest of the evening until now, though he was no closer to an answer than he had been when she'd fled the room earlier that evening.

Fin sidled closer to her door and said softly, "I know you don't want to see me, but you do have to eat, sweetheart."

He could sit her down and demand she speak to him about their situation. Though the direct approach was never a good one with Lissy. She'd be defiant, just on general principle. Even now she wouldn't even open the door for dinner as he was on the other side of it.

He could be patient, like he had been with Georgie. Though he truly didn't relish that particular waiting game again. Besides, the two women weren't the same in the least. He always knew Georgie would come around in the end, but Lissy…Well, a more stubborn girl did not exist.

He could try coercion. He had, after all, spilled his seed deep inside her. She would definitely want any child from their union to have a father, to have a name, for God's sake. That wasn't even up for debate. If she was with child, she'd marry him and that would be it, but…

Well, if she'd only listen to reason.

"Felicity! Open the door," he called, his irritation growing the longer he stood there. Still, she said nothing, the stubborn minx. She'd make Fin stand there, like dolt all night, and she'd wait him out.

Best to retrieve Annie, he decided. Even if Lissy refused to come down to eat, her maid could still bring a bit of nourishment to her.

He started for the servant's room and quickly knocked on Annie's door. "It's Lord Carraway," he called.

A half-second later, the door opened, and Lissy's maid, with a rather large bandage on her head, smiled up at him. "Is everything all right, my lord?"

Things were the furthest they could be from all right. "I can't seem to coerce your lady into leaving her chambers for dinner. I thought you might have better luck than I've had."

"Yes, of course." Annie nodded quickly and then winced as the movement must have hurt her injured head.

"Are you all right?" Fin asked.

"Just the teensiest bit dizzy, my lord."

Fin scrubbed a hand across his face. Annie was in no condition to do his bidding. "Do sit back down, then." He gestured her back inside her room. "I'll get her to eat one way or the other if it kills me."

Annie laughed. "If she's decided not to, it just might."

"Don't I know it?" Fin sighed. "But do feel better, Annie. Chivers' leg has been set and the coach is being repaired as we speak. We'll head out at morning's light."

"I'll be ready, my lord. And I'm certain Lady Felicity will be in better spirits once we arrive. She's been so worried about Lady Juliet."

"I'm certain you're right." He smiled in farewell, though he wasn't certain in the least.

Fin made his way down the old wooden steps into the taproom. He nodded at the barkeeper. "Would it be possible to have a tray delivered to Lady Felicity's room?"

The man blinked at him. "Lady Felicity's room?"

"Yes. First room on the right at the top of the steps."

But the barkeeper shook his head. "The lady is gone, my lord."

"Gone?" Fin echoed, his heart nearly breaking in two. What the devil had she done now? "Gone where?"

The man shrugged in response. "She said something about her sister. Bought a horse from Old Jim, down there." He gestured to a fellow who didn't seem all that old, but he did seem more than foxed.

Fin raked a hand through his hair. Prestwick Chase was only a few hours away. But it was dark as pitch outside. Their carriage had lost a wheel thanks to the uneven road, even with a bit of daylight. One false step by Old Jim's horse and Lissy would twist her pretty neck. "When was this?"

"Not sure, sir. We've been busy down here. At least an hour or so, though, I'd say."

An hour or so. Visions of Lissy's lifeless body along the side of the road flashed in Fin's mind. His heart twisted in his chest. If anything happened to her… "I need a horse," he said, hoping to block any more distressing images from entering his mind.

The crunch of the gravel beneath her new steed's hooves signaled Lissy's approach to Prestwick Chase. Even in the dark she'd know the sound of that particular gravel, as she'd traveled it so often when she was younger.

Not a candle was lit in any window at The Chase, but she could see the manor outlined beneath the dim moonlight. Never would she have imagined Prestwick Chase would be a beacon of salvation for her, but that's exactly what it was at the moment.

Her legs ached, her back was sore, her cheeks still stung from tears. But now that she was home, she'd be safe. Safe from doing something else she'd regret as she didn't trust herself in the least where Fin was concerned. One more protestation of love and she'd throw her arms around his neck, but that just wouldn't do. She had very aptly destroyed her own life. She couldn't destroy his too. She loved him too much to do that to him.

She glanced again at her darkened childhood home. Juliet would be asleep. Everyone would be asleep. She'd wake the whole house at this hour, unless…Her sister *had* spent a small fortune repairing the place, but had she fixed that faulty window in the study? Lissy wasn't certain if anyone else even knew the window was faulty. In her youth, whenever she'd sneak away in the dead of night, she'd always been alone. She'd never been caught back in those days, back when the idea of just a bit of freedom would keep her awake long into the night, and only a walk in the moonlight could soothe her restlessness. If only a walk in the moonlight was all it would take to soothe her now.

The memory of Fin's kiss, his touch, the gentle way he'd made love to her invaded Lissy's thoughts again. There would never be enough moonlit walks to ever soothe her soul, of that she was more than certain.

She guided her horse to the stables, refocusing on the situation at hand, or at least trying to. Pushing Fin from her mind was next to impossible. She dismounted and led the horse to one of the stalls. Though she was exhausted, Lissy made quick work with the saddle, then sponged the horse down while he drank his fill from a large bucket. The fellow deserved to drink all he could, after all he'd done to get her safely home.

Lissy stroked the animal's back. "Thank you," she said softly before exiting the stables and making her way up to the manor house.

With a little bit of luck, she could quietly slip inside and then make her appearance known in the morning. She hoped Juliet was all right. She didn't know what she'd do otherwise. Jules had always been the strongest of them all, the most formidable, the bravest. She had to be all right. She just had to be.

Lissy hastened her step toward her childhood home, heading toward the left side of the manor and the faulty window of the ducal study. A bit of moonlight lit her path, but she didn't need it. She knew this path as well as she knew her own name. She reached the study, sent up a quick prayer that the window would open and then pushed against the bottom of the pane.

Just like all those years ago, the window lifted effortlessly and she smiled to herself. Finally something was going her way.

"One more step, cockchafer," growled a voice from the darkness, "and I'll rip your head from your shoulders and toss it into my hearth."

Heavens! Lissy gasped. What in the world? "Luke?" she breathed out in surprise.

"Lissy?" Her brother-in-law's anguished voice hit her ears. "Is that you?" And then he appeared at the window, staring down at her in mortification. "What *are* you doing here?"

She shrugged. "You sent for me."

Exasperated, he just gaped at her. "Most people don't arrive in the middle of the night. And they use the *fron*t door."

Most people weren't running from their demons or the saintly Lord Carraway either. Though she could never outrun her past, at least she could put some distance between herself and Fin. "Well, I didn't want to wake anyone," she explained calmly.

"No, much better to take ten years off my life instead," he grumbled. "I thought you were a burglar or brigand of some sort."

She blinked at him. "Are there brigands in the area?" Heavens, she'd ridden through the darkness without encountering anyone dangerous.

"Not that I know of. But who else would try to sneak inside here in the dead of night?" He pushed the window all the way up, then offered her his hand. "Come on. Climb inside."

With his assistance, not that she needed it, Lissy stepped

through the window into the darkened study. "I didn't mean to frighten you. I am sorry."

Luke closed the window behind her and said, "I'm — uh — sorry for what I said, Lissy. I'd never say something so vulgar to you."

What had he said? Cockchafer? She hadn't heard the word before, though the meaning wasn't hard to sort out. Of course, she'd heard quite a few shocking terms from Aaron's crews while she was in Boston so she had a higher tolerance for vulgarity than most, not that she'd let anyone know that fact. "I'll forget you ever said it." She smiled and reached a hand out to him. "How is Juliet? I've been worried ever since I received your letter."

He patted her hand on his arm, squeezing it with brotherly affection. "If I'd known it would make you flee into the night, I'd have crafted it with more care." Then he began leading her towards the corridor. "She's fine. Uncomfortable, irritable and beyond bored since Doctor Perkins ordered her to stay abed, but she's fine."

Lissy released a relieved breath she hadn't known she'd been holding. "Thank heavens. Fin said that was probably...." Blast it all. Could she not get him off her mind even now?

"Probably what?" Luke asked.

She heaved a sigh, remembering that day in her parlor back in London. Fin had been so kind, so caring, so...Well, so very much like Fin always was with her when he wasn't in the midst of a lecture. Even then, even when he lectured her, there'd always been concern and affection behind his words. Lissy's heart squeezed in her chest. If only things could be different. "He thought I was overreacting."

"If so, it's only because you love your sister." She could hear the smile in Luke's voice as they navigated the corridor.

She did love Juliet. She loved her honesty, her strength, her confidence. There was no better example of a strong woman than Jules. "She's irritable, you say?"

Luke chuckled softly. "She's been ordered to stay in bed for the foreseeable future. What do you think?"

Lissy thought that all of Prestwick Chase was probably walking around on eggshells. Her sister in a temper was not a sight most wanted to witness. No wonder Luke was hiding in his darkened study. "I'll just see her after she's had her tea in the morning, then."

"Coward," he said softly.

"I believe the word you're looking for is 'brilliant'."

He laughed again. "You'll help restore her mood, I'm certain."

"Papa?" Came a tiny voice from inside a set of rooms as they entered the family wing.

Luke scrubbed a hand down his face. "Sweet Lucifer, he's the lightest sleeper ever born." He released Lissy's arm and quietly pushed open the door, poking his head inside. "Go back to sleep, Ben."

"I want milk," Lissy's three-year-old nephew whined from his chambers.

Luke heaved a beleaguered sigh. "If I get you some warm milk, will you go back to sleep?"

"Uh-huh," the child promised.

"Stay there, then. I'll be right back." Then he quietly closed the door and turned to face Lissy. "Luckily, your chambers were already prepared for whenever you did arrive. Can you find them in the dark?"

"I know the way." Lissy nodded. After all, she'd navigated the darkened corridors of Prestwick Chase long before Luke had lived there. "Kiss Benton for me."

Luke nodded. "See you in the morning."

Lissy parted ways with her brother-in-law and continued down the corridor until she reached the set of chambers that had been hers all her life. She slid from her slippers and then padded across the rug to her bed and dropped across the four-poster without even attempting to toss her dress off.

She was too tired, too sore, too unmotivated to do anything

other than climb under the counterpane and drift off to sleep. In the morning she'd see her sister, kiss her nephew herself and try to forget the all-encompassing joy she'd felt in Fin's arms.

Just as she fell asleep, or at least it seemed like she'd just fallen asleep, a ruckus somewhere else in The Chase roused her slightly. Was that Ben? Was he awake and roaming the hallways? Was—

"Felicity!" Came Fin's bellow, some distance away.

Fin! She sat bolt upright in bed. Heavens! What was Fin doing here?

Nineteen

"What the devil are *you* doing here?" Lucas Beckford hissed, standing just inside the threshold of Prestwick Chase, glaring at Fin as though he was a madman.

Of course, Fin *was* a madman, banging on the door, shouting Lissy's name, barely knowing his own. She'd somehow turned him into a stark-raving idiot. "Tell me she's here," he breathed out, praying to hear those words more than anything else in the world. He hadn't come upon her lifeless body anywhere along the road, but she could have stumbled across a highwayman's path. She could have fallen to her death and he hadn't spotted her in the dim moonlight. She could have —

"She's asleep!" Beckford growled. "Just like the rest of The Chase was until two minutes ago. Do you have any idea what time it is?"

She was asleep. For the first time in hours, Fin took a relieved breath and every tense muscle in his body relaxed perceptibly at hearing those words. Thank God she was safe. At least until he got his hands on her. Riding across Derbyshire in the dead of night like a Bedlamite. She could have gotten herself killed, for God's sake.

"Have you lost your mind?" Beckford continued. "Have you completely forgotten that my wife is expectant? The last thing she needs in her condition is to be startled awake in the middle of the night by your bellowing."

He was right, of course. At one point he'd been a fairly well-respected noblemen, though he doubted he even resembled himself anymore. A twinge of regret pricked Fin's heart. Poor Juliet. He hadn't thought about anyone or anything else other than Lissy. "I am sorry, Luke." Fin raked a hand through his hair. "When I realized she'd taken off on her own in the dead of night, I thought…" Damn it all, he didn't want to finish that sentence. He didn't want to relive the awful thoughts that had plagued him during his entire mad dash to Prestwick Chase.

Luke Beckford's eyes narrowed slightly as though he could tell there was something Fin was keeping from him. "Between the two of you, I'll be lucky if I get even five minutes worth of sleep tonight. I hope you're happy."

"Sir?" Keeton, the butler, in his nightdress and cap appeared in the entryway behind his employer. "Is everything all right?"

"It will be if this is the last of our midnight visitors," Beckford grumbled. Then he glanced over his shoulder at the servant and added, "I'll deal with Lord Carraway, Keeton. Do go back to bed. I have a feeling tomorrow is going to be a rather long day."

"If you're certain, sir."

The gentleman nodded. "See you in the morning."

"Sorry for waking you," Fin called as the butler made his way back towards the servants' quarters.

Beckford gestured Fin over the threshold, then shut the door behind him. "What the devil is going on, Phineas?"

Nothing Fin could reveal to Lucas Beckford, not if he didn't want to sport a blackened eye and to be tossed unceremoniously on his arse outside the gates of Prestwick Chase for seducing the man's sister-in-law. Luke wasn't Lissy's guardian, but he was rather protective of his wife's younger sister. "I am sorry about the late hour."

Even in the darkness, he could see Beckford's brow lift in disbelief. "I am surprised to see you at all, honestly. Lissy didn't mention you. I thought she must have traveled alone from London."

Of course she hadn't mentioned him. She'd run all the way across Derbyshire to avoid him. If Fin wasn't completely certain it was fear of marriage spurring her forward, he'd feel a bit rejected by the whole thing. But she *was* afraid. He'd seen that terrified look in her eyes before she'd fled the inn chambers, and the memory of her expression still twisted his heart. "We would have made it much earlier tonight if my carriage wheel hadn't found a nasty hole in the road. We were going to depart first thing in the morning, but being this close to Prestwick Chase, I suppose Lissy didn't want to wait any longer than she had to."

"Mmm." Beckford shook his head and then said, "I think I'm going to need some whisky." He started down the darkened corridor. "You're welcome to join me."

"I'll take you up on that." Fin followed in the gentleman's wake. After all, he could use a dram himself after the night he'd endured. Perhaps more than a dram. Perhaps a whole damned bottle.

A moment later, Fin stood in the middle of the ducal study as Beckford lit a lamp on the desk, casting a warm glow throughout the room. The gentleman dropped into an overstuffed leather chair, tilted his head toward the sideboard and said, "Help yourself, Carraway. And pour me a glass too."

Fin lifted the crystal decanter from the sideboard and quickly poured two glasses. Then he turned back towards his host, offered the gentleman one of the drinks and assumed the spot opposite him. "I'm hoping Lissy was unharmed when she arrived."

Beckford snorted. "Do you know she tried to sneak into the house—" he gestured towards the window "—through there? Said she didn't want to wake anyone. She's damned lucky I didn't have a pistol in the room.""

Dear God. Fin pushed that awful image from his mind and scrubbed a hand down his face. "She will be the death of me, on my word." Then he downed the contents of his glass in one gulp.

"She'll get remarried at some point and then she'll be the death of *that* fellow." Beckford took a healthy swallow from his own whisky glass.

Which amounted to the same thing. She'd be the death of Fin one-way or the other because if she was going to marry anyone, it was going to be him. Though saying as much to Lucas Beckford probably wasn't the best idea, especially considering the man's mention of a pistol just a moment before. "Perhaps," he began conversationally. "But she doesn't seem to be in a hurry to replace Pierce."

"She'll meet the right fellow, I'm certain. Then God help the poor man."

God help the poor man, indeed. Fin pinched the bridge of his nose, hoping to stave off a headache. Life with Lissy would never be dull. But it was much better than life would be without her, of that he had no doubt. If only he could persuade her of the same thing.

"I suppose it's your fault she arrived in the dead of night all alone," Beckford remarked, breaking Fin from his reverie.

"Beg your pardon?" Fin managed to keep from squirming in his seat at the accusation. A rake, even a reformed one like Luke Beckford, would notice such a thing. "My fault?" he echoed, hoping he sounded innocent of the charge leveled against him.

"You couldn't keep her from running off in the dark? For God's sake, she's just a mere slip of a girl."

Oh. That's what he meant. Fin supposed he was guilty of that charge. Still, he shook his head. "I didn't even know she was gone. The St. Claire sisters are quite determined when they get their mind set on something."

At that, Beckford laughed and lifted his remaining whisky up as a mock toast. "Truer words were never spoken."

"Speaking of determined St. Claire sisters, how is Juliet?" Fin asked. Truly he should have asked before now, and would have if he hadn't been so singularly focused on Lissy.

A bemused grin spread across the gentleman's face. "Bound and determined that this child will be born on Georgie's birthday. If it kills her. Fairly certain she's been holding off contractions with sheer will."

Georgie's birthday. Damn. Fin hadn't even realized the date was so close.

His expression must have said as much because Beckford's grin grew wider and he said, "Forgot, did you? I only ever remember Juliet's because a sennight before she starts reminding me. 'My birthday is in six days, you know?' Or 'Just five more days until my birthday, Luke.'" Then he laughed. "I missed the date *one* time and she's been adamant ever since that I'll never do so again."

"That does sound like Juliet," Fin said softly. It sounded like Georgie too. He still missed her. Part of him always would. Fin heaved a sigh and stared most pointedly at his would-be brother-in-law. "You don't think Georgie would mind if I found someone, do you?"

Beckford's eyes widened in surprise. "Have you? Found someone, that is?" He downed the last of his whisky.

Fin shrugged slightly. "Fallen rather hard, I'm afraid. Even asked the girl to marry me."

"Good for you." The twinkle in Beckford's eyes said better than words could how truly happy he was for Fin. Of course, he didn't know all of the details. Who knew what his reaction would be to the truth?

"Don't congratulate me yet. She didn't say yes and the girl is more than stubborn."

But Beckford shook his head. "They all are in their own way." An earnest smile lit his lips. "But, no, I don't think Georgie would mind. I think she'd be happy for you. Juliet, Felicity, Edmund. They'll all be happy for you."

Felicity. What was he going to do about her? "I hope so."

"You've always been there for all of them. They want you to be happy, I can assure you." He frowned just a bit and continued, "Things do change when you get married, though. You'll see her family all the time and your own hardly at all. I can't remember the last time I saw my brother, actually. Caroline is a different story because…Well, she's Caroline and if she didn't have her fingers in everyone else's business, she wouldn't be my sister." He shrugged. "So just do be cognizant of that. I think the three of them wouldn't know what to do with themselves if you just up and vanished from their lives."

That was hardly a concern. "I *am* Edmund's guardian," he said instead of revealing the truth about his feelings for Lissy.

"And Juliet's confidant and Lissy's savior. The many hats you wear, Fin." He grinned widely. "You'll have to warn your lady about the madness she'll be marrying into. Do try not to scare her off."

Fin couldn't help but laugh. Under any other circumstances, the warning would be most apt. But not in the one Fin actually found himself in. "I hardly think that will be a problem at all." Though scaring her off was, very clearly, a problem. One that needed to be sorted out.

"Papa?" came a tiny voice from the doorway.

Luke winced just a bit. "Benton Beckford, what are you doing out of bed?"

The little blond boy scampered across the Aubusson rug and threw himself against his father's legs. "I want milk."

"You've already emptied one entire cow this evening." He placed his now empty glass on the desk not far away and then scooped his son up into his arms. "You will be exhausted in the morning and then your nurse will come to yell at *me*. Hardly fair, if you ask me. But that's what will happen."

The little boy giggled, which was, even at this hour, one of the sweetest sounds Fin had ever heard. Lucas Beckford clearly adored his son. Even through his exhaustion and annoyance, his love and adoration shone through. Someday…

Someday Find would like to have his own son in his arms, Lissy by his side, doting on the child. In fact, he wanted that all of suddenly more than he'd ever wished for anything in his life. If only—

"All right, Ben." Beckford pushed out of his seat and jostled his son in his arms. "Let's go see if Uncle Fin's room is prepared. It should be, but these days you never know."

Fin placed his own glass on the ducal desk and followed the gentleman into the corridor. His room would be ready, however, Fin had no doubt. His room was always ready and had been ever since Juliet had taken up residence at Prestwick Chase, declaring that Fin was and always would be welcome as any member of the family. He hoped that would still be true the next morning.

Twenty

Lissy didn't think she'd slept even a wink after Fin arrived the night before. And with the sun now shining brightly into her chambers, attempting to get anymore was a lost cause. But how *could* she have slept? Fin was just down the corridor, as he always was at Prestwick Chase, his presence calling to her as strongly as a flame called to a moth.

She'd cried until she had no tears left and then just lay awake, staring up at the canopy over her bed, like she had in her younger years when the call of freedom and distant shores always seemed to beckon. If only she'd never gone to Boston to visit with her mother's family. If only she'd never met Aaron. If only she was free to love Fin the way he deserved to be loved. She did love him. She loved him quite desperately. If she hadn't known that before her dash across Derbyshire, she certainly knew it now. She'd had nothing but her own thoughts to keep her company the night before. Perhaps it was the clear country air or perhaps she just didn't have the strength to deny what she knew in her heart any longer.

But none of that mattered. She wasn't free, after all, and wishing she was wouldn't change the situation. Even still, that didn't make her heart hurt any less. She doubted anything ever would.

She should get up, throw on a clean dress, head into Juliet's chambers, visit her sister and —

Just then, the door to her chambers was unceremoniously tossed open and her little blond-headed nephew raced across the floor and hurled himself onto her bed. "Aunt Lissy!" he cried, wrapping his arms around her neck.

She couldn't help but laugh. The boy was such a little scamp. "Good morning, Ben." She hugged him tightly to her and kissed one of his rosy cheeks. "I have missed you."

"Benton," Fin's voice came from the threshold, "your nurse is waiting for you."

Lissy clutched her nephew a bit tighter to her as though the boy could shield her from having to face Fin, but that was silly and not terribly effective in the long run. Besides, she couldn't use the child that way. It was hardly fair to him. So she kissed Ben's cheek once more, loosened her hold on him and said, "Go see nurse and we'll play later, all right, sweetheart?"

He nodded quickly, scrambled from the bed and stopped right in front of Fin. "See. I found her for you."

"That you did." Fin didn't even have the decency to look contrite for manipulating the three-year-old. "You are the best scout, Ben." He tousled the boy's hair before turning his pointed attention on Lissy. "Good morning." His brown gaze nearly scorched her where she sat.

Without a look backwards, Ben took off down the corridor like a tiny tornado, leaving Lissy to fend for herself.

She folded her arms across her chest, and glared at the viscount who looked as though he had enjoyed a very restful sleep. Blast

2

him. "I cannot believe you used that little boy to gain access to my chambers. You should be ashamed of yourself."

Fin shrugged a bit, completely unrepentant. "I've been a politician all my life, Lissy. One should have as many allies as one is able to possess, even those found in very small packages. And one should know the best time to ask for favors."

"I hardly think Juliet would appreciate you using him in such a way."

"I hardly think Juliet would appreciate the fact that you risked your life racing across the county last night. But I didn't come here to discuss what would or would not make your sister happy."

No, of course not. He'd want to talk about what happened between them, and Lissy would rather do almost anything else in the world. "I'm not even dressed, Fin," she complained, even though she was still wearing her clothes from yesterday and was perfectly decent.

He stepped into her chambers and shut the door behind him. "I've seen you in less."

Hardly a gentlemanly thing to remind her of. "Phineas," she began, adopting Juliet's most haughty voice, "open that door at once."

His brow lifted perceptibly. "Do you really want all of Prestwick Chase to overhear our conversation?"

She didn't even want to hear it herself. "This is all highly improper. And I know how you pride propriety above all else, so—"

"I think we're beyond propriety, Lissy." He shook his head, his warm brown eyes boring into hers as though he knew exactly what she was up to. Of course, he probably did, as he'd known her most of her life. "We need to talk."

The hard line of his jaw made it quite clear that he wouldn't be dismissed very easily. But talking wouldn't solve their predicament, and having him alone in her chambers only made the memories of yesterday stronger in her mind. If she could only put him off a few more minutes, give her sleep-deprived mind a little bit of time to figure out what she could say. Lissy feigned a smile and said, "Give me time to change and we can talk in the breakfast room, then."

"You mean give you time to bolt somewhere else, don't you?" He crossed the floor in a few strides and stopped at the foot of her bed. "Do take pity on me, Lissy. No more running. Let's just talk, shall we?" And then he sat on the very edge of her bed.

Lissy gulped. The nearness of him invaded her senses and should have sent her fleeing for safety; but it was Fin – kind, dutiful, noble Fin. A more honorable man didn't exist, or at least she hadn't met anymore more noble than him.

He captured her hand in his and tingles raced across her skin from the contact. "Sweetheart," he began.

But Lissy pulled her hand from his grasp and shook her head. "Don't, Fin. Whatever you're about to say, please don't. I don't want to lose you and if you —"

"You're not going to *lose* me."

"If you say anything else, I will. If you say anything else then things will never go back to how they were, and I —"

"I don't want things to go back to how they were." His eyes seemed to warm even more. "I want *you*, Lissy, for now and for always. I meant what I said last night at the inn."

And what she wouldn't give to make all of that a possibility. But it wasn't. And it couldn't be. "I can't get married again, Fin. I just can't. You can talk about it all you want, but it won't change that fact."

He heaved a sigh. "You know I'd never hurt you."

She did know it. Fin would never hurt anyone, but... "That doesn't have anything to do with this."

"Doesn't it?" His brow lifted in question. "I saw the fear in your eyes, Felicity. Just like I used to see it in Georgie's."

Lissy snorted. "I am *not* Georgie." She was the furthest thing from her sainted sister.

"No. Two sisters couldn't be more different," he agreed. "But in this you are the same. I know that particular look, Felicity. I know it better than most. Every time I saw it in her eyes it broke my heart and seeing it in yours nearly killed me. How could anyone mistreat you? How could anyone steal your lightheartedness, your sweet nature?"

How had he possibly seen all of that? Feeling vulnerable and quite exposed all of a sudden, Lissy tugged the counterpane closer to her chest as though she could somehow keep him from seeing anything else. "Don't, Fin."

"Don't talk about it?" His eyes bore into hers once more. "It's the only way to dispense with the ghosts of the past, Lissy. Face them head on. Take away the power they have over you. And I'll help you. I'll be right there with you, every step of the way, because I love you. I love you with all my heart."

Lissy didn't realize tears had started to stream down her face until Fin retrieved his handkerchief and softly pressed it to her cheeks. She could only stare at him. Gentle, honest, honorable Fin. He deserved so much better than her, and if she'd done things differently…

Lissy's eyes dropped to her lap. She couldn't look at him, not with his uncanny ability to see so clearly into her soul. When had he developed that skill?

"There's no need to rush anything, sweetheart. We can move as slowly as you need. I'm not going anywhere."

"I'm not marrying you, Fin," she whispered. She wouldn't be a bigamist, no matter how badly she might wish the future he painted in her mind was a possibility. "And that is that. So please do leave. You shouldn't be in here."

He heaved a frustrated sigh. "Felicity," he began in his most placating tone, "I know you felt the same as I did yesterday. I know it wasn't just me."

And she would relive that night for the rest of her life. But that didn't change the situation in the least. "Go, Fin."

"Not until you hear me out." He slid a tiny bit closer to her on the bed and his voice softened to a whisper, "It is quite possible that you're carrying my child, you know? And—"

A strangled, mirthless laugh escaped Lissy. "I can't have children, Fin." Her voice sounded weak to her own ears as the memory of her miscarriage began pushing at the corners of her mind. "So if that's what has you so concerned, there is no reason."

He sucked in a surprised breath, but Lissy still couldn't look at him. He'd see right through her if she met his gaze. "I'm concerned about *you*," he said most earnestly, nearly breaking her heart once more.

Of course he was concerned about her. That's who he was, what he did. Always trying to make certain those he cared about were fine. And he cared about her. He loved her. He'd said so a number of times, but even if he hadn't said the words, she'd know he loved her. She could hear it in his voice.

It must have become clear that she had no intention of saying anything else because he pressed forward with, "What do you mean you can't have children?"

Lissy shrugged. "Doctor Watts said it just isn't possible for me," she replied. In truth, the London doctor had explained quite some time ago that the trauma she'd suffered in Boston would make it nearly impossible for her to conceive or carry a child to term, but she wasn't about to tell Fin any of that. She'd never breathed a word to anyone after hearing that truth, and the last thing she wanted to do was remember the heartache she'd felt upon hearing those words. "Now do, please, leave me be."

Fin seemed to reach a hand in her direction but then thought the better of it and let his hand drop to the counterpane beside her instead. "I love you, Lissy. I just want to help. I wish you'd explain everything to me."

But that was the one thing she couldn't do.

Fin wanted to brush his hands across her cheek, to comfort her, to love her. But her back was straight as a board and she refused to even look at him. Staying in her chambers at the moment wasn't going to earn him any rewards.

So he slid from the edge of her bed, walked slowly towards her closed door and then opened it. Standing in the hallway, leaning his large frame against the wall, was Lucas Beckford. His arms were folded across his chest and he wore a bemused expression. Damn it. That didn't bode well.

"Fell rather hard, did you?" the man echoed Fin's words from the night before.

Fin quickly shut Lissy's door and then turned to face her brother-in-law. "Don't know what you're talking about." Damn it all, he'd rather not have this particular conversation just now, but there was no avoiding it, apparently.

"Come now, you can do better than that. Besides, Ben isn't really old enough to keep secrets and you *did* enlist my son's aid this morning."

Not that Fin had said anything to the child other than to ask for the boy's help in locating his Aunt Lissy.

Beckford chuckled and gestured towards Lissy's door with the tilt of his head. "You were in there quite some time and I didn't hear any of the usual lectures come filtering through the door."

"I don't always lecture her." Fin started down the corridor, away from her chambers, towards the staircase. If they were to have this conversation, he'd rather do it somewhere else, somewhere she couldn't possibly overhear.

"Apparently not." Beckford met his pace. "You seem quite distraught, though. Everything all right?"

Fin scoffed. Nothing was all right and he didn't even have a damned clue as to why. "If she'd just talk to me…"

The gentleman clapped a commiserating hand to Fin's back. "You did enter her chambers without invitation. Women, in my experience, are never very happy about that. Well, not usually."

Fin stopped in his tracks and turned to face Beckford. Strange as it was, the one-time rake might be the closest thing he had to an ally at The Chase. "Everything was perfectly fine, everything was perfect until I mentioned marriage and then she bolted across Derbyshire in the dead of night as though the devil was chasing after her."

Beckford's brow lifted as though he'd just found the final puzzle piece he'd been searching for. "I never knew the old duke. He must have been quite the bastard to terrify each of his daughters from ever wanting to marry. Juliet wore her fortune as though it was some sort of magical cloak that could protect her from the parson's noose." He shook his head. "She was in love with me, Carraway. She loved me as much as I loved her, but she never would have married me, not if Albert St. Claire hadn't been coming for her, not if she didn't need the protection my name offered in that moment."

That was probably true. Juliet had most definitely had an aversion to matrimony. She had witnessed more than one of her father's unhappy unions. "Prestwick was mostly remote, distant," Fin began, starting again for the breakfast room in the hopes of a much needed coffee. When Beckford matched his stride, he continued, "He didn't care a thing about his daughters, nor any of his wives, from what I understand. He certainly didn't give Pamela a second thought except in terms of her providing him an heir." And Fin's older sister had deserved a second thought. She'd deserved love and admiration, not a disinterested man, old enough to be her father, even if he was a duke. "I never saw him be cruel to any of them. Honestly, I don't think he cared enough." He shrugged. "Except for Edmund. His son, his legacy." Prestwick had been over the moon when his son was born, but the man hadn't even shed a tear over the death of his young wife the very same day.

"The boy is better off with you as his guardian than he would have been raised by his father," Beckford grumbled.

Fin did adore Edmund. The boy looked so much like Pamela.

He was a constant reminder of Fin's beloved sister. Even so, he shook off the compliment. He couldn't take credit for Edmund, much as he would like to. "Georgie and Juliet are responsible for the wonderful boy he is."

"Always so modest." The gentleman smiled. "If left up to Juliet, Edmund would be a spoiled little devil, and you know it. *You're* responsible for the duke he is, Phineas, instilling honor and duty in him."

Like he'd hoped to do with a child of his own one day. Lissy's revelation of her bareness had crushed part of Fin's soul, but it didn't change the way he felt about her. He loved her. He loved her with all his heart and nothing would change that. "I like to think he inherited that from my sister. Pamela was dutiful and kind. I wish she could have known him. She'd be so proud of her son."

Beckford heaved a sigh as they reached the breakfast room. "What are you going to do about Lissy?"

"I haven't the faintest idea. She won't even talk to me. How can you reason with a lady who won't even talk to you?"

A bit of wickedness flashed in Beckford's eyes. "Well, you *were* in her chambers a rather long time. I could demand you do the honorable thing."

At that, Fin laughed. He couldn't help it. "If I thought that would work, Luke, I'd take you up on it." He settled into a chair at the table and gestured for a cup of coffee, which a footman delivered right away.

"I can be quite demanding when I set my mind to it." Luke began to fill his plate from the sideboard. "I'll just sit her down and explain things to her."

"It wouldn't matter." Fin should probably break his fast as well, but the idea of food made his stomach turn. "She's built some wall up around her." He took his first sip of coffee. He'd need a lot more before the day was through, he had no doubt. "I'm not sure what Aaron Pierce did to her, but it was something.

Something that still strikes terror in her heart. I've only ever seen that look in Georgie's eyes before, whenever the subject of Teynham arose."

Luke turned around, his plate in hand, staring at Fin. "Pierce physically harmed her?" A vein pulsed in his neck. "What did he do?"

That was the question, wasn't it? Fin shook his head, trying to make sense of it all, to no avail. "I wish I knew. Much easier to slay a dragon when you know which dragon it is you need to slay."

Luke dropped into a seat across from Fin, his brow creased with concern. "But you're certain it's something?"

"More than certain." Fin frowned. "I just feel like a bloody fool for not realizing it before now. How the devil was I so blind for so long?"

Twenty-One

Lissy strode into her sister's room. At least focusing on Juliet, she wouldn't have to think about Fin. Her older sister was reading some leather-bound book in bed, propped up against a mound of pillows, her dark hair unpinned and down about her shoulders. Juliet always had demanded the most comfort, and Lissy couldn't help but smile upon seeing her look so well.

"Jules!" She rushed towards the large four-poster, relieved beyond measure to finally see her sister.

Juliet dropped her book to the counterpane, and true joy shone in her dark eyes. "Lissy!" She reached both of her arms out, an invitation to be embraced if there ever was one. "Luke said you and Fin arrived separately in the middle of the night."

Lissy hugged her sister gently, careful not to hurt her. "I

couldn't wait to see you."

Juliet laughed, hugging Lissy a bit tighter. "Next time, be less anxious. You could have gotten hurt."

Lissy pulled out of her sister's embrace and grinned. "So little faith in my skills as a rider?"

Juliet rolled her eyes. "I'm not even going to respond to such a ridiculous question."

"How are you, Jules? Ever since I got Luke's letter I've been out of my mind with worry."

"Hot." Her sister patted a space on the bed beside her. "And uncomfortable. And miserable. Do tell me everything I'm missing in Town. I am bored out of my mind, stuck in this bed."

Lissy climbed onto the bed beside her sister and rested her head on Juliet's shoulder, just like she used to when they were much younger. She' always idolized Juliet, who was always so brave, so confident, so headstrong. Lissy had often wondered during those awful months in Boston what Juliet would have done in her place. Her sister had such a commanding presence about her, she always had. Would Jules have intimidated Aaron from the very beginning? Would she have put him so perfectly in his place that he wouldn't have dared to lay a finger on her? Or would even the bold and courageous Juliet have buckled under Aaron's viciousness? Would any woman have ever stood a chance against him?

Beside her, Juliet sucked in a breath and grabbed a handful of counterpane. Her features, at once, all looked quite strained.

"Are you all right?" Lissy whispered, wishing she had some clue what to do.

Juliet released her breath, though her pretty features were still tinged with pain. "Just a contraction."

"A contraction!" Lissy touched a hand to her heart. Good heavens! The baby was coming now? "I'll send for Doctor Perkins," she said, and would have scrambled off the bed, but her sister grasped her hand and squeezed.

"Don't go," she pleaded. "He'll be along soon enough, but you just got here. And you were going to tell me all the news from Town."

Was she? It was hard to remember anything at this point.

"Truly, Lissy, it wasn't even a painful one. Do give me something else to think about. What did I miss this Season?"

Lissy sat a little taller, trying to focus on the most interesting news from London, something her sister might be interested in. "Well," she began, "let's see. Lucinda Potts ran off to Gretna with the new Lord Brookfield."

"He has to be better than the old Lord Brookfield, doesn't he?"

On that they could agree. "Even with his scandalous reputation, I don't imagine he could be worse." Lissy smiled. "What else? Oh, speaking of rogues, Olivia and Kelfield are in Town for the season this year. And she was welcomed more warmly than she has been in the past."

"That is good." Julie smiled. "Poor girl has had a rough time of it."

And had ever since a certain house party at Prestwick Chase a few years back. But that was what happened when one did foolish things like fall in love with notorious rakes, one's reputation took a beating, something the new Lady Brookfield would soon find out. Even so, it had to be a much better choice than running off and marrying a sadistic ship's captain on the other side of the world, so Olivia Kelfield and Lucinda Brookfield had Lissy there.

She shook her head, determined not to focus on that last bit. "Cordie and Clayworth are in residence too, but…" But she probably shouldn't mention her friend's miscarriage, at least not during her sister's current state. Foolish, foolish thing to say.

"But?" Juliet's brown eyes widened expectantly.

Lissy frowned. Changing topics was most certainly necessary. "Jules, do you know of any gentlemen who owe Clayworth a large debt?"

"A gambling debt?" her sister asked. "Luke might know, but

I—"

"I didn't get the feeling it was gambling related." Lissy shook her head. "You remember Bella Winslett? My friend from that ladies' academy Georgie had insisted upon?"

"Of course. Shy girl." Juliet's brow furrowed as though she was trying to remember more clearly. "Her brother is Lord Gillingham, isn't he?"

Lissy nodded, then told her sister everything about Bella Winslett, her awful Prussian cousin, Lissy's plan for a pretend betrothal, and Cordie's mysterious mention of a fellow who owed Clayworth a rather large debt. By the time she was through with her tale, Juliet was giggling and protectively holding her belly with both arms.

"Heavens, Lissy!" she laughed.

"Well, I had to do something," Lissy replied. "It's not fair that Bella should be forced to marry some horrid Prussian against her will. And Gillingham is no help at all. Foxed all the time. He even cast up his accounts upon some fellow at the Astwicks' not too long ago."

A look of horror splashed upon her sister's face. "That is awful."

Indeed. Poor Bella. Hopefully she was faring well with Cordie back in London. "At least you're amused. Fin was…" Lissy's smile faded.

"Fin was what?" Juliet asked.

Heavens, it would be easier if she didn't think about Fin every few minutes. "Fin was Fin. Quite angry about the entire thing."

Her sister draped an arm around Lissy's shoulder and squeezed her affectionately. "Well, I think you're brilliant. You might even put Caroline Staveley to shame with your genius."

"High praise, indeed." Lissy grinned in response. After all, Juliet's sister-in-law was known for her wildly successful scheming over the years.

"Oh, for God's sake, don't encourage her," Fin said from the threshold, and Lissy's merriment vanished in an instant. "It was all I could do to keep her from embroiling Edmund in this madness."

"Fin!" Juliet reached out a hand towards him, completely unaware that his presence made Lissy's heart race and break all at the same time. "I am so glad to see you. Thank you so much for bringing Lissy to me."

"It was my pleasure," Fin replied, stepping further into Juliet's chambers.

His eyes strayed to Lissy and heated her skin anew. Blast it all. How was she supposed to behave normally when just a glance from him could set her aflame?

"How are you feeling, sweetheart?" he asked her sister as he reached the edge of the bed.

Juliet winced and said, "Perfectly miserable. But I'm having this baby today, no matter what. I am glad you're both here for it."

That was a thing to say. Lissy couldn't help but laugh. "Fairly certain it doesn't work that way, Jules."

But her sister sat straight up in bed, or as straight as she was able in her current state. "I dare the gods to defy me. I've been suffering contractions all week long. And this baby is coming today." Then she focused all of her attention on Fin and said, "You do know what today is, don't you?"

He frowned for just a moment and then bestowed Juliet with his most charming smile. "Georgie's birthday," he replied, and a twinge of jealousy stung Lissy, which was ridiculous. Why shouldn't Fin remember Georgie's birthday? And why should she feel jealous that he did? For heaven's sake, she was Lissy's sister. But he'd said he loved Lissy, and...Well, he'd loved Georgie too. She'd always known that. But none of that was neither here nor there. She couldn't have Fin anyway, so what did it matter if he knew without a moment's hesitation that today was Georgie's birthday or not? It shouldn't matter. It shouldn't bother her in the least. But it did.

Juliet clapped her hands together. "Your memory is much better than Luke's."

His brown eyes twinkled with mirth. "Would you think less of me if I admitted that he's the one who reminded me?"

"Fin!" Juliet's mouth dropped open.

"Sorry, Jules. I have been preoccupied of late." He shrugged and then continued, "Do I get credit for my honesty?"

"An honest politician." Juliet laughed. "Such a novelty." And then she sucked in a swift breath of air and squeezed Lissy's hand so hard, Lissy thought her fingers might break off in her sister's grasp. "Fin," Juliet said through clenched teeth, "would you please get Luke for me? And ask someone to send for Doctor Perkins?"

Lissy sucked in a quick breath of her own. The baby *was* coming! Oh, good heavens! Panic gripped her heart and Juliet squeezed her hand even harder.

"Of course. Of course." Fin nodded quickly and then rushed from Juliet's chambers.

"Jules," Lissy said, trying to retrieve her hand from her sister. "You are hurting me."

"Oh!" Juliet instantly released Lissy's hand. "Sorry." She looked so frightened all of a sudden, which did nothing to calm Lissy's nerves. Heavens! Juliet had been through this before. Why in the world did she look frightened now?

"Are you all right?" she asked, for lack of anything intelligent to say.

Juliet nodded tightly. "I'm just so glad you're here."

Though Lissy would do anything for Juliet, she did wish she was anywhere but here right now. She wasn't a good nursemaid, not as far as birthing babies went. She never had been. And the panic that was coursing through her veins made it more than clear that she wouldn't start being a good one today. Actually, breathing was becoming a bit difficult. And the little flashes of light circling her vision made her a bit…light headed. And…

"L−i−ssy?" Juliet's voice sounded so far away…

Twenty-Two

Fin's heart squeezed in his chest at the sight of Lissy's limp form on the bed. Beckford had, of course, raced from his study to Juliet's chambers as soon as Fin found him. The man had bolted through The Chase in record time, though Fin was right on his heels the whole way.

As soon as they crossed the threshold, Luke had rushed to Juliet's side; but Fin had only been able to gape as his eyes landed on Lissy, in a lifeless heap beside her sister. "What happened?" he breathed out.

"She's having the baby!" Luke barked. "What do you think?"

"He means Lissy," Juliet said between gritted teeth. Then her dark eyes met Fin's, and she added, "Smelling salts. She fainted."

Fainted? "Oh, good God!" He started for the bed. Where the devil did Juliet keep her smelling salts?

"Take her to her room, Fin," Luke called. "Juliet should have all the space she needs."

Without another thought, Fin scooped Lissy up in his arms, jostling her just a bit. Then he started for the corridor, promising to have Keeton send for Doctor Perkins at once. But his sole focus was on Lissy.

She'd fainted! How truly strange. She'd tended to Chivers as quickly as any army field surgeon, tearing her nightrail into usable strips, binding his broken leg without so much as a blink. But the early stages of her sister's child labor had caused her to faint? She was, without a doubt, a complete dichotomy. He could spend the rest of his life with her and he'd never figure her out. Honestly, life with her would never be dull. But then he'd known that already. Life with her would also be immeasurably happy and maddening and completely joyous.

A little maid darted in front of Fin and he called, "Do have Keeton send for Doctor Perkins. Lady Juliet does appear to be having her babe today."

"Oh!" the girl exclaimed. "Right away, my lord." Then she bustled down the corridor as quickly as her feet would carry her.

In his arms, Lissy squirmed a bit and her brow crinkled as though she was in pain or starting to come to. Then her pretty blue eyes fluttered open. She sucked in a surprised breath when she looked up at him, as though she wasn't certain why he was carrying her, but she didn't struggle against him and she didn't say anything at all. She just held his gaze and Fin was certain that he'd never been so enthralled by so innocent an expression before in his life.

"Are you all right?" he finally asked.

"I think so." She nodded slowly. "What happened?"

"You fainted." He rounded the corner towards her chambers.

"I'm certain I can walk on my own, Fin."

Truly, she could do anything she set her mind on, but that didn't mean she should. "And yet I'll carry you the rest of the way anyway."

"You are stubborn," she returned without heat, resting her

head against his chest, making him yearn for her anew.

"And the raven chides blackness," he teased.

Lissy tilted her head upwards to see him better. "Don't think to charm me with Shakespeare."

"No Shakespeare?" He jostled her in his arms again, lifting her higher against his chest. "How should I charm you, then, Lissy? Any advice is more than welcome."

She glanced away from him. "And don't think to take advantage of me in my weakened state."

"Is your state weakened?"

Her gaze slowly lifted to his once more. "My state always seems to be weakened with you."

That was a good sign. Fin couldn't help but smile.

"Now you're going to be all arrogant about it," she complained. "Do put be down, Fin."

But they were already at her door. So Fin waited until after he'd stepped into her room, and then he lowered Lissy down to her feet. She stared up at him with her cerulean gaze, and Fin brushed his fingers across the apple of her cheek. "Beautiful," he whispered.

She pressed her cheek against his hand, like a kitten wanting to be stroked. Then she sighed. "You are making quite the habit of entering my bedchambers without an invitation."

Fin shrugged just a bit. "A habit I'm in no hurry to break." He dipped his head down and pressed his lips to hers.

Lissy grasped the edge of his jacket as though to steady herself, kissing him back ever so softly.

Fin slid his arm around her waist, securing her against him, reveling in the feel of her softness pressed against his chest. He could stand there with her like this for a lifetime. No quarreling, no pretenses, just the two of them, clinging to each other as though they were the only two people in the world.

He tangled his tongue with hers, delighting in the soft mewling sounds that escaped her every so often. He gently sucked her plump bottom lip and the memory of holding her naked form, of joining his body with hers, washed over Fin and he deepened their kiss.

But then she pressed slightly against his chest and took a step away from him. At once Fin felt the loss. What he wouldn't do to have her back in his arms right now. "Lissy, I know I'm not the only one who feels this."

Of course he wasn't. But what was she supposed to do, encourage him? Lissy shook her head. "Please don't, Fin."

He heaved a sigh, studying her as intently as a student preparing for an examination. "Tell me you don't love me, Lissy. Tell me that and I'll leave you be."

But she couldn't tell him that. He'd see right through her, like he always did. "Why are you making this so difficult?"

"Because I love you," he said. "Because I'm trying to understand."

There was nothing to understand. There could never be anything between them and that was that. "You don't want me, Fin. I'm not any good for you."

"I do want you. I want you more than anything." He took her in his arms once more.

Lissy shook her head, no longer able to look at him. "I'm damaged. I'm not who you think I am. Please just leave it at that."

He scoffed. "Leave it at that? You mean leave *you*, don't you? I love you, Lissy. I adore you. I'm not going to leave it at that. Help me understand. Tell me what this is about. Tell me what happened with Pierce."

She would have pulled away from him if he wasn't holding her so tightly. The last thing she wanted to do was relive her life with Aaron. But she was tired of fighting Fin over this. He truly was a most stubborn man. So she sagged a bit against him instead. At least with Fin she'd always been safe. "He wasn't who I thought he was," she breathed out.

He said nothing, almost as though he was holding his breath, afraid she wouldn't continue if he made a sound. Perhaps he was right. She'd never uttered these words to another living soul. She hadn't ever even spoken them aloud to herself.

"I thought him the most handsome of men," she admitted, even smiling a little as she remembered how innocent she'd been at that time. Heavens, she'd been just an idiot to marry Aaron. "He'd been so attentive, so charming as he courted me, and I was young and foolish, easily duped. I fell for his entire performance and by the time I realized what and who he was, it was too late. I was already married to him."

Memories started to play about the corners of her mind and instead of pushing them away as she usually did, Lissy let them rush into her thoughts, almost as though she was seeing herself in a play on the stage.

She took a staggering breath as long held off emotions swamped her. "O-on our wedding night, he bound me to his bed. He was so very strong and cruel and violent. I'd never seen any of that in him before." And the things he'd done to her that night and the nights since… She hadn't known such pain existed. But she didn't want to think about those particulars. Certainly, Fin would allow her that privacy. "When he was through with me, he left me bound there for days. I begged him to free me, but he wouldn't." He'd told her when she pleased him, she could go free, his cold and heartless voice striking terror in her young, innocent heart. His eyes that had once seemed to dance with mirth were nearly vacant in expression, almost as though he couldn't even see her, that she was nothing more than an object meant to be toyed with for his own personal amusement.

"He left you there?" Fin's horrified voice filtered into her thoughts. "For days?"

"Many, many times." Lissy nodded. Begging and pleading never did her any good. Doing so only proved to anger him more quickly.

"And what about your cousins? The ones you'd gone to visit? They didn't lift a finger to help you?" He sounded angrier with each word he spoke.

Lissy shrugged. It was so hard to explain. If she hadn't lived the life herself, she doubted she'd understand it. "No one knew. If I ever looked at anyone and wasn't smiling the way he wanted, he'd be furious later." She heaved a sigh. "And the threat of his punishment was enough to ensure my silence at all times. You don't understand what he was capable of." She'd kept all of this a secret for so long. Now that she was saying the words, they just seemed to spill free.

Fin grumbled something under his breath, the word punishments, perhaps.

"If it hadn't been for Sally, an indentured chambermaid, I think I might very well have died in his bed more than once. She always managed to get me a bit of food and cup of water...salve for my injuries after he was gone. But the bindings were too much for her, expert sailor's knots, of course. And I suspect she feared for her own life if she were to free me."

"Sadistic son of a bitch," he muttered under his breath, his hold tightening just a bit.

"I had thought," she continued, lost in horrible flashes of memory from those days in Boston she'd once feared would never end, "things would be easier, that he would be kinder, gentler with me after I was carrying his child."

Lissy didn't even realize she was crying until tears fell to her bodice, dampening the material. She swiped at her tears with the palm of her hand.

"But he only got worse, and..." A sob she was unable to hold back finally escaped her throat. "There was so much blood. So very much."

"Dear God, Lissy." Fin pulled her closer in his arms. "He made you lose your child?"

She nodded once, pain and anguish twisting her heart anew.

She had wanted that child so desperately. A tiny, little person who would love her no matter what. A child she could hold and dote on, adore for all of her days. But that wasn't to be. Another sob wrenched from her soul and Lissy couldn't catch her breath. She couldn't stop shaking and she couldn't speak.

Fin's hand smoothed up and down her back. "Shh," he soothed. "I'm here. I'm here, sweetheart. Just take a breath."

But all she could do was cry. Tears flooded down her face, soaking his jacket and cravat through. But still the tears kept coming, the tears she'd tried so hard to never shed, the tears she'd tried so hard to pretend weren't always right beneath the surface, the tears for her child who had never had a chance. "Tr-trauma," she struggled to get the words out. "Th-tha's what Doctor Watts said."

"Trauma?" Fin echoed, still caressing her back, still giving her whatever peace he could.

Lissy nodded against his chest, trying to remember exactly what the London doctor had said. "The trauma I suffered—" she took a staggering breath "—would make it nearly impossible for me to conceive." She stared at Fin's tear-soaked cravat, but all she saw was nothingness. "He said the word so many times that day I never wanted to hear it again. B-but I still do. At night, when no one else is around I hear it in the recesses of my mind."

"Oh, Lissy." He peppered the top of her head with soft kisses as though they could erase the memories plaguing her. "My dear, sweet Lissy, I'm so sorry." Then he simply held her against him, gentle but firm, offering his love and comfort in the most quiet of ways.

Goodness, she loved him, with every bit of her heart and soul. There was no better man in all the world. She could have stayed there forever, wrapped in the safety of his arms. The only time she'd ever truly been safe, she'd been with him. He'd comforted her after Papa had passed, he'd comforted her when she'd returned home and learned of Georgie's death, and now he comforted her once again.

"My poor, sweet Felicity," he cooed after what seemed like a lifetime. "My darling girl. I am so sorry about everything. If I'd known…"

"There's nothing you could have done," she said softly, pulling herself back together a bit. "There's nothing anyone could have done. He was my husband."

"Husband?" Fin scoffed. "He bound you to his bed. He was your captor and tormentor."

"That too," she agreed.

"He's damned lucky he's dead. I'd—"

"He's not dead." The words flew from her before she could stop them. She hadn't meant to tell him that part. She'd never meant to tell him any of it. But really, what was the point in keeping that secret any longer? Perhaps now he'd understand.

"I beg your pardon." He pulled back slightly as though to see her better. Anger and disbelief flashing in the depths of his brown eyes.

"That's why I can't marry you, Fin." She looked away once more, unable to see the pain and fury flashing in his eyes. "I'm not free. I'll never be free."

"Aaron Pierce is *alive*?" Fin's fingers tightened on her shoulders. "Is that what you're saying?"

Twenty-Three

Fin's mind was awhirl. Damn it all, the things she described where truly beyond comprehension. As hard as it was to believe, Lissy had endured an even worse fate than Georgie had. Until this moment, he hadn't known it was possible to hate anyone more than he'd hated the late-Marquess of Teynham. But Aaron Pierce was an even more despicable villain. Binding her to a bed and leaving her for days on end, doing God knew what to her in the meantime. And causing her to lose her child!

If Fin hadn't been holding Lissy, he would have balled his hand into a fist. That damned bastard was *alive*? Was that true? If Fin ever got his hands on the monster, he wouldn't breathe another breath, there wouldn't be a safe corner in the world for Pierce to hide. How quickly could he get to Boston?

He glanced down at Lissy in his arms, who'd begun trembling again. Truly, he could not have heard her correctly. It wasn't possible that Aaron Pierce was alive. It just wasn't.

26

"Sally helped me," Lissy said softly, not even daring to lift her gaze to meet his, but staring instead at the onyx pin in the middle of his tear-drenched cravat. "When I lost the baby, I was beside myself. All I could think about was finding a way home, anyway I could. Something I'd thought about many times before, of course. But at that moment there wasn't anything I wouldn't have done." She shook her head as though memories were flooding her thoughts. "Aaron went to sea that very afternoon. He wasn't supposed to be gone long. A week or so at the most, but it was my chance to escape. And I wouldn't have made it without Sally."

"How did you escape?" He had no idea how she could have managed it.

Lissy took a deep breath and finally lifted her gaze to meet Fin's. "She sawed through the bindings with a blade, then we left it in the middle of the blood stained bedclothes so it would like I'd managed to free myself. I wrote Aaron a letter saying that my will to live was gone. I told him I was going to slash my wrists and leap from a bridge into the bay so I could join my child in the next world."

Good God! Fin's mouth dropped open in horror at the image she painted in his mind.

"He had to think I was dead," she continued, blinking back another deluge of tears, "or he would have come after me, Fin. I left him the note so he wouldn't look for me," she explained, though her voice sounded so distant all of a sudden. "Then I fled to New York with just the clothes on my back and sought passage on the first ship destined for England that I could find."

"And then told everyone here that your husband was dead," Fin finished for her.

Lissy nodded. "I didn't have any other choices. Everyone knew I'd gotten married. I had to say something."

So she chose an enormous lie over the truth? "Why didn't you tell *me*?" he asked, his mind still spinning. He hadn't been in love with her then, but he'd always loved her. There wasn't anything he wouldn't have done to keep her safe. Surely, she'd always known that.

Lissy pushed out of his embrace and turned her back to him. "I couldn't risk anyone sending me back to him."

Sending her back to him! Of all the damned things to say! "You think Luke and Juliet would send you back to him?" His voice raised an octave in frustration. "You think *I* would send you back to him?" The idea that she thought he would do something so terrible made his blood nearly boil. Didn't she know him at all?

She spun around to face him once more. "He's my *husband*. I belong to him, Fin. You wouldn't have had any say in the matter."

"The hell I wouldn't," Fin growled. "If he had taken a step in your direction I'd have slayed him where he stood." At her frightened expression, Fin heaved a sigh and tried to soften his voice. "I know powerful people, Felicity. Liverpool is an ally. We can...Well, we can do something. We'll get the marriage dissolved, annulled, something."

"I hardly think an annulment is possible."

Why was she being so damned difficult? He was trying to help her. "Anything is possible with the right allies. No one even consulted your guardian for permission for your marriage, for God's sake. We can certainly use that to our advantage."

She began to shake as though a tremor raced through her. "But then he'll know I'm alive," she said so softly he barely heard her. Terror flashed in her eyes and Fin's heart ached for her all over again.

One way or the other, he'd free Lissy from that union if it was the last thing he ever did, no matter the cost, be it financial, personal or political. "He'll never touch you again, Lissy, I swear it." If Aaron Pierce ever stepped foot on English soil...

"You don't know him, Fin." She shook her head. "If he knows I'm alive..."

"Trust me, Lissy." He stepped towards her and grasped her hands, bringing them to his lips. "I'll never let him hurt you again.

That is a promise."

Her blue eyes blinked back more tears, but she looked to be wavering a bit, which was the first bit of hope for a future together she'd given him since they'd made love.

"And when this is through, tell me you'll marry me."

"I want to say yes," she said quickly. "But I don't know if I'm ready for that, Fin."

"Then I'll wait until you are," he vowed. After he was done with Aaron Pierce and once Lissy was free, he'd do whatever it took to win her hand.

"And what if I'm never ready?" she asked. "I may *never* be ready, you know? You shouldn't waste your life waiting for me."

"Waiting for you would never be a waste." He brushed his fingers across her soft cheek.

She smiled sadly. "But I may never be ready, Fin. I don't want to lie to you. Marriage…Well, it's so permanent and more than bit frightening."

It would have to be after what she'd endured. But their life together would be vastly different. "If you're never ready, then I suppose I'll settle for loving you and—" he winked at her "—living the rest of my days in sin."

A laugh escaped her, which did warm his heart a bit. "Be serious."

"Have you ever known me to be otherwise?"

"You *are* mad." She shook her head, but she was smiling so Fin simply nodded in return.

"Apparently." He leaned forward and pressed a kiss to her brow. "But I'll take you any way I can have you." Then he dipped his head lower and kissed her again, ever so gently. She tasted like the sweetest, purest heaven, though a bit salty from her tears. Damn it all, she didn't deserve what she'd suffered. If there was a way for Fin to ease her pain and calm her fears, he'd do it without hesitation.

After a moment, Lissy pushed back from him. "But, Fin, odds

are I'll never be able to give you an heir. You deserve someone who can give you that."

And if they never had children, his heart would be heavy; but there was no point in worrying about something that might or might not be. "Then I suppose a distant cousin will inherit, because I'm never giving you up, Lissy. So stop worrying about things we don't have control of."

A sob burst free from her, and Lissy threw her arms around his neck once more. Fin held her trembling body close, caressing her back, murmuring words of love and adoration against her ear and vowing to care for her all of his days.

But first things first. Her marriage had to be dealt with sooner, rather than later. "Just as soon as I can, I'll start for London."

"London?" she echoed, gazing up into his eyes.

"Today. Now." He nodded. "The sooner I get there, the sooner I can sort out what can be done, sweetheart."

"Now?" She frowned. "But your carriage isn't even here yet, a- and the baby..."

The baby. Now he knew, or suspected he did, why she'd fainted in Juliet's room. Who knew what awful memories would plague her the rest of the day while she waited for her new niece or nephew to finally emerge in the world? "Or tomorrow." He caressed her cheek. "Do you want me to stay today, sweetheart?"

Her blue eyes lightened a bit as though a fog had been lifted from them. "Please."

Fin smiled. He could deny her nothing. He didn't suspect he'd ever be able to. "Tomorrow it is, then."

"Do you want me to come with you tomorrow?"

Fin's smile widened and his heart lifted at her eagerness to stay with him. "More than anything, but it might be better for you to stay here with Juliet and Luke."

"But you'll hurry back?"

He nodded quickly. "As quickly as I possibly can, Lissy."

Ben squealed with joy as Fin tossed him into the air, and Lissy couldn't help but laugh. They were a pair. Ben had always made Fin seem so carefree, so boyish. It would truly be a shame if he never had children of his own. Her heart twisted a bit at the maudlin thought. Doctor Watts hadn't said it was impossible for her to bear children, just that the odds were unlikely she could do so. But she'd beaten the odds before, hadn't she? Escaping Aaron's clutches had certainly been unlikely. She pushed all of those awful memories away, however, as she didn't want to dwell on them at the moment.

Fin was right. There was no use worrying about something neither of them had control of. Besides, with Ben giggling and Fin looking so happy, living in the moment seemed a much better choice.

From the nursery threshold, Annie cleared her throat.

Lissy rose from her seat and grinned at her maid, so very happy to see her. "Oh, Annie! You made it. Are you feeling better today?"

Her maid nodded and stepped into the nursery. "Chivers is resting in his quarters, but I am good as new, my lady."

"I am glad to hear it."

"How is Chivers?" Fin asked, catching Ben about the middle and stepping closer to the maid.

"His leg is bandaged, but he's in a fair amount of pain. The innkeeper's son drove the carriage today. I hope that was all right."

"Of course." Fin nodded. "I'm so sorry to have abandoned you both."

Lissy's cheeks warmed a bit. It was, after all, her fault Chivers and Annie had been abandoned. "As am I."

The look Annie cast Lissy said better than words could that she knew something had transpired, but she'd never say so aloud. "Keeton saw the man was well compensated and has returned him to the inn."

"Good of him to do so," Fin replied.

Annie glanced back at Lissy and said, "Lady Juliet is asking for you."

"For me?" Lissy's voice was so soft she barely heard it herself.

"Apparently, she'd like for you to meet your niece."

Lissy released a breath she hadn't known she'd been holding. It was almost as though a heavy weight had been lifted off her shoulders with those words. Thank heavens Jules was all right! Lissy was a terrible sister to have abandoned Juliet in her time of need. If her sister never forgave her, she'd be well within her rights.

"A girl?" Fin said, and though Lissy wasn't looking at him, she could hear the smile in his voice.

"Georgina," Annie confirmed.

Georgina. A sob lodged in Lissy's throat. Oh, dear God. It was Georgie's birthday. And now… She glanced over at Fin to see him brush a tear from his cheek. Her heart stung a bit. Not from any jealousy over her departed sister, but just from the void Georgie's absence still was.

But now there was a little girl, born on her birthday, bearing her name. It was almost as though Georgie was there with them in spirit.

"Thank you, Annie," Lissy managed to find her voice. "I'll be right there."

"A girl?" Ben sounded most dejected.

Lissy turned slightly to see her nephew in Fin's arms. A laugh escaped her. "Sisters are the most wonderful things in the world, I'll have you know. " At least hers were. Kind-hearted, dutiful Georgie, who had only ever wanted the best for Lissy. Brave Juliet who would take on the world if it was required of her. And they'd been saddled with…Lissy in return. All of a sudden, she felt very small and unimportant, filled with remorse for things she hadn't done, filled with regret for things she had done.

"Well, I'll be certain not to mention that bit to Edmund." Fin quirked a grin at her, and Lissy's spirit lifted just a bit.

Who knew he had the ability to make her feel better when darkness threatened to encroach upon her? She tipped her head back regally like any good duke's daughter had been trained from birth to do and said, "I'm certain Edmund is quite aware of the fact already."

Fin laughed. "I'm certain he is." The look he cast her, so filled with adoration, warmed Lissy from the inside out.

She wasn't certain how her fortunes had changed, but she knew they most definitely had. Phineas Granard was the most wonderful man she'd ever known and by some grace of God he loved her, was determined to right the wrongs in her life, even the ones she'd caused herself. She was, without a doubt, the luckiest girl in all the world. She hoped that if Georgie could see the two of them, that she'd wish them well. Knowing Georgie as she always had, Lissy was certain that her sister would be happy for them.

She brushed away a tear that had come for nowhere, took a deep breath and said, "I'll make certain to tell your little sister what a wonderful big brother she has." Then she left the nursery and started for her sister's bedchambers.

Once she reached Juliet's domain, there was no need to knock. The door was open and Luke's laughter drifted out into the hallway. Lissy poked her head inside to find Juliet propped up against pillows in bed. Luke was sitting in the chair nearby, bouncing a little bundle in his arms, staring at the child as though all of the answers to life's mysteries could be found right there in her depths.

"You called for me?" Lissy asked from the threshold.

Juliet and Luke both glanced to the doorway and both smiled in welcome. Jules, though she looked exhausted and paler than she had earlier in the day, reached her arms out towards the doorway and said, "Come here, Lis."

Lissy stepped into the bedchambers and Luke pushed out of his chair. "Do come meet Georgina. I daresay she is the prettiest little girl in all the world."

Lissy couldn't help but laugh. Luke truly was a proud papa. She crossed the floor and peered into the bundle in Luke's arms. The bluest eyes she'd ever seen blinked up at her. The baby didn't look a thing like Georgie. She had her father's nose and the shape of his eyes. It was probably a blessing to not resemble one's namesake, however. "She's beautiful," she said softly.

"Do you want to hold her?" Luke asked.

Lissy nodded quickly. She'd never held a newborn. Ben had been a couple months old before she'd ever laid eyes on him. And Juliet had played nursemaid to Edmund all those years ago.

"Sit where I was," Luke directed.

Dutifully, she moved to her brother-in-law's vacated chair and took the seat. Then Luke turned and gently placed baby Georgina in her arms.

"Just be careful with her head," he advised as he rose back to his full height. "They're wobbly at this age."

Lissy stared down at her niece. She was a pretty little girl. Georgina's eyes fluttered shut and she was instantly asleep. How wonderful it would be to fall asleep so easily.

"Do you need anything, princess?" Luke asked, stepping closer to Juliet's bedside.

"I'm fine now that Lissy's here."

"On that note—" he smiled at his wife "—I am suddenly feeling outnumbered. I think I shall go find our son and see how he is."

"He's in the nursery," Lissy said, "With Fin. Or at least they were a few moments ago."

"Perfect." The expression Luke cast her made it quite clear he was very aware of everything that was going on between her and Fin, which should have sent her fleeing for safety but it was, instead, oddly reassuring. "He'll help even out our numbers if you don't run him off."

Lissy's cheeks warmed, but she refused to be baited by Luke.

He might suspect or even know what was going on, but Lissy wasn't prepared to discuss the situation with him, at least not right now.

"Go on with you," Juliet urged. "I want to talk to my sister."

Luke nodded in farewell, then took his leave.

"How are you?" Juliet asked as soon as they were alone.

An embarrassed laugh escaped Lissy. "I should be asking you that. I'm so sorry I was no help at all to you. I'm the worst sister alive." She lifted her gaze to meet Juliet's. "If you never want to see me again…"

Her sister scoffed in response. "Always so dramatic. You *fainted*, Felicity. I don't think you had control over that."

"No," she agreed. "But I was hardly any help."

"Luckily, I've done this before. I didn't need help. I just need to make certain you're all right."

Lissy nodded quickly. "I'm fine now. Fin—"

"Yes, Fin," Juliet interrupted. "What exactly is going on with Fin?"

"Everything." Lissy's cheeks heated anew. Was she so easily seen through? She supposed it didn't matter, not with Juliet. "Everything is going on with Fin. I'm not even certain how it started, but I am most in love with him. And he is quite in love with me."

The broadest smile Juliet had ever worn stretched across her face. "I had wondered how long it would take for the two of you to come to your senses."

Lissy's mouth fell open. "I beg your pardon?"

"Oh, don't make me laugh," her sister said on a chuckle. "It hurts to do so."

"What do you mean you wondered how long it would take us to come to our senses?" She got the feeling all of a sudden that something else was going on that she didn't know a thing about.

Juliet's brown eyes twinkled happily. "You've bickered like a married couple forever, Lissy. He's always trying to protect you from whatever scheme you've concocted and that's exactly what he needs to bring a little excitement and levity to his life. And while you have complained endlessly about his staid and steady nature, you'll never let anyone else utter an unkind word about him. You are the opposites of each other, but you balance each other out perfectly. You always have."

Lissy could only stare at her sister.

"Why do you think I urged you to attend this season alone?" Juliet asked. "We thought…Well, truly, *Caroline Staveley* gets the credit for the plan. She —"

"Caroline Staveley?" Lissy breathed out. "I barely even saw her in London." The famed matchmaker couldn't have plotted this all out. She just couldn't have. Wouldn't Lissy have realized if Caroline Staveley was behind all of this?

"I'm sure Fin did. You don't think he'd suddenly start showing up at social functions on his own, did you?"

An uneasiness washed over Lissy. "You all played us."

Juliet shook her head. "We eased the way for the two of you to see each other in a new light. The rest was up to you." Then her brown eyes twinkled once again. "Do tell me everything, Lissy. He is such a wonderful man. Do tell me you're happy."

And she was happy. Happier than she'd ever been. But she was annoyed with her sister and Luke and Caroline and anyone else who sought to interfere in her life too. There was, after all, a rather large reason she'd never sought another match. And that reason had yet to be dealt with. "There's something I should tell you, Jules," she began, not certain how much she would tell her sister in the end. She certainly didn't have it in her to tell her everything, not for the second time in one day.

"What is it?" The twinkle in her eyes dulled a bit and her brow furrowed.

But there was one thing she would learn anyway at this point. "You'll find out one way or the other. And I'd rather you hear it from me, than from someone else."

"I don't like the way you said that."

Lissy looked back down at little Georgina, asleep in her arms. Such a sweet little girl. She was much easier to look at just now than at her sister. "I'm not widowed," she admitted. It was a bit easier to say that now that she'd told Fin everything. "My husband is an awful man. Three years away from him and I still have nightmares."

"You're not widowed?" Juliet breathed out.

"He is quite alive." Lissy shook her head. "Fin says he can do something, I'm not sure what. But something to gain me a divorce or dissolve the marriage somehow. I don't hold out a lot of hope for that, but I am willing to let him try."

"How are you *not* widowed?" her sister asked, shock and uneasiness lacing her voice.

"It's a very long story and I truly don't want to dwell on the facts at the moment. Someday I'll tell you all of it, but for now, please believe me when I say that if I didn't escape when I did I would most likely be dead now."

"He hurt you?" Indignation seemed to rise up inside Juliet. "I'll kill him myself."

Lissy couldn't help but smile. "You don't know how often I wished for your bravery, Jules." She shook her head. "But that's all in the past." She heaved a sigh. "If Fin isn't able to free me from this marriage, I'll have to let him go. It wouldn't be fair to him otherwise. And when that time comes, I'm going to need your bravado then." If she wasn't holding her niece, she'd have swiped at a tear that trailed down her cheek. "He's so honorable, he'll never leave me; but I couldn't live with myself if my past foolishness stole his future."

She lifted her gaze to meet her sister's once more just in time to see Juliet swipe at a tear of her own. "Why don't we cross that bridge when we come to it, Lissy? If Fin says he can free you from this marriage, then he can. I would never bet against him."

Lissy nodded in response. "But if he can't, I'm going to need your support, more than I've ever needed it."

A sad smile settled on her sister's face. "Lissy, you have always had my support. There is nothing I wouldn't do for you. But don't count Fin out."

Twenty-Four

"I have a daughter." Luke Beckford's face was slightly pale as he stepped just inside the nursery.

Fin glanced toward the threshold from his spot in one of the chintz chairs and said, "And a son." He gestured to Ben, stacking a pile of blocks on the floor at his feet.

Luke glared at Fin as though he was most inept. "A *daughter*, Phineas." He stressed the word as though there was some sort of secret meaning in it.

"Yes," Fin agreed, not knowing what was suddenly wrong with the man.

"A daughter who is going to grow up and…And there are men like *me* out there." Luke scrubbed a hand across his brow, then crossed the floor in just a few strides. "I have no idea how I'll protect her."

Ah, now it made sense. A reformed rake might be a bit terrified at the prospect of raising a daughter versus a son. "That is a long time off, my friend."

"Not long enough." Luke raked a hand through his hair and then dropped into the chair across from Fin.

"I'm sure when the time comes, you'll be prepared."

"I wanted a boy." Ben dropped his block and scrambled over to his father's chair.

Luke tousled his son's hair. "That would have made things easier," he muttered, but then he plucked the boy off the ground and settled him on his lap. "But girls can be delightful, Ben. Mama's a girl, you know?"

"And Aunt Lissy," Fin tossed in.

At that, Luke's gaze shot to Fin's. "Speaking of Aunt Lissy..." he began; his ever-knowing green eyes seemed to assess him. "She seemed well, just now."

He couldn't help but grin widely in return. "We had a productive conversation today."

"And?" Luke prodded.

"And," Fin continued, "I'll leave for London tomorrow. She's in a bit of a predicament, but once I untangle her from all of that..."

"Then you'll be Ben's Uncle Fin in more than just name?"

Fin chuckled. Who would have guessed Luke Beckford was as much of a matchmaker as his sister? "I am hopeful she'll agree to that, but it may take some time, and perhaps a fair amount of convincing."

"Still, that sounds more promising than it did this morning."

So much had changed since that morning. Lissy had finally confided in him. He'd learned about the awful existence she'd suffered in Boston, which was far worse than anything he could have ever imagined. And he'd vowed to help her in any way he could. It felt like much more than just one day had passed. "Our path isn't without its pitfalls, but I am more confident than I was at breakfast that things will turn out like I hope."

A genuine smile lit Luke's face. "I am glad, Fin. You deserve happiness. You both do. And while a St. Claire girl can drive you to distraction, they are worth it."

But that Fin already knew.

Lissy smiled as Fin's hand landed on the small of her back as she ascended the staircase, headed to the family wing. Spending the day with him, with Juliet, Luke, Ben and little Georgina had been the balm her soul had needed. But the small pressure from his fingers warmed her from the inside out and her sister's words rushed to her mind once more. She'd always loved Fin, but had she been *in love* with him for longer than she'd realized?

She reached the top of the stairs and spun around to face him. With him a step lower than her, she was almost his height, as close as eye-to-eye as they could be. Surprise lit his dark eyes and Lissy's heart overflowed with love for him. "You are *the* most remarkable man. Do you know that?"

His lips tipped up to a most charming smile and his hands slid around her waist pulling her to him. "Flattery will get you everywhere, Lissy." Then, ever so gently, he pressed his lips to hers.

Her eyes fluttered closed and her hands settled on his shoulders. It was so hard to believe that her life was turning out so well, better than she could have possibly imagined. But she was starting to believe it, starting to picture a future with Fin, starting to hope that ugly shadow of Aaron Pierce would vanish forever.

She pulled back slightly from him. "Will you stay with me tonight?"

He looked rather smug all of a sudden, but then he was still a member of the male of the species. "Can't live without me now, hmm?

She quirked him a smile and said, "I'm certain I can hold out longer than you, Uncle Fin. Shall we put it to a contest?"

His dark eyes narrowed perceptibly. "Felicity, if you ever call me that again…"

"Yes?" she prodded. "What will you do, *Uncle Fin?*"

"I will tickle you mercilessly, until you beg me to stop and even then I won't. Not until I secure your promise to never call me that again."

Well that hardly sounded so bad, especially when it was such a simple way to get under his skin. Besides, she had the upper hand, at least right now. Lissy stepped slightly away from him, shot him what she hoped was her most impish smile and said, "You'll have to catch me first, Uncle Fin." And then she turned on her heel and bolted down the corridor towards her room.

She almost made it. But just as she reached for her handle, Fin caught her about the waist and rasped against her ear, "You are in trouble now, my little minx."

He pushed the door open and scooped her up into his arms. Lissy squealed as he kicked the door closed behind them and then dropped her into the middle of her bed.

His brown eyes flashed playfully as he yanked at his cravat. "I will show you no mercy, Lissy."

She giggled in response. "You don't like 'Uncle Fin', is that what you're saying?"

"You're only going to make it worse for yourself." He tossed his jacket onto the floor.

"It's not formal enough, is it?" she teased. "You prefer Uncle Phineas, don't you? Honestly, you should have mentioned that long before now. I am quite embarrassed."

A smile played about his lips but he said nothing else as he dropped his waistcoat onto the floor and tugged his shirt over his head.

The sight of Fin's bare torso made Lissy's breath catch in her throat. He was handsome. His straight nose and strong jaw. His broad shoulders, his strong muscles and the light dusting of brown hair across his chest. Much more handsome than Michelangelo's David. Much more handsome than any man in the world, she was most certain. "I love you, Fin," she said softly, and she'd never meant anything as assuredly as she did those words.

Fin shook his head, a most boyish expression on his face. "Oh, it's too late for words of love to save *you*, Lady Felicity." And then he dropped onto the bed beside her, grasped her waist in his hands and tickled her most feverishly.

Lissy twisted and turned to get away from him, but she was laughing too hard to truly escape. "I pr-promise! I pr-promise!" she giggled.

"What do you promise, my darling?" Fin returned so smoothly as though he was asking her to dance at a ball.

She tried to catch her breath, but his assault didn't lessen in the least. "I won't c-c-call you Uncle Fin. I won't."

He stopped tickling her. "What will you call me?" He rolled her beneath him and hovered over her, his dark hair falling across his brow.

Lissy stared up at him. Her wonderful Fin, the most honest and true man she'd ever known. Her heart nearly overflowed for him. "My love?" she asked.

The smile he brandished could have lit a hundred ballrooms. "I do like the sound of that," he said before lowering his head and capturing her lips in a searing kiss.

Tingles raced across Lissy's skin and before she knew how he'd done it, Fin had tugged her bodice downward, freeing her breasts from their constraints. His gentle fingers caressed her bare flesh and Lissy ached for more. She groaned against his lips, and then those clever fingers of his teased her nipples until they were hard peaks, straining upwards.

"Once again," he whispered across her lips, "you are overdressed, Lissy."

But she wasn't for long. Together they made quick work of her dress, her slippers, his trousers, his boots and were joined as one.

Fin's languid strokes were so careful, so loving, Lissy was in complete heaven. She might as well have floated right up to the clouds. And when she fell over that invisible precipice, Fin fell right along beside her.

Then he dropped onto the bed, pulled her into his embrace and simply held her close.

Lissy toyed with the bit of hair across his chest. "How long will you be gone?"

His hand tightened on her waist. "I'm not sure, but I won't be gone a moment longer than is absolutely necessary, sweetheart."

She smiled at that and then pressed her lips to his chest. "Do you want to see Edmund…Tell him about…us?"

"I probably should," he agreed. Then he kissed the top of her head and smoothed his hand down her side. "But I might just send him a note instead."

Lissy couldn't help but giggle. It was such a wonderful feeling, knowing that he wanted to be with her as much as she wanted to be with him. It was a feeling she hadn't expected to ever experience in her life. She pushed up against his chest to look down on him and said, "I will miss you."

"I should hope so," he returned before pulling her down for another kiss.

Twenty-Five

Traveling back to London wasn't nearly as enjoyable as the trip to Prestwick Chase had been, but that was to be expected as Fin was traveling this leg alone. Borrowing Beckford's driver, Fin had departed The Chase at dawn and traveled a good distance.

When the carriage finally stopped at a coaching inn for the night, Fin entered the taproom, and was beyond surprised to hear his name called across the din.

"Carraway!" Lord Staveley rose from his spot at a table in the far end of the taproom, waving his arm in the air. "Is Lady Felicity with you?"

"Staveley?" Fin could hardly believe his eyes. Of all the people he thought he might encounter along the road, Viscount Staveley would never have topped his list. The man rarely left his own study. Fin pushed his way through the drunken patrons to Staveley's table. "What are you doing here?"

"Caroline said Felicity was traveling with you," the man

replied, gesturing to an empty seat at his table.

"She was. I left her at Prestwick Chase. I'm on my way back to Town to attend to some business." He slid into a seat across from the bookish viscount.

"Ah." Staveley nodded. "How is everyone at The Chase? Caroline's been so worried about Juliet."

Fin couldn't help the smile that spread across his face. Everyone at The Chase was fine. Especially a maddening little blonde that he couldn't wait to get back to. But Staveley had asked about Juliet, and so Fin adjusted his thoughts accordingly. "She is quite well. She had her babe yesterday. A girl. Georgina."

"Georgina?" Staveley smiled as well.

Fin laughed. "Born on Georgie's birthday, actually." And while in the past, even mentioning Georgie's name would twist his heart, that wasn't the case now. Oh, he'd always love her. She'd been his first true love. She was kind and compassionate. Honest and sincere. Perfect in nearly every way. But Lissy had somehow healed his broken heart, made him feel things he never thought he'd feel again. And for the first time in what seemed forever, the future didn't seem as bleak as it once had. Just as soon as he dealt with the business of Lissy's marriage, their lives together could truly begin.

"I think this calls for a little celebration." Staveley motioned towards a tavern wench. "Your best whisky," he called. Then he turned his attention back to Fin. "Luke must be over the moon."

Fin nodded. "Though suddenly having a daughter in his arms seems to have struck a bit of fear in his heart."

Staveley chuckled. "Years ago, I never thought I'd see the day he'd be a responsible parent."

Fin hadn't either. But the rakish ne'er-do-well that Lucas Beckford had once been had certainly led the way to the devoted husband and father that he was now. "The only one befuddled by the whole thing is Ben. He can't understand what all the fuss is about. Wrinkly baby girl who can do nothing but cry, but everyone seems enthralled over her."

Staveley laughed heartily. "Rachel was the same when Adam was born, and he was the same when Emma came along." The tavern wench placed a couple glasses of whisky before the men and Staveley said, "Thank you."

"Pamela probably thought the same about me."

"Probably. Such is the way of things." Staveley agreed with an incline of his head. He lifted his glass in the air and said, "To our new niece Georgina Beckford. May she make her namesake proud and her father regret each and every last one of his past sins."

"Here. Here." Fin lifted his glass as well before downing the oaky drink in one large swallow. Then he lowered his glass and smiled at the studious viscount. It was so strange to be sitting in the middle of a taproom with him. "Now what *are* you doing in the middle of Northamptonshire, of all places?"

Staveley dropped his own glass to the table, his smile vanished quickly and was replaced with a rather serious expression. "Heading to Prestwick Chase to find Felicity."

"Oh?" Fin's brow furrowed. He couldn't imagine a scenario that would lead to Staveley searching out Felicity in Derbyshire.

"It's all very convoluted, honestly."

"I have the time." Fin shrugged, his interest more than piqued. "Besides, when is anything having to do with her *not* convoluted?"

Staveley scoffed in an apparent agreement, then a frown settled on his face. "Well, it seems a fellow claiming to be her not-so-dead husband has come to Town and is looking for her."

A chill raced down Fin's spine. "I beg your pardon?" he breathed out.

"My thoughts exactly." Staveley nodded. "It's completely ridiculous. Not-so dead husband. Sounds foolish to even say. I might very well be on some wild goose chase concocted by that blackguard Haversham just to get me out of Town."

"Haversham?" Fin's head began to pulse with pain. "What the

devil does he have to do with this?"

"He went to Caroline. Said this Pierce fellow was looking for Felicity and thought someone ought to warn her. Said he thought the fellow would find his way to Prestwick Chase very soon and that she should be prepared."

Oh, dear God! Why now? Why after all these years would Aaron Pierce suddenly get it in his head Lissy was alive? Had that indentured girl finally broken and revealed the truth? Had Lissy somehow slipped up and Pierce had recently found her out somehow? The fact that Haversham was involved didn't bode well for anyone. "Why would *he* care one way or the other?"

At that Staveley snorted. "The only thing I'm certain about as far as that man goes is that he's bound and determined to capture my wife."

"Not that she's willing to be captured." Fin smiled at the man. Honest, dutiful Staveley. The last thing he deserved was that scoundrel Haversham chasing after his wife's skirts.

But thoughts of Staveley, Caroline and Haversham quickly fell aside as panic once again gripped his heart. Dear God. Was Aaron Pierce *truly* in London? If so, should Fin race there and put a ball in the man's chest? Or race back to Prestwick Chase instead and keep Lissy safe? He didn't even have to think about that for more than a second. He could easily pass Pierce on the road to London and never see the villain, leaving Lissy defenseless. So The Chase it would have to be.

Staveley rose from his spot, completely unaware of the turmoil encompassing Fin. "Do excuse me, Carraway. Nature calls." Then he started for the staircase at the back end of the room.

Fin's mind was awhirl. He'd traveled so much distance today. It would take quite some time to return. He'd need a fresh steed. "Actually, I'll be on my way, Staveley," he called to the man. "I'll see you soon, I'm sure."

"Godspeed," Staveley called back over the din, then hurried up the staircase when he noticed a man waiting behind him.

Fin pushed his way through the taproom and out, once again, into the coaching yard. He hailed a young groom and said, "I need your fastest, most rested horse."

"R'ght away, sir." The lad raced towards the stables.

To everything there is a season, and a time to every purpose under the sun. At least that was the verse from Ecclesiastes that Aaron Pierce's father had always pressed upon him as a child. And for all of Aaron's life, he'd found those words to be quite poignant.

John had encountered Thurlstone just as Heaton and Pierce Shipping was at the precipice of financial ruin, bringing the Englishman and his investments into the business at the precise moment to keep them afloat.

Aaron had been in the right London club at the right time to learn that his wife was somehow miraculously alive.

Thurlstone had gladly offered Aaron and John use of his traveling carriage to take them to Derbyshire, which was kismet as Aaron didn't have one of his own in this godforsaken country and his funds were particularly low.

But just now, those old words of his father's had never been more true. If he hadn't been seated at exactly the right spot in the raucous taproom just now, he'd have never overheard that bespectacled, scholarly looking Englishman mention Felicity or of the fellow's plan to warn her of Aaron's imminent arrival.

Across the taproom table from Aaron, John scratched his head. "Why do you think that Haversham fellow sent him to warn Felicity?" he asked softly.

That Aaron didn't have an answer for. He hadn't cared for Haversham at all upon meeting the man a few days ago, though he hadn't seemed the interfering sort. The prick had seemed self-serving and smug, mostly. But he also seemed cleverer than he tried to let on. Though Aaron had noticed that, no one else seemed to. Regardless of the reason, however, Haversham would be dealt with once Aaron had taken care of the Felicity situation.

"Do excuse me, Carraway," the scholarly looking fellow at the next table said as he pushed up to his feet. "Nature calls."

To everything there is a season, and a time to every purpose under the sun.

Aaron glanced towards the man tasked with warning Felicity about his presence, then turned his attention back to John. "I'll find out though." Aaron pushed out of his chair and followed the bespectacled man towards the back staircase.

"Actually, I'll be on my way, Staveley," the scholar's friend called to the man. "I'll see you soon, I'm sure."

Perfect! No one would even realize the scholar was missing then.

"Godspeed," the man replied, then seemed to notice Aaron and hastened up the steps.

Aaron followed the scholar, at a much slower pace. There was no reason to attract attention in the taproom. After reaching the top of the staircase, the corridor that met him smelled of dank ale and was dimly lit, but Aaron could make out his quarry perfectly well. He retrieved his dagger from the scabbard he always kept strapped just inside his boot, then he rushed after the scholar, who was easy to catch, as he had no idea he was being followed.

Aaron quietly wrapped his left arm around the man's neck from behind, which made it very simple to thrust his dagger into scholar's back and twist it just a bit, puncturing the fellow's lung, making it impossible for him to call out for any sort of help, a nice little trick he'd learned a while back. After a moment, Aaron released the man who fell to the floor in a heap, gasping for air.

"Nothing personal," he said into the darkness, retrieving his weapon from the fallen man's back. "But I would rather surprise my wife in my own time, if you don't mind."

The scholar grasped into the darkness as though that was going to help him somehow. Then his arm went limp and Aaron wiped his blade clean before replacing it in the scabbard in this boot.

Now, where to put the body?

He was able to make out what looked like a doorframe in the corridor and Aaron moved quietly towards the door. Sure enough, there was a handle and he pulled it open. Supply cupboard.

The space looked just large enough to place the scholar for the night or at least until someone found the fellow. But by that time, Aaron would be long gone. He turned back to the lifeless form in the middle of the corridor, bent at his middle, hefted the man over his shoulder and then made quick work of depositing the fellow inside the cupboard.

To everything there is a season, and a time to every purpose under the sun

He dusted his hands across his trousers and then started back for the taproom. John was looking anxiously in his direction, but there was no reason to look anxious. Their problem had been easily dealt with.

Aaron descended the steps, resumed his spot across from his old friend and lifted his pint to his lips.

"Well?" John prodded. "What did he say?"

"Man of few words," Aaron replied.

"He had nothing to say?" John frowned. "Seemed talkative in here."

Indeed he had. Still, Aaron shrugged in response, as it seemed to be what John was expecting. "The fellow has problems with his own wife, apparently. So I simply explained that it would be best for him to return to London to deal with *his* wife and let me deal with mine."

"And that worked?"

In a manner of speaking. Aaron smiled. "Very reasonable fellow, actually."

John nodded as though that made sense. But then John had always been easy to appease. He never looked any further than the most simple of explanations, and at times Aaron had the feeling that his friend and business partner didn't want to look any deeper, and that suited them both perfectly.

"I still have a hard time believing that she's alive." John scrubbed a hand across his brow. "That note and all of that blood..." He heaved a sigh. "I am sorry, Aaron. I searched every inch of the bay, hoping for some sign of her. I was certain she'd been washed out to sea."

Which was exactly what she'd wanted them to think. Aaron tipped back his pint once more. Felicity was much more crafty than he'd given her credit for. A mistake he wouldn't ever make again.

Twenty-Six

The sun was just coming up over the horizon of the Peak District as Fin rode up to Prestwick Chase. Exhaustion had set in over an hour ago, but he couldn't stop. Any delay could mean dire consequences for Lissy. So he'd pushed on, changing horses when necessary, but never stopping for longer than just a few minutes.

He handed the horse off to a groom and then made his way to the manor entrance. Keeton greeted him at the door, surprise splashed across his face. "Lord Carraway?"

"Lady Felcity, Keeton. I need to see her right away," he said, stepping over the threshold and wishing he'd gotten at least of wink of sleep the night before. "Find her as fast as you can."

"Good God, Fin!" Luke Beckford said, rounding the corner into the foyer. "This is like *déjà vu*. You arriving unannounced and bellowing for her. Except it's not the middle of the night this time."

And neither was Fin bellowing, but he was in no mood to argue the semantics with Luke. He sent the butler his most formative glare and said, "Find her quickly."

"Of course, sir." Keeton started down the corridor at a spritely clip.

"What's wrong?" Luke asked, all traces of humor from his voice long gone.

"She's in trouble," Fin replied. "And we have to keep her safe."

"Keep her safe?" Luke echoed. "What sort of trouble is she in?"

But before Fin could answer that question, Lissy's voiced filtered down the corridor. "Fin!" she nearly sang, appearing a moment later. "You are quick when you put your mind to it." Then she rushed forward and threw her arms around his neck. "How are you possibly back already?"

Fin caught her about the waist and held her against him. Just having her in his arms was a relief. He didn't truly think it was possible for Pierce to arrive at The Chase before he did, but that niggling thought had plagued him the entire journey back to Derbyshire. Thank God she was safe!

Fin inhaled her soft lilac scent, relishing the calm before the storm. But he couldn't foolishly waste whatever lead they did have. So, he pulled back from her and said very calmly, "Aaron Pierce is in London, or was. He's apparently headed this direction."

Lissy's mouth fell open and she began to tremble like she was freezing, though Fin knew her reaction had nothing to do with the temperature at The Chase.

"Aaron Pierce?" Luke asked. "What are you talking about?"

Fin squeezed Lissy's hand. "It's all right, sweetheart. I won't let him touch you ever again."

"Did you say Aaron Pierce?" Luke asked once more.

Lissy met Fin's eyes and nodded perceptibly, silently accepting the fact that they had to confide in Luke, that the tale she'd told for so long was about to unravel before them.

Fin turned his attention to her brother-in-law. "He's alive," he confirmed. "Dangerous and cruel. And he's headed here."

Luke's brow furrowed as though he was trying to sort through this sudden development. After a moment, he gestured in Lissy's direction with his head. "Take her somewhere, then. Somewhere he won't find her until we can figure out how to handle the situation."

"No!" Lissy almost screamed. She was shaking even worse, her teeth nearly chattering, but she shook her head. "I'm not leaving. I'm not leaving Juliet and the children. If he got here and I'm not—"

"You think he would hurt *children*?" Luke's jaw hardened and his green eyes darkened dangerously.

Lissy's arms wrapped around her middle as though she could stop herself from shaking. "I don't think there's anyone he wouldn't hurt."

"Who exactly is this man?" Luke breathed out.

"A nightmare," Lissy returned. "The worst man I've ever known, and I'm so sorry that I've put everyone in danger."

Fin slid his arm around her shoulders, hoping to comfort her. "This is not your fault, Felicity."

But she shook her head most stubbornly. "No, Fin, it's all my fault. I should have—"

"You should have what?" Fin asked. "Let him continue to torture you? Let him kill you?"

"I made the mistake in marrying him, not anyone else." Tears began to trail down her cheeks. "It isn't fair that I've put the rest of you in danger."

"The treatment you suffered at his hands isn't fair. Nothing is your fault."

"I don't care who he is." Luke started in the direction of his study. "He's not entering my house and he's not putting anyone in any danger." Then he bellowed, "Keeton!"

"Sir?" The butler fell into line behind Luke.

"Send for Sir Nigel. Tell him to come at once and to bring those burly sons of his."

"Sir Nigel?" Lissy echoed, looking up at Fin in alarm, the remaining color in her face draining away. "Is that necessary?"

Fin nodded. Luke's plan was actually a good one. Of course, his would-be brother-in-law had already dealt with one murderous villain in the past. It would stand to reason Beckford would have a good idea of how to begin. "Having the local magistrate on our side *before* I threaten to kill Pierce can only be to our advantage."

"Fin!" She shook her head. "Please don't do that. If Aaron hurt you—"

"He's not going to hurt me or you, not ever again."

She didn't look convinced, however; and she shook her head once more. "You don't know what he's capable of. I—"

"I won't lose you," Fin vowed fervently. And he wouldn't, no matter what he had to do or what it would cost him. He loved her completely and facing life without her wasn't an option.

<hr>

Lissy's belly twisted in panic. Every fear she'd had over the last three years was coming true. So many questions flooded her mind. How had Aaron discovered her deception? How did he know where to find her? And what would he do to her once their paths crossed again? She suppressed the tremor that washed over her.

She glanced up at Fin, at the dark circles around his blood-shot eyes and his pained expression. Poor, dear Fin, the best man she'd ever known. He looked as though he hadn't slept in a fortnight.

She forced a smile she didn't feel to her face and slid her hand into his. "You need to rest, Fin."

His hand tightened around hers, a silent promise of love and devotion. However, he shook his head. "I can rest later. I can—"

"You won't be any good to anyone if you don't get some rest now," she interrupted, hoping to appeal to that sensible side of him that she loved so dearly. "Come on. " She tugged him in the direction of the staircase. "I'm rather tired myself. I'll stay with you." At least until he fell asleep.

"Lissy," he complained, even though he kept his pace even with hers down the corridor.

"You always take care of everyone else, Fin. Now it's my turn." And one way or the other, she *would* take care of him. She'd take care of Juliet and Ben and little baby Georgie too. It wasn't fair for everyone else to suffer because of her foolish mistake all those years ago. One way or the other, she would have to face the choices that she'd made, but she'd need to face them without putting anyone else's safety in jeopardy.

Luke had mentioned his dueling pistols the other night, and though Lissy's father hadn't been a terribly attentive parent, he had taught her how to shoot at a very tender age. She didn't imagine, however, that Fin or Luke would be in favor of her retrieving either of the pistols. So she'd just have to figure out how to get her hands on the weapons without anyone else being the wiser. Aaron would, after all, come for her, and she would need to be prepared.

"You'll *stay* with me?" Fin asked as they reached the steps, as though he was afraid to let her out of his sight, and she wondered if he had any idea of the inner workings of her mind.

"For the rest of my life," she vowed. No matter how short that might be, just as long as she took Aaron with her.

She led Fin up the steps, slower than normal, as his legs did seem rather wobbly. Heavens, had he ridden all night long to return to her? He truly did mean to keep her safe even to his own detriment. Noble, honorable Fin. Lissy led him down the corridor towards her chambers, then she opened her door wide for him.

Fin's brown eyes speared her where she stood. "Felicity St. Claire, I have a feeling all of a sudden that you've set your mind on something."

Felicity St. Claire. Heavens, it had been a hundred years since anyone had called her that. St. Claire was preferable to Pierce, however. Her life would be so different if she'd only ever been a St. Claire. "The only thing I've set my mind on, Phineas Granard, is making certain you get some rest."

"And you won't leave me?" He seemed able to stare right into her soul. "Promise me you won't leave me."

"And go where?" she hedged, laughing just a bit. "Everyone I love is right here at The Chase."

"I have a feeling." Fin shook his head. "An ominous feeling that if I don't secure your word right now, I'll be sorry for it the rest of my life."

"My word?" she echoed.

"I can't lose you, Lissy." His voice seemed caught in his throat all of a sudden. "After everything, I can't lose you too. I'll never survive it. So promise me you won't leave my side. Give me your word."

He hardly seemed like himself, exhausted and nearly broken. So Lissy nodded, she couldn't help herself. "I promise, Fin. I won't leave you."

"Thank you." He seemed to sag forward a bit as he stumbled over her threshold.

Lissy hurried to his side and slid her arm around his back, steadying him. "You almost killed yourself with that ride, didn't you?"

"I'm fine," he said. "I got here first, that's all that matters."

Stubborn man. He could have killed himself. "Take off your jacket and waistcoat, Fin."

"Are you going to take advantage of me in my weakened state?"

Lissy snorted in response. "You are mad."

"Wishful thinking, then" he said as he slowly shrugged out of his jacket.

At that, she couldn't help but laugh. Though it might be the last time she'd laugh in quite a while.

Twenty-Seven

Afternoon light poured into Lissy's room and she blinked her eyes open. Heavens, she hadn't intended to fall asleep but with Fin's large, warm body wrapped around hers, sleep had come quite naturally. She started to slide towards the edge of the bed, but Fin's arm tightened around her waist.

"You promised," he whispered.

Lissy turned back and stared at his handsome face, his eyes closed and his brown hair mussed against his brow. She could happily stare at that face the better part of most days, but today wasn't most days. "For heaven's sake, Fin." She sighed. "I can't stay in bed all day."

"Why not?" he asked, cracking open one eye. "You have somewhere else to be?"

It really was rather frustrating how well he knew her, but then he had known her the better part of her life. "I'd like to check on Juliet, if you must know."

"Very well." He opened both eyes. "I'll go with you, then."

He was maddening! "Meaning you don't trust me?"

Fin pushed up to his elbows, his dark eyes peering right into her soul. "Are you not the same girl who bolted from that inn in the dead of night, making me chase you across Derbyshire?"

"You didn't have to chase after me," she grumbled.

"Yes, I did," he said softly, tucking one of her curls behind her ears. "If anything had happened to you, Lissy, I'd—"

A scratch sounded on her door, halting whatever else he meant to say. Lissy glanced from the mussed counterpane to Fin. "You will scandalize Annie, you know?"

"I *am* fully dressed," he countered.

Mostly. His jacket, waistcoat and cravat *were* draped across her chair, rather neatly, a few feet away.

"Besides," he continued, "since I have every intention of marrying you, Annie will have to get accustomed to finding me in your bed."

Meaning he didn't have any intention of leaving her bed at the moment. A scratch sounded once more and Lissy heaved a sigh. "Come," she called half-heartedly.

Her maid strode through the door and stopped in her tracks when she spotted Fin and her cheeks pinkened instantly. "I—I," she began. "I am sorry, my lady. I—"

"Lord Carraway was just napping, Annie," Lissy explained, though it explained very little.

"U-um, well, Mr. Beckford was asking for you in his study."

"Staveley must have arrived. We'll be right there," Fin said, swinging his legs over the side of the bed.

"We?" Lissy echoed.

He reached for his discarded waistcoat. "Until Aaron Pierce has been dealt with, I don't intend to let you out of my sight."

Her heart warmed at his words, even if he was being his overbearing self. "You are very stubborn, my lord. Do you know that?"

He shot her a smile that warmed her to her toes. "Which makes us the perfect match, does it not?"

The perfect match? Aside from their stubbornness, they were as different as night and day.

With her arm draped around his, Fin led Lissy through Prestwick Chase until they reached the ducal study. He released her arm and directed her over the threshold of Luke's borrowed domain. He expected to find Staveley sitting before Luke, explaining about Pierce's presence in England; but the local magistrate Sir Nigel Mycroft, a thin man with graying hair and soft eyes, occupied the seat instead. The man's three not-so-thin sons lined the walls, all sporting rather serious expressions.

Luke and Sir Nigel came to their feet and the older man smiled in Lissy's direction. "My lady, always so nice to see you." Then his eyes met Fin's and he nodded. "Carraway."

"Has Staveley filled you all in?" Fin asked.

"Staveley?" Luke frowned. "What the devil does he have to do with any of this?"

Fin shook his head. He must have done a rather poor job of explaining things this morning. "So he hasn't arrived here yet?"

"I can't imagine my brother-in-law anywhere other than his own library," Luke continued. "What is this about, Phineas?"

Damn it all, Fin would have to start at the beginning. He gestured towards one of Luke's empty chairs. "Do sit down, sweetheart," he said to Lissy. "I think this might take a while."

She was shaking just a bit, but she did as he asked. Fin followed after her, and grasped the back of the chair in his hands, hoping his presence would offer her any support she needed.

"Lady Felicity is in trouble," he began.

"Beckford said as much," Sir Nigel replied. "It's the sort of trouble she's in that we don't understand."

And Fin had to find a way to explain the situation without revealing too much of Lissy's most private torment. "Well, you all know she married an American captain several years ago, while she was in Boston, visiting her mother's family."

"Yes," Sir Nigel agreed. "That is what Lady Juliet said at the time."

Fin took a deep breath. "What Lady Juliet didn't say, what she didn't even know, was the terrible circumstances Lady Felicity found herself in while in Boston. Aaron Pierce is the most vicious and evil man I've ever heard of."

All eyes shifted to Lissy but she didn't even squirm in her seat. Good for her.

"Vicious and evil?" Charles Mycroft, the magistrate's oldest son asked.

Fin nodded. "I have seen quite a bit of the world, but nothing prepared me for Lady Felicity's horrific tale. To have survived her ordeal, she is the strongest lady of my acquaintance. And I am simply in awe of her resilience."

Luke frowned at hearing these words. No doubt the man would want a better explanation than that at some point, but not in front of Sir Nigel and his sons. The general brushstrokes would have to do for now.

"She was tormented and tortured," Fin continued. "In order to survive, escape was her only option. She rather ingenuously tricked him into believing she had died and then she fled home to England."

"Tricked him?" Sir Nigel asked.

"I left him a suicide note," Lissy said, her voice small and timid in this group of men. "There was so much blood in the room, I imagine the story was easily believed."

"Until now," Fin added. "Pierce has somehow arrived in London, looking for Lady Felicity." He met Luke's gaze. "I happened upon Lord Staveley last night at a coaching inn. He was headed here to warn you of Pierce's imminent arrival."

"How the devil would Staveley know any of this?" Luke shook his head.

"He said your sister…" Fin let his voice trail off when Luke snorted.

"Well, that explains it." Luke heaved a sigh. "So what do we do, Carraway? Just wait for Pierce to show up at The Chase?"

"I'm certainly not going to ever let him harm her again. I think waiting for him here, being ready for him, is our best chance."

"I do not relish getting involved in any man's marriage, Carraway," Sir Nigel heaved a sigh. "That's between him and God."

Which would be most people's feelings on the matter without hearing the horrific details, Fin was certain. But he wasn't quite ready to concede that point. He turned his attention to the magistrate and said, "I was on my way to London to see what could be done about the marriage. Her guardian was never asked for permission for her to marry, sir, and I believe there are grounds for an annulment."

"Meaning you plan to use your influence to gain her one," the magistrate said.

Fin would use anything and everything at his disposal. "You were a friend of her father's. He isn't here to protect her."

"But we are," Sir Nigel finished for him.

"But we are," Fin agreed.

"Very well." The magistrate sighed. "What do you want from us, Carraway?"

"I would like each entrance of The Chase to be guarded by one of our rifles or pistols. I don't want Pierce to get past us or take us by surprise."

"You think that's necessary?" the magistrate's youngest son, Howard, asked. "Pistols and hunting rifles? You think this American fellow can siege the castle, as it were?"

"I only wish there were more of us."

"I thought we were just going to see her," Heaton said, as he crouched down beside Aaron in a copse of trees not far from

Felicity's family seat.

Against the backdrop of the waning light, Aaron gestured towards a burly fellow with a rifle, leaning next to a side door of the manor house. "The place doesn't look very welcoming."

"Odd," Heaton agreed. "The English I've met so far have seemed much friendlier than that. Do you think that fellow from last night lied to you? He said he was going to return to London but he could have started for here instead."

That was one thing Aaron was certain hadn't happened. The scholar from last night had been quite dead when Aaron deposited him in that cupboard. The fellow he'd been talking to, however, was another matter. Aaron had been foolish not to realize that the night before. "Perhaps," he replied instead of discussing the possibilities with Heaton any further. "But it's of little consequence. If my wife is truly holed up in there, a few men with rifles aren't going to stop me."

His business partner sighed. "We could try the diplomatic approach. Drive up to the house and simply ask to see the lady."

Was Heaton really that naïve? If there were armed men at the manor's entrances, they'd most likely shoot Aaron on sight. Still, the suggestion might get the man out of Aaron's hair. "Why don't you wait for me back at the inn, and I'll try that."

The inn where they'd acquired rooms this afternoon was certainly within walking distance of Prestwick Chase.

"You'd rather see her alone." Heaton frowned.

"Well, she is *my* wife." Even if the man had been sweet on Felicity in those early days.

After a moment, his old friend agreed with a nod of his head. "All right, then. I'll wait for you back at the inn." Then he pushed back to his feet, dusted his hands on his trousers, and left Aaron alone in his hiding place.

Twenty-Eight

Lissy felt like a specimen in a traveling circus. Sir Nigel and his sons kept glancing at her across the dinner table as though she was an unnatural curiosity that hadn't yet been explained. They could look all they wanted to. They could think her the worst sort of liar, if they liked. They could never understand what she'd endured and she didn't owe any of them an explanation for her choices.

"You're certain Staveley said Captain Pierce was headed to Prestwick Chase?" Juliet asked Fin, lifting her turtle soup to her lips.

"More than certain," Fin replied. "He said Caroline sent him to warn us."

"Where the devil *is* Staveley, I'd like to know," Luke complained, leaning back in his chair and shaking his head. "I would have thought the man should have been here hours ago."

"Perhaps he encountered trouble on the road like Fin and I

did," Lissy suggested.

"Or got a late start," Fin added in. "Though he did seem anxious to arrive when I saw him last night."

Luke scrubbed a hand across his jaw. "So odd she would send *him*. Doesn't make any sense at all."

Truly, Lissy was surprised at that too. Lord Staveley was such a nice man, with a generous heart; but he spent more time in his library than he did out of it. He hardly seemed the sort who would race through the countryside on a mission.

Juliet sighed a bit. "I do hope he's all right."

"I'm sure he's fine," Luke replied. "I just wish he'd hurry along."

"Well—" Sir Nigel cleared his throat "— my boys and I can stay through the night, but we can't stay forever, Beckford."

"We can re-evaluate the situation in the morning." Luke nodded toward the magistrate. "But for now, we appreciate you being here with us."

"Yes," Juliet added. "I'm certain my father would appreciate everything you're doing, sir."

"I appreciate it too, Sir Nigel," Lissy said softly. And she did. Even though the magistrate and his sons didn't seem to understand how Lissy had ended up in this particular situation, and even though they seemed uncomfortable about lending their support, they were still lending it just the same.

"You know," the magistrate began, a wistful smile on his face, "I still remember that little blonded-headed imp who ran around this place with more energy than sense." He laughed at some memory floating about his mind. "You didn't have a care in the world. You even made your father laugh more often than not in those days." He heaved a slight sigh. "I wish you still didn't have a care in the world, my lady. We'll do what we can to help in that regard."

Lissy's heart lifted, and she brushed a tear from her cheek. How kind Sir Nigel was.

The Peak District was blanketed in darkness, and though Fin had slept many hours that afternoon, he was grateful when the second footman relieved him of his post at The Chase's front door. He'd sleep a few more hours at Lissy's side, then relieve the servant, just as Luke, the magistrate, his sons and the rest of the male staff would be doing at their respective posts to ensure that a fresh pair of eyes would keep watch on every entrance.

He navigated the darkened corridors of the manor and descended the steps that led to the family wing. He didn't bother knocking, for fear that he'd wake her. But as he stepped into her chambers he stopped in his tracks when he heard...

"One more step, cockchafer," Lissy growled, "and I'll shoot you right between your eyes."

"Felicty!" Fin's mouth fell open. He'd never heard her utter something so vulgar in all of his days.

"Oh, Fin!" She dropped something heavy onto her bed and then rushed across the floor to him, throwing her arms around his middle. "I thought you were him."

He held her trembling body against his and kissed the top of her head. "Where the devil did you learn such a vile word?"

She looked up at him in the darkness and said very meekly, "Luke. But I think I'm supposed to have forgotten that he taught it to me."

"I should say so." Fin shook his head, then focused on the next part of the threat she'd issued. "Do you have a pistol in here?"

"Just in case," she admitted, dropping her eyes to his chest.

"Sweetheart, Pierce won't make it this far. There are armed men at each entrance."

She nodded in agreement. "I know. I just needed that bit of security, being alone in here."

"Well, I'm here, now." Fin kissed her brow. "I won't let anything happen to you." Then he directed her back toward the bed and retrieved a dueling pistol from the top of her counterpane. Damn it all, he was lucky he hadn't shot him or herself, for that matter. "We are *not* sleeping with this, Lissy."

"But, Fin," she started to protest.

"I won't have one of us wake up without a head in the morning." That sounded perfectly ridiculous. He hadn't gotten a ton of sleep however. "I mean, I won't have one of us never wake up again." So he put the pistol on a nearby table, then climbed into bed bedside her.

"You're going to sleep in your clothes?" she asked around a yawn, rolling over in the bed to snuggle against him.

"I have to be up in a few hours to relieve Martin at the front door."

Her delicate hands slid around his back, holding him against her. "I love you, Fin," she said against his cravat.

His arms tightened around her. "I love you too, Lissy."

Aaron waited until well after all the candles in the manor had gone dark and well after there'd been a changing of the guards before he started towards the door that led to the gardens. As he approached the garden gate, he glanced up at the window, the third from the left, where he'd spotted his errant wife that evening. It was one thing to hear she was alive, one thing to realize that he had been duped for quite a while, and another to actually see her with his own eyes. His blood was still boiling over that deception. No one made a fool of Aaron Pierce. No one.

He crept through the garden gate, careful to stay in the shadows so the man at the door couldn't catch a glimpse of him. He edged his way closer to the entrance but stopped when he brushed against a hedge, which made a rustling sound.

The guard stepped slightly away from the door, peering into the darkness. It was a blessing that only a sliver of the moon was out that night or Aaron might have been spotted. He crouched down and retrieved the knife from his scabbard. No one was going to keep his wife from him.

⸎

"Papa?" Ben's tired, little voice in the distance hit Lissy's ears, jarring her slightly from sleep. "Milk."

She twisted a bit in Fin's arms and must have made a sound because he whispered, "What is it, sweetheart?"

"Ben," she mumbled back. "It sounds like he's awa—"

Something wrenched her from the bed before she could finish her sentence. She fell onto the floor thud and bumped her head on the nearby table.

She screamed, or at least she thought she did, as she saw a large figure looming over Fin in the darkness. Someone was holding him down on the bed.

"Fin!" she screamed for certain that time.

"Shut up, you whore," a vicious voice growled back. "I'll deal with you next."

Aaron.

Lissy's heart plummeted as every fear she'd ever had was right there in her chambers. And he had Fin by the throat. She caught a tiny bit of moonlight reflecting off a...knife.

"Fin!" she yelled again, pushing up to her knees. "Fin!"

Oh dear God! The pistol. Where had Fin put the pistol?

Aaron's knife thrust downward and Fin cried out, but then he reared upwards. The two of them struggled on the bed and Lissy could barely see anything other than two darkened beings thrashing against each other.

The table. Fin put the dueling pistol on the table. The table Lissy had bumped into.

She scrambled to her shaky feet, retrieved the heavy weapon from the table and pointed it at her bed. Heavens, she could barely make out one man from the other as they wrestled for dominance.

"Shoot him, Lissy!" Fin cried out.

His words halted the attack on Fin, and Lissy could make out Aaron's face as he turned his attention on to her. Memories of every horrible thing he'd once done to her flashed in her mind and she pulled the trigger.

A small burst of light lit the room, and Aaron's astonished expression before he dropped onto the bed was an image Lissy would never forget.

She dropped back down to her knees and struggled for breath.

"Aunt Lissy?" Ben's voice from the corridor nearly stopped her heart.

"Go find your papa, Ben," Fin called out rather calmly, though how he could be calm, Lissy had no idea.

Tremors raced through her and though she opened her mouth to order Ben away, nothing came out.

"Uncle Fin?" Ben asked. "What are you doing in there?"

"Helping Aunt Lissy with something. Go find your papa. Go quickly, Ben." Fin was at Lissy's side, though she couldn't recall him having left the bed. Then his hand was on her shoulder, steadying her. "Sweetheart," he rasped. "Are you all right? Did he hurt you?"

He had hurt her for so long and now... Now his lifeless from was draped across her bed. A gurgled cry escaped Lissy and she couldn't hear or think or speak to save her life.

Lights from candles suddenly filled her room and a flood of men filtered in. Keeton. Sir Nigel. It was all a blur.

~♦~

"We heard a shot!" Sir Nigel said from the threshold, gasping for breath as though he'd run a foot race.

Fin's shoulder throbbed like the devil, his shirt was soaked through with blood, and a number of men were crowded into Lissy's chambers, their candles and lanterns filling the room with light; but all he could focus on was the dark red splotch at Lissy's temple. "Oh, sweetheart," he said, dropping to his knees beside her. "Your head."

"Dear God," Luke muttered from the threshold as he arrived at the scene.

"Papa?" Ben said from the corridor.

"You don't want him to see this, Luke," Fin said quickly.

"No, I don't," his friend replied, stepping out into the corridor. "Come on, Benton, I'll take you to Mama for a while."

"But I want milk," Ben said, his voice getting softer as Luke must have ushered the child away.

Fin turned his attention back to Lissy. Tears streamed down her face and she couldn't seem to keep from shivering. He pulled her into his embrace, holding her against him with his good arm. She trembled and cried and Fin just held her. At least Aaron Pierce couldn't torment her any longer.

He glanced over at the man's lifeless form on the bed. There was a hole where his neck used to be, but...Fin stared harder at the man. He knew that face. He'd seen it somewhere before, he was quite certain. But where?

And then it hit him.

The coaching inn. Pierce had been at the table next to Staveley's and could have easily overheard their conversation. Then the man had followed Staveley up the stairs. Damn it all. That did not bode well at all, and dread settled in Fin's belly, though he kept his fears to himself. Lissy was in no condition to hear them now.

He held her tighter and whispered in her ear. "It's all right, sweetheart. Everything is going to be all right."

Twenty-Nine

Lissy blinked her eyes open, finding the chambers filled with light. Her lids heavy, she closed her eyes once more and would have been perfectly happy to drift back to sleep.

But her sister's voice from just a few feet away pushed through Lissy's foggy brain. "Finally awake?"

"My head," Lissy groaned. Why was opening her eyes so difficult?

Her bed dipped as Juliet sat on the edge of it and took Lissy's had in hers. "Doctor Perkins gave you some laudanum. Do you remember?"

Lissy slowly opened her eyes to meet her sister's concerned expression and wished the fog in her brain would lift as well...And then it began to recede.

She gasped as memories began to flood her mind, and she wished that she could forget everything.

Aaron.

Fin.

He'd been stabbed, hadn't he? In their struggle? "Fin!" She bolted up and realized she wasn't in her chambers. She was in Georgie's old set of rooms.

"He's fine," Juliet assured her. "Though he'll be put out with me that I didn't rush to retrieve him as soon as you woke. He's been sitting vigil here all night long until I made him leave a little while ago."

"He's fine?" Lissy's pulse began to slow to its usual rhythm again. "But he was injured. I heard him scream."

Her sister nodded slowly. "Doctor Perkins sewed him up in the middle of the night, right after he gave you a dose of laudanum."

Why did she need laudanum? Was she sick? Feverish? "What's wrong with me?"

"Nothing." Juliet smiled and squeezed Lissy's hand. "Well, other than jumping feet first into things without thinking everything through." She shook her head. "You were shaking so badly last night, you couldn't even talk. He thought it would bring you some rest and some needed peace. I hope he was right."

Lissy did remember the tremors that had racked her body. She remembered the fear that had spread through her like wildfire when she realized Aaron was in her chambers. She remembered the terror that took root in her soul when she realized he meant to kill Fin. She remembered pulling the trigger of Luke's pistol. And she remembered Fin wrapping his arms around her a few moments later. He couldn't be injured too badly with that being the case. Still… "I'm not sure if peace will ever find me."

Juliet heaved a sigh. "Time will help. Sometimes it's the only thing that will."

Time. There would never be enough time in the world to erase last night or Lissy's culpability. "I'm so sorry, Jules. I'm so sorry about everything. If I could do things over…"

"We'd all make different choices if we could do things over," her sister replied evenly. "But you can't go back. You can only ever move forward." Then she moved closer to Lissy and wrapped her arms around her in a very motherly fashion, the way Georgie used to. "You are free now, sweetheart. Free to start over. Free to do things differently this time."

But Lissy wasn't certain that was the case. "I killed him last night, didn't I?" she asked, just to make certain. With as horrifying as the previous night was, she needed to make sure she wouldn't ever have to face Aaron Pierce again.

Juliet pulled back from her slightly. "You did."

"So I'll have to face a trial." Lissy winced at the idea of baring her soul in an open courtroom. How would she ever be able to do so? She hadn't even told Fin or Juliet all of it. But a room full of strange men?

"Sir Nigel isn't charging you," her sister softly interrupted her thoughts. "He never would have, as you were clearly defending yourself and Fin, but when he realized Captain Pierce had murdered Charles Mycroft last night to gain entrance…" her voice drifted off.

Sir Nigel's eldest son? "Oh no!" A sob was wrenched from Lissy's soul and she fell back onto the bed, staring up at the ceiling above, the weight of her guilt weighing down on her.

Juliet fell into place beside her, grasping Lissy's hand. "Oh, sweetheart."

"It's all my fault," Lissy said through her tears. Charles Mycroft would still be alive right now if it wasn't for her. No amount of time in the world would ever bring the man back to his father and brothers.

"It's not your fault at all. Pierce's actions were his alone, Lissy."

But she shook her head. "He came here because of me. I put all of you in danger. You, Luke, Ben…" Oh, good heavens! Ben! Had he been in her chambers the night before? She seemed to remember he was there. "Oh, Jules, did Ben…?"

"Ben is fine. He's safe."

"But did he see anything?" Lissy would never forgive herself if that sweet little boy was plagued with those awful images for the rest of his life.

"He didn't see a thing. Luke brought him to me, and he stayed with me through the night."

Thank heavens. Lissy closed her eyes and wrapped her arms about her middle. "He could have been hurt. You could have been hurt."

"And you *were* hurt, Lissy," Juliet said softly. "You were hurt for a very long time and you certainly didn't deserve such treatment at his hands."

"I chose to marry him. I—"

"You were too young to make such a decision. He took advantage of your age, and naivety, and the fact that you didn't have a guardian looking out for your best interests. It is not your fault. You didn't make him the man he was. You didn't make him do the things he did. You fell in love with the image he presented to you. It's not your fault he wasn't who he pretended to be."

How could Juliet so easily forgive all of Lissy's sins? Lissy couldn't do the same. Her conscience wouldn't allow it. Charles Mycroft was dead. Fin had been injured. And the rest of Prestwick Chase had been put in danger all because of her. She wasn't blameless and Lissy's guilt couldn't be wiped clean with just a few words. "I should have been smarter. I should have realized he wasn't who he seemed. I—"

"You were *fifteen*, Felicity. And barely that," Juliet stressed. "You are not to blame and that's the end of it."

A mirthless laugh escaped Lissy. "You may be more stubborn than me."

At that, Julie laughed in earnest. "Are you just now realizing that? You should have asked Luke, he'd have told you."

"Well, Fin might disagree with him." Fin. Lissy had the overwhelming need to see him just then. "You promise he's all right?"

Her sister nodded. "The dagger went through Fin's shoulder.

As long as infection doesn't set in, he'll be fine."

"I need to see him."

"I imagine you do." Juliet squeezed Lissy's hand once more. "He loves you, Lissy. Injured, he sat vigil at your side all night as though he was afraid you might disappear if he looked away.

~~~✦~~~

Fin's entire right arm throbbed, from his shoulder right on down to his wrist. Of course, Doctor Perkins said it would be that way for a while since his muscle in his arm had been sliced open. He lifted a coffee cup to his lips with his left hand, which did feel a little awkward, but he'd make do.

"Sir Nigel just left," Luke said as he entered the breakfast room.

The poor man had been more than grief-stricken all night after the loss of his eldest heir. But he hadn't returned home until he'd removed Charles Mycroft and Aaron Pierce's bodies from Prestwick Chase. "Something has been worrying me all night, Luke," Fin said, lowering his coffee cup back to the table.

"Just one thing?" The man dropped wearily into a chair across from Fin, looking much older than his thirty-seven years.

"Staveley," Fin replied. "I saw Pierce at that coaching inn in Northamptonshire. Didn't know who he was at the time, of course. But I'm fairly certain he overheard what Staveley told me that night. And if I was a betting man, I'd wager he's responsible for whatever has delayed your brother-in-law's arrival."

"Dear God." Luke's brow creased in concern, a look he'd worn most of the night. "I'll travel there straight away, then. What's the name of the place?"

"The Kettering Arms. I'd go with you but..." Fin gestured to his bad arm. Traveling would only open up his wound, Doctor Perkins had explained.

"No need." Luke waived him off. "I just hope you're wrong."

"When has Fin ever been wrong about anything?" Lissy teased from the threshold, sounding more like her cheeky-self than she

76

had in a while, clearly having only overheard that last sentence. Her pretty blue eyes twinkled as she met Fin's gaze, touching something deep in his soul.

Damn it all. She took his breath away and Fin didn't know what he would have done if the previous night had turned out differently, if she'd been taken from him by that madman. "Lissy," he breathed out as he stumbled to his feet, as did Luke.

"Tell me, Luke," she said as she navigated around the table to slide into the seat beside Fin, "what is he right about this time?"

Luke and Fin exchanged a glance, both silently agreeing not to mention Fin's theory about Staveley at the moment. Lissy had been in such a state of hysteria the night before, and it was such a relief to see her looking so well this morning. Neither of them wanted to see her crumble like that again.

"That the coffee tastes like tar this morning," Luke lied, forcing a smile to his face. "I had been looking forward to a decent cup."

"You are looking well," Fin said to her, dropping back into his seat.

She touched his wrist and smiled, heating him from the inside out. "Juliet said you sat by my bedside all night."

After almost losing her, there was nowhere else he would have been, but he simply nodded instead of saying as much.

"Do excuse me," Luke said, pushing out of his seat. "A lot to do today." He didn't wait for any sort of response before quickly exiting the breakfast room, headed most likely for Northamptonshire without delay.

"How is your shoulder?" Lissy asked, her blue eyes focused so intently on Fin, he wasn't certain he could even remember his own name.

Damn it all. What had she asked?

"Fin?" she prodded when he hadn't uttered a sound.

"Yes?" he said quickly.

"Your shoulder. Juliet said Doctor Perkins stitched you up. How is it?"

His shoulder hurt like the dickens, but Fin feigned a smile for her benefit. "Tender, but it'll be right as rain in no time, I'm sure."

She heaved a sigh and her gaze drifted to the table. "I nearly lost you," she said so softly it was almost a whisper. "I don't know what I would have done if I'd lost you."

Fin tucked one of her stray flaxen curls behind her ear and let his fingers linger against her cheek until she met his eyes. "You won't be rid of me that easily."

"Easily?" A gurgled laugh escaped her. "How can you make a joke about that?"

"Because it's easier to do so than to think about losing you, Lissy."

"Oh, Fin." She slid closer to him in her seat and gently pressed her lips to his.

For the first time since he'd raced back from Northamptonshire, Fin felt the world was right, even if his right shoulder throbbed like nothing else. It was worth it. Freeing her from Pierce's clutches was worth any amount of pain he endured. And she was free now. No need to race to London. No need to utilize his contacts to obtain her an annulment. No need to do anything other than kiss the woman at his side and beg her to never let him go.

Someone cleared his throat from the threshold and Lissy quickly broke their kiss. Keeton, who looked as though he hadn't slept in a week, stood just inside the breakfast room and said, "Lady Felicity, a Mr. Heaton to see you."

At her gasp, Fin grasped her hand in his. "Who's Heaton?"

"Aaron's friend. His business partner."

"What the devil is he doing *here*?" Fin pushed out of his seat. After all the hell Pierce had brought down upon Prestwick Chase last night, there was no reason for his friend to ever show his face there.

"I don't know." Lissy shook her head. "I thought I saw him, Fin. Back in London. I caught a glimpse of someone who looked like him but had convinced myself it was just my imagination."

So he was Pierce's spy. He'd come to The Chase to finish off what his friend had started. "I'll deal with him," he said, starting towards the butler. "Where did you put him?"

"The white parlor, my lord."

"Fin!" Lissy called from behind him. "Mr. Heaton was always very kind to me."

"I don't think it was very kind," he bit out, "to lead that murderous beast right to you."

Thirty

Lissy had no idea how or why John Heaton had showed up at Prestwick Chase, but she wasn't going to let Fin throttle the man, not with his bad arm, and not considering that the Bostonian *had* always been kind to her. She followed in Fin's furious wake, trying to make him see reason.

"Phineas Granard! Do stop."

But he didn't. He strode right into the white parlor and only stopped after he'd crossed through the doorway. "I don't know how you can even dare to walk through these doors, asking to see Lady Felicity, but—"

"Oh, dear God." John Heaton rose from his spot at seeing Lissy. "It really *is* you."

She stopped at Fin's side and slid her hand into his, hoping to calm his temper just a bit. Then she nodded at her one-time neighbor. "It really is me."

"How?" The man's face contorted into disbelief. "I searched the bay for you until I couldn't see straight."

So he'd been the one to search? She suspected as much, but felt quite guilty all of a sudden for the anguish he must have gone through in trying to find her, the anguish she could see reflected, even now, in his eyes. "I'm so sorry, John."

"I'm just so glad you're alive." He raked a hand through his hair. "I—"

"Yes, well," Fin began, his tone rather clipped, "that's no thanks to Aaron Pierce."

John Heaton's gaze flashed from Lissy to Fin. "Where is Aaron? He never came back to the inn last night, I expected he would."

"He won't be going anywhere ever again," Fin replied before Lissy could say anything.

"I beg your pardon?" The American frowned. "What do you mean by that?"

"I mean he's dead." Fin heaved a sigh. "He slaughtered the magistrate's son in the middle of the night, slashed my arm open and intended God knows what for her ladyship if he hadn't been stopped."

"Oh, dear God." John dropped back into his seat, his face as white as a ghost. "I-I had no idea." He shook his head in disbelief. "I knew he was angry, but—"

"Angry!" Fin roared.

"Fin," Lissy broke in. "None of this is Mr. Heaton's fault. He—"

"He what?" Fin glanced down at her. "He didn't know what sort of a monster his friend was? He traveled with the man from London to Derbyshire and had no idea what the man had in store for you?"

"I-I didn't," the American protested. "I had no idea. I thought he meant to talk to his wife, find out what had happened. I had no idea he meant to harm anyone."

"Who knows how many he's harmed along the way?" Fin

muttered enigmatically. "How could you not know?"

"No one ever knew what happened to me," Lissy said, hoping Fin's anger would dissipate a bit. "Aaron could be very charming, he was always whoever anyone ever needed him to be in any given moment." She glanced down at her floor. "He certainly pretended well enough with me until after our vows were spoken. No one could see through him, not unless you knew what to look for."

She felt John Heaton's eyes on her, but she couldn't lift her gaze to meet his.

"No," the American said softly. "There were times I thought I'd caught a glimpse of something else beneath his surface, but I never looked hard enough to see anything I might not like. I don't know what he did to you, Felicity, but you can't wipe away my complacency so easily. I should have done something."

At that, she did look up, finding her one-time neighbor with an expression that tore at her heart. Aaron's actions were certainly not John Heaton's responsibility. "You did." Tears pooled in her eyes. "You searched the bay for me until you couldn't see straight." In his own way, he'd helped her gain her freedom. He'd added the credibility that her suicide story had needed.

He blinked at her in apparent wonder. "You are amazing. I'm not sure how you managed all of that. The blood, the note, the escape. But I was quite certain you were gone." A breath seemed wrenched from his soul. "I am so glad to discover otherwise." John pushed back to his feet and added, "I suppose I have some arrangements to make if you can point me in the right direction. He may not deserve any sort of service, but my conscience requires I give him one anyway."

Without a doubt, John Heaton was an honorable man, if nothing else.

"I'll point you in the right direction," Fin said, his tone softer than it had been thus far. "Or rather, I'm certain Keeton can do so."

And then the two of them were gone and Lissy was alone in the white parlor wondering at how much had changed in her life in so little time. For years, she'd been certain her future was etched in stone, without a thing she could do about it. But now her future was what she could make of it.

She could spend the rest of it afraid to move forward, or she could take the second chance she'd been given and live the life she truly wanted. Juliet's advice echoed in her ears. She *was* free to start over. Free to make better choices than she had so long ago.

When Fin returned to the parlor, she spun on her heels to face him. Noble, honest Fin. The man she loved more than she could have ever imagined. "Do you still mean to marry me?" she asked, hoping his answer hadn't changed.

A bemused look spread across his face. "Do you think me so fickle, Lissy? I've told you I love. I've showed you I love you. And I will love you until my final breath."

She didn't even try to keep the tears from streaming down her face now. "Then I suppose we should have the banns started, Fin; because I mean to hold you to your word on that."

The smile he flashed her lit up the room. He pulled her into his one-armed embrace and kissed her for all she was worth.

Epilogue

May 1821 – Carraway House, London

Giddiness bubbled up inside Lissy. But she was afraid to move. Afraid to find out she was dreaming. So she just sat in bed, and would be perfectly happy to stay there in that exact spot for the next eight months. She wouldn't eat anything unusual or laugh uncontrollably or raise her voice or...anything. She wouldn't even suck in a breath if she could help it. And she *could* help it. She would do anything and everything in her power to make certain Fin's baby came into this world.

She glanced down at her flat belly and touched a tentative hand to it. Was she really going to have a child? She had long since given up hope and so had Fin, not that he ever said as much. True to his word as always, he had never made her feel less than for her inability to give him an heir. He doted on Luke and Juliet's brood as an adoring uncle. He continued to guide Edmund with the wisdom and love of a father. But she knew there was nothing more he would love than to cradle his own child in his arms. And now…

Now that was an actual possibility.

If she wasn't dreaming.

But should she tell Fin? That was the real question plaguing her even as excitement welled inside her. She might feel better about telling him if *old* Doctor Watts had attended her this morning and not his son. The younger Doctor Watts hadn't been at this as long as his father. What if he was wrong? What if he had no idea what he was doing? She couldn't let Fin get his hopes up only to have them dashed.

She shook her head, even though there was no one in her chambers to see her do it. But she'd have to wait. Make certain before she told him.

A knock came at her door and Lissy glanced toward the sound. "Come," she called.

Her door opened and Fin strode through the door, his brow furrowed in concern. "Ames said Doctor Watts was here." He crossed the floor and was about to touch a hand to her head when his frown deepened. "Good God, Lissy, you're green."

She was still a bit nauseous, but she hadn't thought about any of that ever since the young doctor had left that afternoon. "I'm sure I'll feel better tomorrow," she lied.

Fin didn't seem so sure. He sat gently on the side of her bed. "Is there something I can get you, sweetheart? Did he leave anything for you to take?"

"I'm fine, Fin." Lissy shook her head. "Tell me how things went with Liverpool."

His dark eyes narrowed perceptibly. "There's something you're not telling me. What did Watts say, Lissy?"

She shook her head once more. "It *wasn't* Doctor Watts, it was his son, and I—"

"His son?" he interrupted her. "You mean the fellow who was the top of his class at Edinburgh and is a leader in medical research? That son?"

She shrugged in response. Just because young Doctor Watts was heralded as a brilliant mind, didn't mean he was right about this.

"The man has even consulted the King, Lissy. Now what did he say?"

"Fin," she complained. "I think I'll just lie down a bit. I'm certain I'll feel better after a nap."

"Felicity Corinna St. Claire Carraway," he began rather sternly. "What did the renowned doctor have to say? You *are* scaring me."

Lissy winced. She hadn't meant to scare him. That was the last thing she ever wanted to do. So she heaved a sigh and said very softly, "He said I'm expecting."

Fin's eyes rounded in surprise. "Expecting?" he echoed cautiously. Then he swallowed.

Lissy nodded, unable to take her eyes from her husband. "I didn't want to tell you. I wanted to be absolutely certain first. But you—"

Fin leaned forward and pressed his lips against hers. Lissy slid her arms around his shoulders and held him close. Joy radiated from him and she couldn't help but be caught up in his excitement.

He pulled back slightly from her and looked her up and down. "How are you feeling? Can I get you anything?"

Lissy laughed as she shook her head. "You already asked me that, silly man."

He nodded in agreement. "Silly, indeed. I shall be silly from here on out." His smile could light up a darkened room on a moonless night. "We're going to have child."

"If Doctor Watts is right and—"

"He's right," Fin declared. "I'd put more weight on his words than his father's."

Lissy heaved a sigh. "All that aside, Fin. I don't want to take any chances. I—"

"No chances, indeed," he cut her off. "I'll hire a doctor today. We'll bring him in fulltime and he'll see that you get care around the clock. And—"

Lissy laughed. She couldn't help it. His exuberance was more than contagious. "So you are happy, then?" she teased.

His warm eyes focused on her so intently, she barely dared to breathe. "Felicity, you have made me happy everyday of our lives together. Never doubt that."

And she never had.

About the Author

The author of several Regency Noir Romances, Ava Stone first fell in love with Mr. Darcy, Jane Austen and Regency England at the age of twelve. And in the years since, that love has never diminished. If she isn't writing Regency Era romance, she can be found reading it.

Her bestselling Scandalous Series is filled with witty humor and centers around the friends and family of the Machiavellian-like Lady Staveley, exploring deep themes but with a light touch. A single mother, Ava lives outside Raleigh NC, but she travels extensively, always looking for inspiration for new stories and characters in the various locales she visits.

Ava can be found at www.avastoneauthor.com and at Lady Jane's Salon Raleigh-Durham, where she is one of the salon's directors.

Also Available...

The SCANDALOUS world continues in...
A Scandalous Wife
A Scandalous Charade
A Scandalous Secret
A Scandalous Pursuit
A Scandalous Past
My Favorite Major
The English Lieutenant's Lady
To Catch a Captain
An Encounter With an Adventurer
In the Stars
Promises Made (Encounter With Hyde Park)

And the Regency Seasons Novellas...
A Counterfeit Christmas Summons
By Any Other Name
My Lord Hercules
A Bit of Mistletoe
The Lady Vanishes (One Haunted Evening)

Printed in Great Britain
by Amazon